Man Overboard

TIM BINDING

Man Overboard

PICADOR

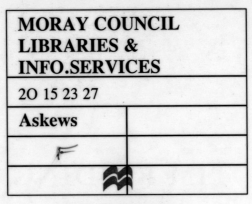
First published 2005 by Picador
an imprint of Pan Macmillan Ltd
Pan Macmillan, 20 New Wharf Road, London N1 9RR
Basingstoke and Oxford
Associated companies throughout the world
www.panmacmillan.com

ISBN 0 330 48747 7

1 3 5 7 9 8 6 4 2

A CIP catalogue record for this book is available from
the British Library.

Printed and bound in Great Britain by
Mackays of Chatham plc, Chatham, Kent

FOR CHLOE

One

It is cold in here and the windows look out over the snow-capped trees to the hidden town below. I have a blanket over my legs but still the winds of Mother Russia fly under the door and seize the room. Even Rosa's footsteps sound half frozen, as if she is walking across on a floor laid in ice. She hurries over to me, tucking the edges back under my knees with gentle words of rebuke. It is typical of her, to try to add to my comfort, but the truth is, such temperatures hold no fears for me. All my life my legs have been immersed in the cold, the first part of me to be lowered in, the last part to be hauled out, standing on some wet deck with me looking down at their bloodless shivering. Though folded and inert under this scratch of horsehair, I can still feel them kicking against the current. Such a world of cold.

The Imperial Sanatorium sits above the town like a deposed monarch, frozen in attitude, waiting for obeisance. Outside you can almost see the winter air filling the valley like a cold beer in a frosted glass, silver branches scratching against the grey of the flecked sky. Across the way, on the hill opposite, stands the observation point the Mayeruv Gloriet, round and wooden with a conical roof. I've never been there myself but Rosa tells me that everyone living here finds themselves climbing up to it at some point in their lives, courting, carousing, contemplating God's infinite capacity for practical jokes. This afternoon there'd just been this one couple, standing under its hat like a decoration bride and groom stuck on a wedding cake. They didn't move for fifteen minutes, trying to see where their future lay, beyond the reach of the tramlines and the tyre marks, over the wooded hills and far away. Spa visitors haul their bones there too when they're not busy taking the waters. Karlovy Vary is famous for its water. In the centre of the town is the hot spring, the Vridlo; seventy-two degrees centigrade with a spout like the plume of a detonated torpedo head. Take a sip of that and your liver gets back off the floor. Take the plunge and you emerge with a brand-new set of internal organs, at least that's what they claim. Don't believe it myself. If water alone could cure one's ills I wouldn't be here at all. I would be in Venice, the youngest old man alive, crossing the water to Le Vignole, Paola looking at me with her dark eyes, wishing I'd made good all those years. Another might have been.

Rosa tries to talk to me most days, but I do not understand all she says, nor she me. Her Russian is better than my Czech. When I'm alone I speak in English, softly, trying to remember what it was I used to say, and how I said it. I try to keep the two separate but lately the old language has been slipping in unannounced. 'Something to drink, Commander Korablov?' she will ask and I find myself answering, 'Another Gordon's, please, and prudent with the tonic,' and a look of alarm crosses her face, as if I'm trying to catch her out. So I keep conversation to a minimum, a few words of Russian, yes, no, thank you, and leave it at that. It would be discomforting for her to learn of my little secret, an aged Englishman in a Czech sanatorium paid for by the Russian state, secreted away in this vast dormitory, alone and almost silent. She would carry it out the door and down into her little town in no time, and that would be the end of my peace and quiet, and hers.

On days like this, sitting in front of the long pane of glass, staring to the distant hills, I wonder if it's true, that there was another me before this time began. I feel as if there cannot have been, that I am merely a flaw suspended in a perfect crystal of green, raised up in a world bereft of sense. I am submerged, drowned in the shadow of my own enigma, discordant chants my only companions. I hear a multitude of them calling me, muted sounds of admonishment, Minella singing out across the water, the bell chimes of the Holy ministries, voices that grow clearer as I rise up to break the surface, my ears popping with the hiss of the airlock and the click of the door. I stand there dripping with my great black swimfins in front of me.

A man is sitting opposite, thick, squat. There's a look on him, like he's sick and tired of being cooped up inside, the smell of diesel fumes round him, the paleness of his skin. He looks hungry.

'Welcome aboard, Commander Crabb,' he says. 'We've been expecting you.'

He pushes over a small glass.

'Drink,' he says. 'It must have been cold out there.'

Two

My first conversation was a bit awkward. We spoke through a third party, a small man sitting to his side, his chair pulled back slightly, so that his mouth was close to my interrogator's left ear. It was only early morning and yet he was sweating. After a while neither of us took any notice of him.

I drank from my glass, down in one, the warmth spreading out like a coal fire lit in a January waiting room. I had to hold on to the table's edge to keep my balance. The excitement must have got to me.

He held out his hand.

'Director of the KGB, Ivan Sverov. You have heard of me?'

It took the breath away, I must admit, standing in a puddle of seawater looking at that bloodstained paw. Sixteen thousand Polish officers shot and buried in Katyn forest and his hand on the trigger. They'd tried to blame it on the Germans, but the world knew different by then. Oh, I'd heard of Crippen all right. I was there when the plane went down.

He looked at me with eyes fresh from a Russian winter. He had lips as thin as gruel, colourless, protruding from the flat of his face as if they'd been hooked on a fishing line. You could imagine the teeth behind them, tenacious like a pike's. He pointed to the chair.

'You are Commander Crabb, are you not, Commander Lionel Kenneth Philip Crabb, holder of the George Medal, member of the Order of the British Empire?'

We'd always been told not to blow the gaff if questioned, but it's not quite the same when you're confronted by the Grand Inquisitor in person. So I admitted it. Churlish not to. He was a guest in our country, after all, albeit an uninvited one. He'd come over in March to vet Khrushchev's security arrangements and had been given a pretty rough reception all round; press, demonstrations, questions in the House. When he left he'd been told that, come the hour, he was not included on the invitation list. And yet here he was, skulking in the hulking. Sulking in the hulking too, by the looks of it.

'Well, Commander, are you impressed by our new battlecruiser?'

'I'm sorry,' I said, looking all innocent. 'Did I take a wrong turning down there? This is the Gosport ferry, isn't it?'

He scowled.

'You know very well where you are, Commander. You tried to evade our divers, but rest assured there was no possibility of you escaping this time.'

I hadn't stood a chance, the four of them coming out of nowhere, like they'd swum through the walls of the ship. I've only experienced something similar once before in Gibraltar, '43, one of Borghese's men coming at me with a knife, both of us running low. After a couple of lunges he slipped away. His heart wasn't in it. There we were trying to do each other down, and yet there was no real animosity between us. We each had a row to hoe, that's all. This had been different. There was a determination about them, eight arms trying to grab me all at once. We had a brief tussle on the surface, but then I got wedged in from all sides and pulled down again. By the time they got me aboard they were clapping each other on the back, happy as the local soccer team scoring the winning goal.

This time? I didn't like the sound of that at all. I tried to bluff my way out of it.

'It was a pure accident, I assure you,' I said. 'It's the devil of a job, keeping your bearings, swimming through that bilge. As soon as I've got my wind back, I'll push off and not bother you any further.'

I half rose. He gestured me back down with one narrow look, like a cell door slammed shut. Both his eyebrows were slanted in the same direction, as if some cartoonist had drawn them on with black crayon. They gave him an expression of habitual distrust.

'I do not hold you responsible, Commander. You were following instructions, I understand that. But whose? Your Prime Minister, your secret service, the American secret service? Both, perhaps.'

I said nothing.

'It is no surprise to us, Commander, that curiosity should get the better of them. "How do they do it, these peasants from the East, how do they build such ships?" That is what they are asking. And so they send a resourceful man such as yourself to find out. You are like a man in a Gogol story, trying to seduce the farmer's daughter, looking under her skirt without his consent.'

He moved his mouth carefully, repeating the phrase as the translator blushed at his task. He liked that sort of talk, you could tell.

'I assure you—'

He cut me off with a wave of a hand and I understood the pedigree of that gesture, the years of brute authority in which it had been bred. He tapped a white file laid before him on the table. He bit his nails too.

'What are we to make of this, Commander? We come in good faith to further relations between our two countries. Yet we have been here barely twenty-four hours and what happens? It is an outrage that Her Majesty and Her Majesty's government should treat their guests this way.'

I couldn't let him get away with that.

'Now just a minute,' I said. 'Let's get one thing straight. Her Majesty, Queen Elizabeth, had nothing to do with this. I was acting entirely on my own. Rap me over the knuckles as much as you like, but leave her out of it.'

Serov looked at his watch, tapped the glass face.

'The Soviet Prime Minister and the First Secretary will be hosting a lunch in our Embassy at any moment now. What do you think will be their reaction when I inform them of your intrusion? Will it put them off the lunch they will be eating with Sir Anthony Eden, the Prime Minister, Mr Duncan Sandys, the Foreign Secretary, and Mr Butler, the Lord Privy Seal? Do you think – ' he opened up the file – 'the caviar, the smoked salmon, the veal and roast chicken will be enough to assuage their indignation, or will the wine turn to vinegar in their mouths? And after lunch, when the time for speeches has come, what do you think they should say to them, these revered statesmen of the West, who hold out one hand in friendship and slap them across the face with the other?'

For the first time in my life I thought of the world as a globe and me having just kicked it off course. Perhaps it hadn't been such a good idea after all.

'All right,' I said, 'I admit it. I wanted to take a quick peep. Nothing more than the whim of an old frogman who should have known better. It was wrong of me, I know, but when it comes to battle-ships I'm like a schoolboy with his train-spotting. Can't resist it. Chuck me back in the water without a lifebelt if you want, make an official complaint. They'll grovel at your feet and throw me in the Tower, most likely. But no real harm done, except to a foolish man's pride.'

Serov shuffled his papers. I tried not to look, for looking when unasked had already got me into enough trouble, but then I saw them, the edge of my wallet and sticking out of it the photograph, with the crease at the corner and Pat and the little French mutt and the colander on the side of the swimming pool. And I felt cold again, cold and empty, as if the plug had been pulled and every drop of all I knew had been drained out of me. He caught me looking and smiled, a dreadful thing, like something you might find painted on the face of a corpse; nothing but the eyes of the dead.

'We cannot let you go so easily, Commander, not after we have waited for so long. When you didn't come last night some thought that perhaps you had changed your mind, but I told them to have faith. A ship such as this tied to the dock is for Commander Crabb the same as a goat tied to a tree is to a tiger: food for your hunger. And so you are with us now. England is no more. We could be in Sebastopol or Odessa.' He turned his head to one side, inhaled. 'Why, I can almost smell the smoke from the railway yards that run along-side the quayside. Our smoke smells quite different from yours, did you know that?'

I shook my head, trying to make sense of his words and what I had seen.

'Yes,' he said. 'I discovered this during my visit in March. It is something to do with the sulphur content. Your coal is less pure, the smoke more acidic. When I took the air this morning I thought my throat was on fire.' He rubbed his neck. 'But now the air smells sweet to me. Yes, I think we must be in Odessa, or if not, then somewhere in between England and your final destination.'

He lifted the bottle; a shot apiece this time. He looked pleased with himself. From outside I could hear shouts and the scraping of metal. For one foolish moment I thought it was Smithy coming to rescue me. Serov heard it too. He raised a finger to the air.

'Listen. The crowds are gathering outside. Soon they will be invited aboard to gaze at the might of the Soviet fleet. Perhaps amongst them there will be some friends of yours, sent to find out what has happened to you. They will be shown round with courtesy, given glasses of vodka and souvenirs but will leave learning nothing. For nothing has happened. You are not meant to be here and so it follows that you are *not* here. Prime Minister Bulganin will deny it, First Secretary Khrushchev will deny it, and I promise you the British government will deny it. Even your own Queen will disown her most loyal of subjects. Commander Crabb is nothing more than a swirl of dirty water, from which, in ten days' time, this ship and all those on board will sail.'

He stood up, raised his glass and tipped his throat back.

'Come, let me show to you the quarters we have prepared for you. A little cramped, but you are used to dark and discomfort.'

I stood up. I wanted to reach across, snatch up Pat's picture, examine it. How could that be? I'd left it in the wallet on the side table, not four hours ago, along with half a crown for the chambermaid. My head was reeling but I was damned if I was going to let him get the better of me. I peeled off my footwear and laid them out on the table like a pair of overcooked kippers.

'In that case,' I said, 'I'd like a pair of dry socks, if you don't mind.'

Three

If they hadn't come by ship, it would have never happened. If only they had used one of their Aeroflot planes or those new-fangled Tupolevs he was so proud of, Anthony Eden waiting on the red carpet, Duncan Sandys by his side, both wearing their funeral-wreath smiles, overcoats and handshakes and a band playing 'Khrushchev the Beautiful' in the chill April air. Perhaps he was terrified that it would fall out of the sky like Concordski did a few years later. Perhaps he remembered the fate of General Sikorski and thought, if it can happen to a military man, it can happen to an old peasant like me. Perhaps he didn't care much for planes, shared my mistrust of them as a mode of transport. Whatever the reason, he came by this battlecruiser, the one that Whitehall and the Old Cowhands across the Pond were wetting themselves over. Like Margot Fonteyn on water, though not as good-looking, but then your average Russian was never much taken with good looks. You've only got to look at their women. Dumplings in a mutton stew.

But back to the boat.

I was sitting in the Grove, off Beauchamp Place, a neat little cove with a nice crowd of personnel who know how to polish their shoes, when Smithy sauntered in, took a long lanky look around, bought himself a drink and ambled over. Nice chap I always thought, but Pat, Pat she took agin him in a big way.

I waved him into a pew.

'Howdy, stranger,' said I.

I always used that sort of talk with Smithy. Though he tried to sound as English as the next man, there was something about his inflection that was not quite right. He had some Hopalong blood in him somewhere, but he never let on how much.

'Crabbie. Fancy meeting you here.'

Fancy my sweet Fanny Adams. He'd probably been in half the snugs in Kensington looking for me. I waited.

'Still jamming your foot in the door?' said he.

I was working for Maitland by then, selling all manner of tat to all the coffee bars that were springing up in Soho. It might sound odd, a man of my disposition engaged in such activity, but (a) I needed the money and (b) I had rather a soft spot for the frothy concoction, Italian mixed with American. It reminded me of earlier, happier days.

'I don't know if I'm cut out for it, Smithy,' I told him. 'Got the patter but not the suit. Still, idle hands and all that. This is the first Saturday I've had off in a month.'

'Life's a bit of a treadmill, then.'

'On the contrary. Haven't you heard? I'm writing a book.'

'Yes, we did hear something to that effect. Fiction, is it?'

It was skilfully inserted, the 'we', but I took the point.

'You can rest easy,' said I. 'There'll be none of the . . .' I put my fingers to my lip. 'Comprenne? Just a little wartime derring-do. I've got this chappie stringing the actual words together. All I have to do is to slip him the odd story or two and off he goes. It's been fun. Looked up some old friends, chased down some old foes. Belloni came over, fit as a fiddle and twice as stringy. Paola wants me to go back, apparently, for old times' sake.'

Smithy raised his eyebrows.

'I bet Pat was pleased.'

'Those days are over, Smithy, Pat knows that. I told him I couldn't. Silly to raise her hopes.'

'How is Pat?'

'Never lovelier. We're getting engaged.'

'What, again?'

'It's for keeps this time. But don't let on. She doesn't know yet.'

He looked put out. He'd been hoping to keep me to himself.

'Expecting her soon?'

'When and if. A lady's prerogative and all that.'

'It's just . . .' He swallowed his words with his whisky. 'I was thinking, if you've not got much on, you might like to take a trip down to Portsmouth in a couple of weeks, pop into HMS *Vernon*, say hello. It's been a while.'

That's how it's done, see. They don't call you in, hand out orders, the way you might imagine. That's not their way. It's not that they don't believe in a rigid hierarchy, the structure of duty. It's just that once you're in, they simply nudge you in the right direction, let you come to the task under your own breath.

So it wasn't the book, after all. To tell the truth, I was a mite disappointed. It's one thing to be trusted; it's another to be taken for granted.

'Really?' said I.

'Yes, if you're fit enough.'

'Smithy. Don't let's go through that again.'

'As you wish,' said he. 'We're thinking of the week of the 15th. Tuesday the 17th, to be exact. Stay over for the 18th. Possibly the 19th. Two nights max. I'll be there to hold your hand.'

Which meant he needed to keep an eye on me. Meant someone upstairs deemed it important.

'I take it the black suit is required? The webbed feet?'

'That might be an idea.'

I stirred the pink.

'I thought we were going to call it a day, after the last spot of bother.'

'Missed opportunities, Crabbie. Can't afford them.'

'Meaning?'

Conspiracy is a marvellous thing, the way it hunches the body, lowers the tone. He looked over his shoulder once and laid his elbows on the table. Any moment now I thought, he'd starting pulling at his ear. He loved his work, and when his ginger was up, it showed.

'Don't you read the papers any more?' he said, his voice rising despite himself. 'Don't you know what's happening that week?'

'Grace Kelly's getting married.'

'And?'

'And it's not to me.'

'I mean in London.'

'Got me there, Smithy.'

I looked over to Dick, raised my glass, indicating the both of us. Dick saluted, intimating that he'd bring them right away. Smithy knew what I was doing, getting the rabbit out the hole. He rolled his glass between the fingers of his hands.

'Bulganin and Khrushchev? Their first visit to the West? Ring any bells?'

'Yes, and all of them cracked ones.'

'They're coming in on the *Ordzhonikidze*.'

Ah. The *Ordzhonikidze*. The murky waters were clearing.

The thing about the *Ordzhonikidze*, and all the other Soviet ships of her class, was their manoeuvrability. They could turn on a rouble. Me and Sydney had taken a look at one of them, the *Sverdlov*, a year earlier, when it had come over to take part in the Spithead review. It hadn't gone at all well. We'd made a hell of a racket clambering about her underneaths, looking for no-one-knew-what, and came up empty-handed. Rumour had it that the Soviets had found out about our visit and were not best pleased.

Dick set the drinks down on the side on the table. He knew better than to hang around. I waited until he'd gone back behind the bar.

'Are you serious, Smithy? Sounds a bit Harry Tate to me.'

He started to pull on his earlobe.

'It's got to be unofficial, you understand. Eden has given strict instructions to lay off while they're here. Naturally, we're not taking any notice. We've put more microphones in Khrushchev's suite in Claridge's than Doris Day's spat a song at.'

'Oh, I'm sure he'll only be too happy to oblige. I can just imagine him waking up each morning, wondering what state secrets he can blab about over breakfast. You could get the waiters to prod him in the right direction. "If sir would just address his remarks to the kedgeree on the sideboard." '

Smithy smiled.

'You're probably right. We won't learn much there. But the *Ordzhonikidze* is a different story. She's there for the taking, Crabbie. And you're the man to do it.'

'But with all the security that'll be there, they'll be on the look-out, won't they? They won't be wanting their noses rubbed in it a second time. And who's to say I'll find anything, anyway.'

He pulled at his ear again.

'There's got to be something down there,' he said. It was spoken as a wish rather than a statement of fact.

I looked at the snug and everyone settling into the early evening. A couple of drinks, a pleasant chat, dinner somewhere in Soho, Bianchi's maybe, and the Trojan later on. I felt a sudden chill wash over me, as if the Thames had just pulled me in and the tide was running fast. I could feel its grip dragging me out to sea, the land slipping through my fingers like dry sand. I wanted to say no, but the words came out wrong.

'I would need to be here by Saturday. It's the Queen's birthday. Pat and I were planning a bit of a shindig.'

'You'll be back in time for that. How old is she?'

'If you don't know, Smithy, I'm not saying. Every other woman in the land has the right to keep her age a secret and so should she. But she can't. She's the Queen. So we should celebrate the event but draw a veil over the detail.'

'So you'll do it?'

As I once said to Pat, you can make many choices in this life, which master, which mistress to serve, which path to go down; all except one. When it comes to Queen and Country, you have no choice at all. The Italians knew that. That's why I respected them, fought them as men made in my own fashion.

'Pat won't like it, but you leave that to me. It's about time I got my feet wet again.' I paused. I didn't like to mention it, but circumstance dictated. 'Usual rates, I take it?'

He nodded and straightened up, his manner changed, the studied languor of his arrival transformed into the brisk efficiency of his leaving. He'd got what he'd come for. It was just routine now.

'Fifty pounds. You can collect the gear from one of the Clearance Diving Officers. He'll dress you. We'll arrange for someone to take us through, so you'll have a free run. They're due in the 18th. We'll take a recce when she docks in the morning and dive in the evening. A couple of hours later and you'll be on the train back up to London, looking out from the inside of a large gin. Piece of pie.'

'I could take a little surprise down with me if you like, clamp it onto the hull, set the propeller for fifteen knots. She'd be in international waters before it blew.'

'Crabbie.'

'What, getting rid of those two? I'd be doing the world a service. I've got a couple of limpet mines, as it happens, stuffed in a shoebox. If anyone got the blame it would be that old fascist Borghese.'

Smithy stood up.

'April the seventeenth, Crabbie. On your best behaviour.'

'I better pencil it in, then.'

I fished out the pocket diary and turned the pages. 17th April 1780; first action between Admiral Rodney and de Guichen. Not a great success by all accounts. A greedy man who lived for the lining of his pocket rather than for the love of his country. Two days later, the 19th in 1587, Drake's singeing of the King's Beard at Cadiz. That was more like it. This would be a singeing of sorts. A symbolic singeing, I grant you, but doing something untoward to the Soviets' facial hair nevertheless. 1587, 1956. Three hundred and sixty-nine years between them and still the navy coming to the rescue. I took the little pencil tucked down the spine and licked the point.

'Well,' I said. 'The timing seems propitious, if nothing else.'

Four

I was held incommunicado, in a long gunmetal room, metal floors and metal walls. I felt sleepy, half drowned, spoonfuls of meat and potatoes grey in my mouth. Then I was back at the table, before me a packet of cigarettes and a glass of dusty water. I rubbed my hand over my face. My skin was smooth, as if I'd shaved myself. Perhaps I had. Serov sat opposite, with the mouthpiece. He had the same white file in front of him. He pushed the glass towards me. I was thirsty, but I was damned if I was going to take a drink.

'You have been sleeping, Commander.'

'Yes, funny that. I've a terrible crick in my neck. What day is it?'

He ignored my question.

'I have been talking to my superiors. They are intrigued by your arrival. What was he doing there? they ask. What does he want? Is he asking for asylum? Are you asking for asylum, Commander Crabb? Is life in England so terrible?' He chuckled.

'The First Secretary was most intrigued. What does he look like, he wants to know. Tall, short? Young, old? You know what I told him? I said I know what he looks like. I have known for years what he looks like. A little man with a large head.'

'A head that needs examining, I'll give you that.'

'Yes, you may give me that. A head that needs examining. Tell me, what sort of man is it who attempts such a thing, in daylight, with all our sentries posted all around, our guns shrouded, flags of good-will flying from every mast? A clever man, a stupid man?'

'I told you, a foolish one.'

'Possibly. But foolish or not, a man with a mission, a man who has done this many times before; last year, the year before, the year before that . . .' He rested his hand over the file. 'The list is long and tedious. You have made it your life's work. You have swallowed too much sea, perhaps, become addicted to its taste. You are what one calls a habitual offender, a recidivist. In the Soviet Union we have few such criminals.'

'I commend you. The reformed felon is something every civilized country should aspire to.'

Serov leant back on his chair and pressed his lips together. He could speak while barely moving his lips.

'We don't reform them, Commander. We shoot them. Every day they go for a walk in the exercise yard, and then one day . . .' He made a gun with his right hand. 'A bullet in the back of the head.'

'That's one way of dealing with the problem. A bit hard on the persistent pickpocket, though.'

'You British hang your criminals, break their necks like a chicken. Theatre rather than justice, I have always thought. Whatever his crimes, a man should be dispatched with regard to immediacy. Even Beria was shot.'

I took a sip of water. I needed it then. The dust caught on my throat.

'Whatever's most convenient. It makes no difference to me.'

'We will not shoot you. At least not yet. That would be a waste. We are not wastrels. We understand the need for good husbandry. As Mr Khrushchev said, when you catch a prize fish, you don't chuck him back. You set him on the scales, weigh him, see what his worth might be, see what he carries within him that might be of value.' He opened up the file. 'And that is what we are here to find out, Commander. What precious eggs you carry, your weight, your value. And if we find nothing, why then yes, a few days after we leave, we will return you to the sea, cold and without your swimming suit, and that will be the end of the matter. But you are a wise old fish. You have been swimming in these waters for a long time. You have much to impart, I am sure. The First Secretary and Prime Minister are busy in London. Their every waking hour is accounted for. As for me, imprisoned like you on board this ship, I have nothing to do. I twiddle my

16

thumbs. I read the papers. I see pictures of the First Secretary laying wreaths on war memorials, toasting banquets, receiving gifts of books and antiquities from ministers and mayors. And then you come along. It is almost as if the British have sent me a little present of my own.'

He turned his head in the air, struck by the thought.

*

We should go back a bit. How I got into this business in the first place. To tell you the truth, I'm not absolutely certain. Pat would say it was in the stars, and I can believe that. It certainly seemed like destiny, no matter what. Funny that, how one seems to slip into things without taking a bat's eye of the consequences. Not that I didn't want to join the navy. It's what I'd hoped for all my life. The problem was that for most of the time the navy didn't want me.

A brief history of Lionel Kenneth. An only child; father killed in World War One. Nothing special in that. A lot of fathers were. But I took a few knocks in his absence. As a consequence I had a stubborn manner as well as stubby legs, and a nose that was as inquisitive as it was unsightly. A bad thing for a boy, to have a horrid hooter. The best thing about my childhood was when the summer holidays came round and I was packed off to spend a month with my cousins in Eastbourne. We always stayed at the Grand, just down from Beachy Head. I liked the idea of a hotel, even then, how it was yours for as long as you wanted it to be, and then, when you went away, how it wasn't yours anymore. When you aren't there a hotel doesn't think about you for one minute, and you don't think about it either, but when you are there, if it is any damned good, it thinks about you all the time. It wakes you up in the morning and has your shoes ready outside the door. It makes your bed and puts clean bath towels on the rail and if it's filthy outside, it doesn't sulk or complain, but stands there commiserating, with a spread umbrella in its hand. After a while a hotel learns your little ways, good and bad, and keeps its knowledge, like its patrons' jewellery, well guarded, under lock and key. The Grand gave me the taste of something I've hankered after ever since. The very first time I stood in the lobby in my summer shorts,

17

seeing the floor numbers light up above the lift doors, listening to the little bell that the head porter picked up and rang as if it was part of a religious service, I understood the ramifications of a hotel; not simply as somewhere to stay, but as a preferred way of life. There's a philosophy attached to staying in a hotel, living a room that is, as far as you are concerned, disposable. It reminds you of what you are in this life: a traveller and that all ownership is illusory.

The Grand stood (still does, I imagine) back from King Edward's Parade, with lawns and trees to protect it from the crush. You couldn't see much from the ground floor, the lobby, the dining room, the ballroom, but upstairs, in those little bedrooms we would share, oh what sights! While my cousins went swimming I would sit by the window, much as I sit here now, in the playpen of my days, looking down, not at the wind-chased leaves and the huddles of frozen people, but at sailing ships and steamers and the sea sweeping back and forth, like a great hand of time. I would sit there for hours, wondering at all it might bring in, and all it might take away. It held me like a hypnotist's watch, entranced, ready to obey its every wish. Sometimes the three of us would walk up to the cliff and stand on the top, feeling it pulling you towards the edge like a magnet in a schoolboy's pocket. We'd dare each other to see how near we would go, and I always beat them, not because I was braver or more foolhardy, but because I simply accepted the nature of its strength and its hold over me. When I looked down, I looked, not to the cliffs, but to the depth of the sea below, knowing that when I grew up I would find myself within those waters, and somehow contrive to be the master of them. Schoolboys can believe such tomfoolery.

Later, I went to Brighton College. Did nothing and learnt less. As soon as I could I got apprenticed to the merchant navy and joined a packet ship, plying between Buenos Aires and New York. I was a roamer then. I wanted to see the world as any young man with spirit should, with nothing but a few coins in his pocket and a bag to sling across his shoulder. Adventure, that's what I wanted, escape. The merchant navy was all right as far as that was concerned, but it had one great drawback. You had to join a union. Didn't like the idea of that at all. Never have. It's one thing to sign up to an organization that works to serve one's country. It's quite another to sign up to one that works to serve one's self. Topsy-turvy thinking, and I wasn't having any of it. So I tried my luck on dry land, joined the oil business. It sounded enticing enough, what with oil fields and oil wells and untapped gushers waiting to change your life, but it didn't work out that way. I ended up selling petrol in a filling station in Windgap, Pennsylvania. One street, one diner and men who called me partner. I'm so sorry, will you excuse me. I returned to London.

To save money I shared a flat with a young man who, though good company, liked the bottle a little too much. His parents decided to send him to China, as a sort of cure. Pretty daft idea, considering the vices available on that particular subcontinent, but they sent him all the same, and asked me to go along as a sort of chaperone. Another pretty daft idea, but I accepted readily enough. Two suitcases apiece, enough insect-repellent to swab the decks with, and a wind-up gramophone on top of a trunk full of the family's seventy-eights. Puccini with the porthole open, the ship surging over the chords. During the voyage over I gave the stewards strict instruction to serve him only fruit juice and tonic water and whenever we called into port I locked him in his cabin while I took in the sights. We started off friends, but by the time we got to Shanghai he was pretty much my mortal foe, with a nasty craving for morphine. He'd drunk a lot of tonic.

But China. China was endless, another earth. China showed me how hard it was to make sense of it all. China showed me the anonymity of man.

On the way back cabin life became even more combustible. I jumped ship at Singapore, thinking I might stay and learn the lingo, but it was no good. I was keen but I was also tone deaf. If there's one thing you need when you want to talk turkey to a Chinaman, it's a sense of pitch. Otherwise you'll say something you shouldn't and end floating down the Yangtze with your throat cut from ear to ear, and quite right too.

Back in England I found I hadn't a penny to my name. One

of the Eastbourne cousins got me a job modelling a truss for a newspaper advertisement. I had to go to this first-floor room in Soho, above a butcher's shop. I'd never really been to Soho before. It was another foreign land, a different kind of jabbering than in Singapore, but a jabbering all the same, all mixed up, right and wrong. I stripped down to my underwear and got strapped in. The photographer told me that I had the perfect figure for this line of work; to wit, short legs, a compact upper torso, and a head that was too big for my body. It was meant as a complement but ever since school I was sensitive about such things.

'Perhaps that's because I'm still wearing my hat,' said I.

I took it off. He peered through his viewfinder again.

'No,' he said. 'If anything it looks even bigger.'

He told me I should hold my arms like a Greek thinker. I informed him that I was neither a Greek nor a thinker, and what was more I was putting my hat back on. I left with three pounds in my pocket and the job done. I saw the photograph in a paper a couple of months later. Everything but the head. I wasn't asked again.

I tried other oddities, anything that came to hand. I didn't want a normal job, something in an office, running after bits of paper, wiping my shoes on the back of my trousers for fear of what the boss might think. I wanted something out of the ordinary, something that had no right to work, something ridiculous, or downright dangerous. Wasn't that a bit like the world was anyway, a bit ridiculous, a bit dangerous, a bit bloody marvellous? Isn't that how it is for us? The world all in bits? I could see how the rest of London coped, on the trams and buses, sharing the everyday burden, but I couldn't see myself joining in. Not that I thought any the less of them. If anything I thought the less of me. A square peg if ever there was one.

It was about this time I ran into Maitland, again through one of the Eastbournes. He was an adventurer like me, only plumper and jollier and with a lot more brain cells. Always on the lookout for the coming thing that would make his fortune, that was Maitland. Inventions, madcap schemes, new fads, they were his staple diet. When I first met him he was involved with this Frenchman, de Corlieu, who had devised what he called a pair of 'swimfins' that allowed a swimmer to balance in the water, and gave him greater speed. At the time I couldn't for the life of me see why any sane man would want either. Maitland took me up to his office, drew down the blind and unlocked the bottom drawer of his desk. They were wrapped up in newspaper, like a fish supper.

'What do you think, Lionel?'

That's what they did in those days, called me Lionel.

I picked them up. They were black and made of thick rubber. It would be ungentlemanly to tell you what they smelt like.

'They'll never catch on,' I told him. 'Who's going to wander round Eastbourne with these monstrosities at the end of their legs? They'd be run off the beach.'

We went to see a demonstration in the Marshall Street Baths, stopping off for one or two on the way. By the time we got there, I felt quite tropical. We lined up on the side and watched as this woman waddled out in a black bathing cap, a black swimsuit and those black swimfins. All she needed was a ball on the end of her nose. Someone started to laugh.

'See what I mean?' I said. 'It's not what a woman craves, Maitland, unbridled ridicule.'

She jumped into the water and started to thrash about. She wasn't very good, swimfins or no.

"It looks to me as if they hinder rather than help,' I observed.

'We need some personal verification,' Maitland insisted. 'Why don't you try?'

'Why don't I?' I replied and slipping out the door, skipped down the stairs, past the changing rooms and out into the street. Maitland found me, an hour later, trying to explain mah-jong to an Irish barman.

'That was very inconsiderate of you,' he said.

'Since I left school I've only got undressed in front of strangers once. I'll not do it again.'

I made another trip to Singapore, to make another stab at learning the language. If I couldn't speak it properly at least I could learn to write it. Maitland had some contacts out there and set me up with a family who not only found me a job, but took me into their home and their hearts. I became apprenticed to an embalmer. Yes, I know, but that was the whole point of the world then. We hadn't been taken over by career prospects and civil servants and buff-coloured forms. You could walk the crooked mile and no one would bat an eyelid. By day I learnt the art of showing respect; how to honour the dead; to appreciate the dignity of knowing one's place. By night I would sit on the porch and practise conversation and characters with the man and his wife. In the hours in between I would play Grand-mother's footsteps with their little boy. It became my first home, and those three people my first family. I was happy with them in a way I had never been with my own or any other family, and I was old enough to understand why. For me to feel at home anywhere, I needed to be a stranger, a stranger amongst friends. I needed people not to understand me fully and for me not fully to understand them; to get by with winks and nods and a kind of naive trust. To belong but to be an outsider; both joined and separated. It was so simple, the secret of my happiness, and yet the knowledge of it didn't help much, to know that was all I was capable of. It seemed to cast me off from the rest of folk; while they increased their baggage I would always be a one-suitcase man.

I stayed just under twelve months. Before I left, the head of the house gave me a piece of polished jade that hung on a thread of silk. The stone was curved, like the cut of a pirate's sword, and it shone a shifting green, milky, like the colour of their moon. I was uncertain as to what to do with it. I'd never been one for jewellery; it cheap-ens a man. He stood me up and placed it round my neck. It felt light, almost warm.

'Wear it at all times if you can,' he said. 'It is a good piece. It will give you calm, bring you to your strength.'

And I believed him, believed in the power in which he trusted, just as I believed in the delicacy of those brushstrokes and the strength of the Chinese character. But when I got down to the docks

I cut the silk away with my penknife and replaced it with a length of fishline. Not as pretty but a damned sight safer. It was stuck with me now.

I returned to England in 1938. I was twenty-eight years old. When I got off the boat train I tried to find Maitland but he'd moved offices. I made the rounds of his drinking troughs but they hadn't seen him either. It was a wearing business, chasing that plump shadow, so I popped into an hotel on Duke Street, the Cavendish, for some afternoon refreshment. It looked quiet enough and I was tired. I bought a drink and took it to a seat by the window. The next thing I knew it was dark and someone was kicking my leg.

'And who are you?'

A thin woman, with crackly skin and necklaces and brooches and something sparkling in her hair, was standing over me.

'Crabb's the name, Lionel Crabb. I seem to have fallen asleep.'

I picked up the glass, but she took it from my hand.

'Licensing laws,' she said. 'You're three hours outside the limit, unless you're a resident.' She peered down at me. 'You're not a resident, are you?'

'I'm not, more's the pity. I like the way they don't muck you about here, don't you? Damn comfortable too.'

She kicked me again.

'Do you always swear in front of elderly women?'

'Nearly always, yes.'

She seemed relieved. She nodded to the bag at my feet.

'Are you by any chance a vagrant?'

'Pretty much.'

'A vagrant looking for a room?'

'Pretty much.'

She pointed to the ceiling.

'The hotel has rooms.'

'Yes, but I have no money.'

'Then all you can hope for is an unpleasant box room at the top.' She turned to a man standing in the shadows. I hadn't noticed him before.

'Edwards, we do have something nasty and poky that we can offer this young vagrant? Possibly one that smells?'

'We have a number, madam.'

'Good. Pick out our dampest.' She turned back. 'Edwards will bring you a key. You can go up now and finish your sleep. I dare say you'll need a bath afterwards. Hot water is available between half five and six. Dinner will be at eight. You can tell me all about being a vagrant then. Only don't make things up. I don't like that.' She kicked me for the third time. 'I mean it. I don't like that.'

'And I mean it too. I don't have any money.'

She adjusted her tiara or whatever it was.

'Would you be willing to do a few odd jobs around the place, in lieu as they say.'

'Not really, no. I expect to be pretty busy. I aim to join the navy.'

'That explains the unfortunate beard, I suppose. I take it you'll jump ship at the earliest opportunity, then?'

'That's the idea.'

She stood there considering.

'Edwards, perhaps we ought to give the Admiral a slightly better room. But at the back, out of sight from our regulars. We don't want to curdle their custard.'

Edwards shuffled off. I stood up. Bad manners of course not to stand earlier, but a year in Singapore had made me forget the British niceties.

'Forgive me if this offends,' I enquired, 'but do you work here?'

'Work here!' She waved her bangles in front of me. 'Dear boy, do I look like I work here? No, no, no. I own here. I live here. Live I might add in considerable splendour on the third floor, a floor to which you might, one day, be invited, but on which you will never reside.'

Rose Lewis was her name but we all called her the Duchess, the Duchess of Duke Street. I found work soon enough, from one of her regulars, but only as a stopgap. I had a notion that war was coming and I was beginning to be worried. I'd led an erratic, irresponsible life, nothing to be ashamed of, but now I didn't want to be thought of as someone unable to buckle down any longer. I had my sights on the Royal Naval Volunteer Reserve, give that jade something to do. Though Maitland and his merry men turned up soon enough, most evenings I stayed in my room, studying naval gunnery. Maitland would bang on my door and shout, 'Come out for dinner, you old hermit, enjoy life!' and though I gave in every now and again, I was determined. I read my books, I wrote off my applications, I waited.

I've never got the hang of interviews. Anyone can ask half-baked questions when they have a mind to, but if one has an ounce of self-respect, it's hard to bend to their reasoning. When it came, what a farce it turned out to be. The man sat across a table, twitching his nose and firing questions at me like they were bullets. I seemed to spend most of the time avoiding them. I can remember some of them and his rat-trap face.

'Skills?'

'I would like some, yes.'

'Do you have any skills.'

'Most definitely.'

'And what would they be?'

'Embalming and modelling, though not in that order.'

'Can you swim?'

'Only in water. However, with swimfins I anticipate a considerable improvement.'

He sniffed the air.

'Swimfins?'

'A new invention. You strap them over your feet. They assist balance, increase speed. An acquaintance of mine is thinking of manufacturing them. If you like, I could secure you a batch for a trial run. At very reasonable rates, I am sure.'

His face grew to a point, and he started to nibble at his questions.

'You are a sales representative of this firm?'

'No. Just a disinterested bystander.'

'It is quite improper for you to use this interview as a sales opportunity. If you have something to sell you should make representations to the proper purchasing authority.' He squirmed, as if his tail was giving him trouble.

'Let's leave it, shall we. I assure you I am not a salesman.'

'And by the look of things perhaps not a member of the Royal Naval Volunteer Reserve either.'

'Oh?'

'Your age. Twenty-eight.'

'A very proper age for a twenty-eight-year-old, wouldn't you say?'

'It may be proper for you, Mr Crabb, but it is far too old for a Royal Naval Volunteer.'

He held his paws out as far apart as he could and smiled; two neat little pointed rows of pure savagery.

'By about this much.'

Thank you so very much.

*

The war came. I managed to wangle a post as a merchant-seaman gunner on a tanker bound for Aruba, then negotiated a transfer to the Royal Naval Patrol Service. Most of the chaps I trained with ended up petty officers, but they took one look at me and sent me out an able seaman. I sailed with the trawlers and learnt a fisherman's trade. I worked harder than I'd ever worked before, thrown onto a sea I had only heard about, terrible and vast. I think it was Sherpa Tensing who once said that the Himalayas put the human being into perspective, but avalanches excepted, at least mountains stay put. Two years in, 1941, I got my commission. Now, I thought, I could show them what I might be capable of. I checked in for the medical; just a formality, I was told. I stuck out my tongue, held in my breath, and introduced them to parts of my body that rarely see the light of day. They poked and prodded and pounced on my one weakness. My left eye. There's nothing wrong with it, really. It just wanders about a bit from time to time and consequently finds it hard to fix on things, particularly at a distance. They tut-tut-tutted and wrote it down on their little forms. I said that Nelson only had one eye and it hadn't held him back much. They smiled and debarred me from further service at sea.

Thank you so very much.

I volunteered for special duties down at Dover. During the day I was Drainage Officer and lorded it over picks and pumps. At night I hung around the bars, like a judy touting for business. Buy the right man a drink, I reasoned, and I might strike lucky, find a kindred spirit willing to help me in my quest. After two months and my wages blown and eight pounds on my bar tab, I struck lucky. I found that kindred spirit, a captain. On day one I introduced myself. Day two I told him of my plight. By the end of the week he had wangled me a transfer to Mine and Bomb Disposal. I was in. I never thanked that man properly. His name was Malcolm. He had a beard like mine. He claimed he could do the *Times* crossword while his morning egg boiled and I believed him. For ten days he was my best friend, the man I waited to see at the end of a gruelling day. When it was time for me to go, we promised to meet up when it was all over. He gave me his address. I gave him mine. On the day I left he drove me to the station, and just before I boarded the train, presented me with a lavatory brush as a going-away present. I laughed and waved it out the window at him as the train pulled out. I never saw him again and when the war was done, never once tried to get in contact with him. I don't even remember ever thinking about him until these blanket days and the regime of recollection they have imposed. How could I have wiped such a selfless gesture from the blackboard, when it led to the rest of my life? I cannot even recall his surname. Malcolm, perhaps you were the one link that I should have kept, who might have moored me to Queen Bess's shores. Perhaps in severing you, I severed my rights as a full-blooded Englishman. And even that is a thought not to be wished. I hang my head, appalled by such a propulsion of egocentricity.

I arrived back in London, late October '41. It was good to be back, despite the bombings and seeing buildings you knew thrown up into a heap of bricks. The city seemed to have come together. Defiance, the papers said, the spirit of London, but it wasn't just that.

Folk were enjoying themselves more, that was the long and short of it; determined to take pleasure in even the simplest of things. Life is a marvellous tonic when there's only one alternative.

That first morning I helped Rose put away the bamboo summer furniture and bring up the heavier, winter stuff. She always changed them over on a given date, whatever the weather. As I set out the last pair in the bay window, I noticed that Edwards was polishing the cups she'd won, shooting big game in Kenya.

'Some special occasion in the offing?' I asked her.

'I was at the Café Royal the other evening,' she said, 'and met some very presentable Poles there. Officers, naturally. They looked a bit down in the dumps, so I've asked them over for a drink at seven. Invite some of your crowd, why don't you. Make a party of it.'

By then you couldn't open an umbrella in Hyde Park without poking some foreign national's eye out. London was chock-a-block with them, Canadians, Belgians, Australians. Some we liked better than others. The Canadians meant well but their social graces were still frozen in the tundra. The French had the manners, but considering they'd already caved in held an unwarranted high opinion of themselves. But we all had time for the Poles. They were like us, from a small country which refused to give in. We took to them before we'd ever clapped eyes on them, and once we had, we took to them even more.

I got hold of Maitland, and armed with a pocketful of petty cash we went foraging at Fortnum's. There was no food shortage, really, if you knew where to go and had the right name. The Duchess's moniker worked just fine. Strictly speaking I didn't approve, but it's difficult to act on one's principles when one of London's finest veal and ham pies is staring back at you. After three-quarters of an hour of selfless sacrifice, we retired to the fourth floor for a couple of gins. Maitland was in good form. Despite the bleak news, the war in the east seemed to be cheering him up no end.

'It's pretty desperate out there, by all accounts,' he said, 'though no one appreciates the size of that country. Their struggle might be titanic, but so is their resolve. Behold the monster Polypheme.' I wasn't sure what he meant.

'I don't wish any one ill in this business,' said I, 'but I can't say I've much time for the Soviets. To my way of thinking, they're just as bad as who we're up against. A bunch of b's, the lot of them.'

Maitland banged his glass down.

'You mustn't say that,' he admonished. 'They're our allies now, fighting a common foe.'

'And what happens afterwards,' I said, 'if Uncle Joe wins?'

'*When* Uncle Joe wins.' He leant forward, with a look suddenly drained of all guile. 'Why, we'll have a new world, Crabbie,' he said. 'Better for you, better for me, better for everyone.'

I held my peace. That was the difference between Maitland and me. I didn't want a new world, a better one. He did. That difference in feeling divided a lot of people, both during the war and after. A lot of us realized we were fighting for a world that would no longer be there when it was all over; others were fighting for the world to come. By rights, the latter should have waded in with greater enthusiasm than the former, but I think that knowing what we did made people like me strive that little bit harder. We knew it would be the last time we'd see the land we loved the way we liked it best.

By six o'clock everything was prepared. Rose had brought the ballroom candlesticks up from the cellar. The lounge bar was ablaze, the lights flickering in the tall gilt-edged mirrors. With the dark red velvet curtains and plates of pies and Edwards dressed in his finest flunkey, the place looked all ready for one of those eighteenth-century orgies. You'd never have guessed it from the outside. It made you wonder what other shenanigans the blackout covered up. Rose stood by the fireplace in a long black dress belted in tightly at the hip and flaring out over a pair of little hand-stitched boots. A proper little Cossack, I said, and to my surprise she blushed. I wasn't used to handing out compliments, but it had never occurred to me that she wasn't used to receiving them. I'd roped in Lofty Gordon and a friend of his, up from HMS *Vernon* on a weekend pass, and Maitland had drummed up a few pen-pushers from some government department or other, older chaps most of them, except for one lanky looking fellow, tall, with a chill, haughty expression, who took himself off to one corner, tapping his fingers at the decor.

'Who the devil's that,' I whispered.

'That? That's Anthony.' There was a certain reverence in his voice. 'Quite a character. Quite an authority on painting, would you believe.'

'He looks like a camel, ready to spit.'

Maitland laughed. 'Hey, Anthony,' he called out. 'Lionel here thinks you look like a camel.'

The man raised his head, and pointed to the ceiling.

'Or a whale, perhaps?'

'Very like a whale,' Maitland replied, and they both laughed uproariously. I couldn't see the joke myself. My remark might have bothered him more than he cared to show, though, for he quickly got up and went to look at the pictures on the stairwell.

'Is he strictly necessary?' I put to Maitland. ' He doesn't look the party type.'

'Oh, don't you believe it. High-spirited young men are very much Anthony's cup of cocoa,' and he laughed again. I understood that one, and didn't care for it. It must have showed, because he added, 'Don't look so put out, Lionel. Actually he's very eager to meet some Poles, sound out their point of view. He takes an interest, you know, in the way of the world.'

Our guests rolled in on the dot of seven, each one carrying a highly polished wooden box held out in their arms, like the wise men of the Bible. They bowed before Rose, clicked their heels and solemnly carried their gifts to the bar. Inside each one lay two bottles of vodka with a dozen little glasses set alongside. They broke open the seals as if they were in possession of the elixir of life. I said as much to Rose. She dismissed the remark with a wave of her hand.

'The Poles take a different attitude to alcohol than the rest of us,' she explained. 'For us drinking is an act of relaxation. To them it's as if they're back in the saddle, leading a cavalry charge. There's no quarter given.' She nodded towards the rank of bottles. 'We'll be expected to drink all that, you know.'

'Well, I'm starting off with a proper pint,' I told her. 'This is England, after all.' I walked to the bar and intimated to Edwards to start pulling. He drew two jars.

'Your good health,' I said to the fellow nearest me and put a glass to my lips indicating that he should follow suit. He lifted the glass, took one look at it and swigged it back as fast as possible. I could tell by the uncomfortable way he swallowed, he abhorred the taste. I'd had the same problem at school, with Thursday's beetroot. I stuck my hand out.

'Crabb. Lionel.'

'Kazhynski,' he said, at least that's what it sounded like. 'Eugene.'

I nodded and pointed to his uniform.

'Air Force?' In those days we thought all Poles were pilots.

'Air Force!' The man pointed to something wavy on his shoulder. 'Navy.'

'Snap,' I said, adding, 'Me too. I work with unexploded mines and such. And you?'

'I am an aide de camp to the best man in the world,' he announced, and pouring two little glasses, thrust one out at me. If it wasn't for the fact he was smiling, I'd have said he was looking for a fight.

'My mother always says that I am the best man in the world,' I said, taking up the challenge. 'But she must be mistaken.'

'Your mother has never met the General,' he said. 'So how would she know? But after the General I am sure your mother is most certainly right. And do not be ashamed. It is a great achievement still, to be the second-best man in the world.'

'You are very generous, though I'm afraid here the phrase "second best" has quite a different meaning to second best. It very much hinders one's promotion prospects, to be thought of as such. Which in my case, explains a great deal.'

'Ah. I have insulted you.'

'Indeed, but more politely than most.' I did to his vodka what he had done to Rose's beer. I was no virgin when it came to knowing my way around the optics, but I never imagined such a trivial amount could pack such a punch. A couple of rounds of that and even Randolph Turpin would be out for the count.

'This General you're so enamoured with,' I said, squeezing the words out as best I could. 'Would that be General Sikorski?'

'You have heard of him?'

Everybody had heard of Sikorski. Fought alongside the French until it was all over, then flew his men to London to fight again another day. A man of honour, dedicated to his country's cause. I nodded.

'Yes, I've heard of him. You are right and my mother is wrong. He *is* the best man in the world.'

He beamed and shouted, 'Jan! I have found a new friend!'

He clapped me on the shoulder and poured me another. I took it as it was meant, for I knew then how this had begun and how this would end. We were tied to each other without knowing why, ropes and knots of unravelled feelings pulling us together. We wouldn't talk about it, but there it was. We took comfort in it. Men can be like that sometimes.

I can only remember the rough outline of what happened that night. The drinking very quickly became more regimented. They'd line the glasses up in long rows and on the command, toss them back. We all joined in. Their laughter and enthusiasm knew no constraints. They were infectious, boisterous, radiating a kind of reckless charm. You could see why, as a race, they made good fighter pilots. Every now and again one of them would stand on a chair and make a speech, shouting to the ceiling and to his compatriots below and they'd all cheer, fling another drink back and start again. Girlfriends arrived; music started up, first an accordion, then a violin. Suddenly couples were dancing, throwing themselves around the room. By the end of the evening they all seemed to have multiplied tenfold. Perhaps they had. Perhaps we all had. Perhaps there was another Maitland in the room, another Lofty, another me. Perhaps it was the other me who led a chorus of the 'Eton Boating Song', perhaps it was another Lofty who demonstrated the rules of rugger with the hotel's ice bowl. The bar grew noisier, and the chatter louder; the wax in the candles started to run freely; coats were discarded, ties loosened, pies devoured; the walls of the Cavendish seem to close in. I shouted first at one man and then another and had no idea what I was saying. I might have even danced, but I have no memory of it, only the giddy feeling that made me step outside and press my face against the cold glass in the foyer doors.

'Quite an evening,' I heard a voice say.

I turned. Maitland was standing at the foot of the stairs, his face quite flushed. A young man was pushing past him, handkerchief to his face, eager to get back to the fray.

'I'll say.'

He lowered his voice. 'Guess what? I've just had one of those girls they brought along, up in one of the alcoves in the first floor. She pleasured me standing up, if you don't mind. You don't get that on a Friday evening whist drive.'

I didn't say anything. Maitland was a married man, but like so many of his ilk, a bar full of pretty young things was a treat he could not lightly cast aside. It happened a lot then, but only if you let it.

I went back inside. Rose was being whirled about from one man to the other and loving every minute of it. I stood back as they all cheered and clapped, with their faces all flushed with an intoxication that seemed to be consuming the very oxygen I breathed. I felt like a witness to something to which I did not belong. What was all this revelry in aid of? The fact that we were at war, the fact that some of us would die; that it didn't do to look too deeply into a fellow's motives, or that we were all faced with living a kind of awe-inspiring nothing? Suddenly I was aware of Maitland's friend, Anthony, standing beside me, his long fingers held to pursed, disdainful lips.

'A conundrum, isn't it,' he said, 'our condition? So commonplace, yet so compulsive.'

I was about to agree when my chap Eugene stood up, clapped his hands and started to speak The room went quiet and everyone stopped drinking. Even the girls they had brought along smoothed down their dresses and took notice. He began quietly enough, but slowly rose in temperature as his mouth grew wider and his face grew darker and small drops of spittle began to form on the edges of his lips. He swayed back and forth, one hand clutching the air. Half the candles had gone out and his long shadow sputtered across the ceiling like an avenging angel swooping down from on high. Then he raised his little glass, yelled one word and hurled it into the fire. Without warning there came a hail of them, flying across the room, everyone shouting the name at the top of their voice. Catherine it sounded like, like the Russian Queen my old history master used to go on about. Normal chatter resumed, somewhat subdued. Eugene stepped down, crossed over to the fireplace and kicked back the shards of glass that had bounced out onto the carpet. We went over to join him.

'That was quite a party piece,' I said. 'Usually we end the proceedings with a couple of rounds of flip the kipper.'

He struck his chest.

'My apologies. But it is very hard for us, this treaty we have made with Russia, when we suspect them of the most terrible thing.'

And he told us. Even now, I find it hard to bring myself to talk about it, for the truth is that I've worked the second half of my life for the country responsible for that crime, worn its uniform, saluted its leaders, and yes, even celebrated its successes (we were all so proud of Gagarin, and his predecessor, that poor unfortunate dog). I'll probably get the facts wrong, but it went something like this. In 1941 General Sikorski met Stalin and later made an agreement with Ivan Maisky, the Soviet Ambassador in London. They were to forget their differences and join forces to fight against the Germans. Polish soldiers on Russian soil, and when the tide turned, Russian soldiers on Polish soil. All working towards the liberation of their lands. As a mark of good faith there was to be an amnesty provided for all the Poles captured by the Soviets in '39. Sixteen thousand men all told. But so far no one had seen hide nor hair of them. When asked, the Russians said they knew nothing about them, they should ask the Germans. The Germans said they knew nothing either. Sixteen thousand men, vanished. Towards the end of '41 the Poles had come to suspect that their compatriots had all been murdered, shot on Stalin's orders, their hands tied behind their back, and buried in mass graves in some forest. And they had the name of the place where this foulness took place. Katyn.

'And the more questions we ask,' Eugene told us, 'the angrier the Russians grow.'

Anthony, fired up, was in argumentative mood.

'And wouldn't you be angry, to be accused in such a manner,' he said. 'To have the word of your enemy believed, rather than your own, an ally?'

Eugene looked him carefully in the eye.

'I do not believe either of them, my friend. All I know is that between them, they have destroyed my country.'

Anthony wagged a finger. They were quite the most delicate-looking hands I had ever seen on a man.

'One invaded your country two years ago on September 3rd. The other is fighting that enemy, not solely on behalf of their own country, but for the good of mankind. It's an aesthetic view of the world they hold. They have no time for detective stories.'

Eugene shrugged his shoulders.

'All we want is the truth, but everyone seems afraid of what the truth might reveal. Even your own country seems reluctant to help.'

Anthony sniffed.

'There have been many truths that should have been told to this world, truths that history has been only too willing to obscure. Why this one, above all others?'

And with that he walked away.

'Your friend,' Eugene said carefully, 'is he in the navy, like yourself?'

'No. I . . .' And then I realized. I didn't know what he did.

I couldn't sleep that night, thinking of what had been said. I'd never thought much about politics before, though I'd never liked the Russians. How could you trust a set-up that had shoved their royal family down the cellar steps, who preferred that praying mantis Lenin to the dignity of a Tsar? It upset me enough when someone sent a letter with the postage stamp the wrong way up. The bank did it once and I chucked it back at them straight away. 'When you put the King's head on the correct way I might read whatever it is you have written,' I wrote on the flap. 'Until then, no show.' I got it back the next day, but the damage had been done. I stuffed it, unopened, in the desk drawer all the same.

Politics seemed rather unnecessary, if you know what I mean. Every four years you voted Conservative. At all other times you simply got on with it; watched the Boat Race, put money on the Grand National, and hoped that England held her nerve when it came to the Ashes. It all seemed rather grubby, wanting more, wanting better, *agitating* for things. Life wasn't about that. At least not the one I wanted to lead. God threw the dice and you took whatever number came up. Complaining didn't do any good. But after that night, I understood what might lead a man to bomb-throwing, to revolution, to anarchy. It wasn't politics. It was justice, what was right. The idea that our lot had been dragging their feet on the issue, and not holding the Soviets to account, didn't sit easily with me at all. The woman with the scales, the one we were so proud of, was blindfolded, remember?

I saw quite a lot of Eugene that week. It made a change to go along to their club and be admitted into their close huddle of comradeship. It was like riding into Sherwood Forest and coming across Robin Hood and his band of merry men. They looked you over, threw you a test or two, and if you passed, you became one of them. It was the nearest I'd got to men at war, and I liked what it had done to them. They were a wild, childish lot, but there was honesty in their infancy, and their love for the mischievous was impossibly contagious. I'd never been to university, but in those seven days I had an inkling of what a rag week must be like.

My papers came through. They sent me to HMS *Volcano* up in Cumberland where I nearly flunked it. It was all so technical. The theory of electricity, positive, negatives, how you could charge a whole ship with one force, I couldn't follow it at all, nor could I remember the details of the enemy bombs, the layout of the gubbins within. Every time I was sent out in front of the class to defuse a dummy I returned to my desk having apparently destroyed most of Lake Windermere. The interviewer had been right all along. I was too old, and incompetent to boot. After a fortnight they washed their hands of me and packed me off to Swansea. Although it had been badly mauled, there were no unexploded bombs there for me to add to the wreckage. I sat on my backside, feeling sorry for myself. Every now and again I'd be called out to examine an old oil drum washed up on the shore, or on one occasion, five footballs tied up in a string bag. I used to sit in the little hut I had, with the table and the telephone, and shout to the teapot, 'You're useless, Crabb. Bloody useless.' In the evenings I would walk the shoreline and stare out to sea, thinking that perhaps there wasn't anything out there for me after all. My time had come and my time had gone and I hadn't been there for either.

Then one morning the telephone rang. There was an excited, breathless voice on the other end.

'Are you the bomb-disposal chappie?'

'I am.'

'Thank the Lord. I am the Mayor. Something's cropped up.'

I sat up. This was more like it.

'It's a matter of some urgency. Could you come over to the Town Hall pronto. Bring your stuff with you.'

The Town Hall!

I got on my bicycle and pedalled over. He was standing on the steps, wearing his chain. He looked grim.

'Have you evacuated the building?' I asked. He shook his head.

'This way.'

He conducted me through a series of panelled corridors and marble stairways. Every time he passed an open door, clerks would jump to their feet and shout, 'Good morning, Your Worship.' In his office two women were standing round looking worried. He led me into a large room with a dais at the end. All around the walls were pictures of former mayors. Same chain, same suit, same florid skin. As a race, they ate well, mayors.

'This is my chamber,' he said.

'I thought it might be. Very nice.'

'That's the problem,' he said. 'There.'

He pointed to the throne on the dais. Apart from the coat-of-arms stuck on the back it was quite empty.

'Where?' I said.

He clicked his mouth, impatiently.

'There. The clock on the wall. It's stopped. I think the clerk must have overwound it. I was hoping you might be able to fix it. You know all about timing mechanisms, springs, that sort of thing.'

I looked down at my bicycle clips. In the excitement I'd quite forgotten to take them off.

'You brought me here to mend your clock?'

Though I'd kept my voice as flat as I thought decent, I think he detected a slight piquancy in the timbre, for he started to finger his chain.

'It's not my clock,' he insisted, 'it's the Mayor's. The Mayor can't hold proper functions if his clock has stopped. Think of the dignity of the office. You can't have a mayor with a stopped clock. I've a meeting this afternoon.'

I reflected for a moment. He was looking at me, tapping his foot.

'No, I suppose you can't. But wouldn't a watchmaker be preferable to a bomb-disposal officer? There must be one in this town.'

He took himself to the window before answering.

'There were two. One's serving in North Africa, the other ran off with his wife.' He span round. 'Anyway, that's hardly the point. You've got nothing better to do, sunning yourself on our beach. Now, can you mend it or not?'

I took it down from the wall and cycled back, with the clock balanced on the handlebars. It was a nice-looking thing. Once at the hut I opened up my bag of tricks and got to work. It didn't take me long. When I was finished I placed the clock thirty yards away on a stretch of shingle, ran the wires over to the hut, then rang the mayor's office.

'Could I speak to His Worship.'

'He's very busy.'

'Tell him it's concerning his clock.'

He came on the line.

'Mr Mayor?'

'Yes.'

'Lionel Crabb here. I think I've solved your problem. Would you care to listen for a moment.'

I held the receiver out the window and pressed the plunger. The bang was more musical than most.

'There. I don't think you'll have any more trouble with it,' I said and hung up.

The call from Cumberland came two days later.

'Your Mayor is not pleased.'

'No.'

'He was going to have you charged with criminal damage until we pointed out that interfering with the duties of the armed forces carried even severer penalties.'

'Interfering with my duties. That's a useful one to remember.'

'The police were pretty browned off too. Explosions like that tend to disturb the populace. The nearby factory had to close, you know. Most of the innards crashed through their skylight. A whole morning's production lost, thanks to you. Not good when you're fighting a war.'

'Yes, I can see that. Well, what would you like me to do?'

'Frankly, Crabb, we wouldn't mind you drowning. Going down and not coming up.'

'Yes, I can see that.'

'We're sending you out to Gibraltar. Unfortunately there's no one else available. Still, there's lot of deep water there. Quite a few mines too. Between the two of them, our prayers might be answered.'

★

I travelled up to London that night and took the next plane out.

Five

Not long ago, dressing myself as usual, my old mess jacket, the checked shirt (something Rosa brought up for me, though it's a little too loud for my liking), the trousers with the loose button, I found I couldn't do up my shoelaces. Just couldn't, the loop of the knot slipping through my fingers. I used to be something of a perfectionist when it came to knots, you needed to be in my line of work; capstan, bowline, triple lark's head, I could do them with my eyes shut. Still do. Yet there I was, stranded on the wreck of a reef knot.

'It's too bloody cold in here, that's what it is,' I shouted, blowing on my hands. 'Put some blood in the radiator,' but I knew it wasn't anything to do with the temperature. I sat on the edge of my bed, staring down at the untied laces lying limply over the leather. The state of man.

Rosa was unreasonably late that morning and by the time she appeared I was heartily sick of the sight of them. She came in with the day-old paper tucked under her arm and the tray bearing my glass of tepid tea and regulation slice of rye bread, but I waved them away angrily, pointing at my boots. At first she didn't understand and started taking out the extra rug stored under the bedstead.

'Shoes, woman,' I shouted, 'I can't . . .' and I waved my useless hands in her face.

'Shoes?' she repeated and I realized I'd been speaking English again. She got the message though and squatting down, hoiked one of my feet onto her lap and starting pulling at the laces.

'Shoes,' she said again, tapping at the leather, 'very good,' and it was true. Russian footwear can be of surprisingly good quality. They deserve to be; they've a lot to keep out. Anything exterior, boots, overcoats, hats, you can't go far wrong. It's the stuff underneath that's so God-awful. Anyway there I was, sticking my legs out one after the other, when I remembered Gagarin telling me the time he was walking down the red carpet after his historic flight in *Vostock 1* and discovered his laces were undone.

'Imagine it, Lev Lvovich,' he said, 'with Khrushchev and Brezhnev and all the other top brass waiting at the other end and me with my bootlaces trailing on the ground. I was terrified. One wrong step and I would have landed up in Khrushchev's arms.'

'You'd have been all right,' I told him. 'He was a great one for bear hugs.'

Yurka liked to talk about that day almost more than the flight itself; the country so proud of him, so proud of itself. I understood perfectly. If there was anything to celebrate, it was the country and the spirit of it that put him there, not the man himself. Only a few knew of his going up, but when he landed it was a different story. Khrushchev had been on the phone to him straight away, insisting on a big parade to the mark the occasion. He rode in Gagarin's motorcade too, couldn't resist it. He just loved the limelight and Yurka was Russia's first film star, perhaps the only one they've ever had. Years later, when Khrushchev had fallen into disrepute, his image was erased from the official photographs, but we all remembered him that day, his arms wrapped around our hero. Sunny skies, cheering crowds, banners flapping in the breeze as the flower-decked cavalcade passed them by; April 14th 1961, nearly five years to the day since they'd taken me. I was Commander Lev Lvovich Korablov by then, holder of the Government Order of Honour, with enough passable Russian to tell a decent joke or two. About a week later we were all gathered in the mess hall to watch a newsreel of it.

'We used to go barefoot and without clothes,' Khrushchev shouted from the podium, 'yet now we have pioneered the path into space! That's what you've done, Yurka. Let everyone who's sharpening their claws against us know, let them know that Yurka was in space, that he saw and knows everything!'

There were tears in his eyes when he spoke and he had to wipe them away with a big white handkerchief. I felt those tears too, not simply for the love of a country I barely knew, but for the need of that love myself. That's what I liked about Mr K. He was a patriot to his bootlaces. He believed in his country, believed in its destiny. He could see it shining in the distance, like one of those stars Yurka had flown up to greet. He might have had blood on his hands and bluster in his brain, but he wasn't afraid of standing up for us, taking off his shoe and banging it on the table, wherever he might be. We saw that one too, Gromyko sitting next to him, looking worried that he might have to follow suit. Later on, they held it against him, behaving like the peasant everyone imagined he was, but we proper peasants loved him for it, defying convention, defending our honour.

When I had got to know him a little better, Gagarin gave me this little booklet they published on his life and his times. He died not long after, on a training mission, just like the British claimed happened to me, only the Russians had a body to prove it, even his head. It always helps, I think, to have the head. And then, thinking of Yurka's sunny smile and looking at Rosa's downcast face, remembering how, despite his fame, he treated people, I felt terrible. Here was I shouting at my poor old nurse, who only wants to look after me the best she can. So I pulled her up and after rummaging in my locker brought the thing out. Yurka had written in it. 'From the man who flew to the top of the world to the man who swam to the bottom!' Not strictly true, but that was Gagarin. Generous to a fault.

'For your son,' I told her. 'He might find a use for it,' and she looked at it, without much interest, until I showed her the autograph.

'Yuri? Yuri Gagarin?' and I nodded. Even in Czechoslovakia, twenty years later, the name carried weight. She carried it away, triumphant, and I thought of her going home that night and bringing it out over their simple dinner. I imagined the conversation they would have about the mysterious Russian naval officer who spoke English, whose insides were giving him gyp and who had a whole dormitory to himself. Why was I banished here? Was I in disgrace, a fallen hero, or did I hold some kind of dread power over them, to be held in such splendid isolation? But whatever my circumstance, she took the gift gladly, and I was pleased. Why I'd hung on to it for so long I don't know, but I know why I gave it up. I'm not going anywhere, not now.

★

When I got to Gibraltar I was thirty-two years old, opposed to any form of exercise and capable of only swimming three lengths of the bath. That's what my official biographer, Marshall Pugh, said of me, and every word was true. I was not much of a haul. And yet for some reason I found my place there, and never left it. Funnily enough I think I'm nearer to it now, landlocked, dried out by radiators and rugs, than I have ever been.

I said was 'sent' out there but that makes it all sound a lot grander than it was. When I arrived I had imagined there would be a diving team with boats loaded with searchlights and equipment, and an operations HQ with staff to run it all. I thought there'd be some semblance of a planned strategy. But the war wasn't like that, at least not the one on the Rock. We had nothing at all, really. Even the depth charges we used were empty tins of bully beef with a pound and a half of TNT stuffed inside. Looking back on it, it was probably just as well. A planned strategy couldn't have coped, couldn't have looked calmly out of the window and seen thirty ships out in the bay to check before nightfall and not a clue as to where or when the devils might come. Yes, all right, better get a move on, that was our philosophy, and we worked with string and sealing wax, and a regular tot of bloody-mindedness. Whatever anyone else says about us British, not giving a hoot is pretty fundamental to the whole show. It's what separates us from the Cowhands. They do not understand the necessity of indifference.

I arrived early November. I can't quite remember the exact date, but whenever it was, I remember leaving Swansea in the cold and drizzle and stepping off the plane into what felt like a spring evening. If all I had to do was to sit under the sun and demagnetize a few limpets every now and again, then I was having it cushier than any fighting man deserved. After a bit of a run-around with officialdom

I was introduced to the diving officer, a chap called Bailey, who wasted no time in taking me down to the harbour. I don't know if you know the layout of Gibraltar, but it's pretty simple from a naval point of view. It guards the entrance to the Mediterranean and our control over it. That's why we've been there all this time, and that's why we hang on to it. You can bang on all you like about Spanish sovereignty, but we'd be seven kinds of idiot to give it up. The Soviets wouldn't, I can tell you that. They'd paint all the seagulls red and turn all the apes into card-carrying party members.

We drove down in an old Studebaker, too big for the narrow streets, but he seemed happy enough with it. I could see he wanted me to ask him questions about it, where it came from, how many miles did it do to the gallon, that sort of nonsense, so I kept my trap shut and feigned interest in the foliage. It always pays, I think, to work against the flow. Keeps one's self trim. The harbour lay on the west side of the rock, its walls, the North Mole, the South Mole and the Coal Pier, forming a slightly squashed rectangle. Within the inner harbour there were three warships taking on fuel, and another two undergoing some sort of repair work. There were flags flying and hooters going and small craft beetling in and out. Bailey took me out along the North Mole and out onto the Coal Pier, the breeze picking up as we came face to face with the open sea. To the north-east, lying dead in the water, lay a string of merchant ships, maybe twenty in all, some of them not four hundred yards from the shore.

'Like ducks on a pond, aren't they?' Bailey said brightly.

'They do look a bit vulnerable. I never imagined . . .'

'That the enemy would be allowed to get so close? Yes, it is a bit of a bugger.' He pointed west, across the bay. 'That is Algeçiras, home to a very active pair of German and Italian consulates. Strictly out of bounds to the likes of you and me. A cafe on every corner and a spy at every table. Also in the harbour there, there's this Italian tanker, the *Olterra*. The crew scuttled it when all this started and there they stay. They're up to something, but we don't quite know what.' He swung me round. 'To your right, a mile or so from our border, is the town of La Linea. Every morning hundreds of Spanish workers cross the frontier, to work in the docks. Every evening, come the curfew, they cross back again, taking all they have seen and heard with them.'

'Tricky.'

'You haven't heard the best bit yet.' He pulled out an old collapsible telescope, the sort a twelve-year-old boy might have at the back of his desk, and directed me to a whitewashed villa at the far end of the bay, almost halfway between the two towns. It stood, isolated, on the bare scrub of a hill, a beach just a stone's throw away.

'See that?' he said, his voice weary with knowledge. 'That's the Villa Carmela.'

'Nice spot,' I admitted. 'Are you planning to retire there?' He shook his head.

'It's already occupied, a charming honeymoon couple, Signor Ramogino, an Italian, and his young Spanish wife, Conchita. See that large window at the front? He put that in on their wedding night. Not what you'd usually expect is it, from your red-blooded Latin? Putty in her hands. They sit there all day, watching everything that comes in and out, aided by all accounts from a pair of binoculars stolen from the British Consulate. That is where they're based.'

I'd already been told who 'they' were, Italians, members of the Tenth Light Flotilla, but Bailey filled me in on the details. There were two parts to them, the Gamma or swimming group, based mainly up at the Villa, and a second, murkier section, charioteers who sat astride two-man torpedoes and rode them, their chins just above water, past the nets and depth charges, to our waiting ships, submerging at the last possible moment. Once under the target ship, they'd sling the warhead on ropes attached to either side of the bilge keel, set the timer and push off home, no one any the wiser. Where they came from no one knew. A submarine? Some isolated spot down the Spanish coast? I was glad I was here. Things were hotting up.

'So when do I meet your team?'

He took the telescope back from me and folded it back into his pocket.

'You're looking at it, actually. Or half of it I should say. Leading

Seaman Bell is the other. Good specimen, even though he can't swim.'

I looked down at the water. It looked surprisingly gentle for the time of year.

'As mine-disposal officer I suppose that if they're underwater, that's where I'll have to dispose of them. Underwater.' Bailey looked out to sea, his voice faraway.

'Yes, I suppose that might be an idea. How are you, would you say, in the swimming stakes?'

He sounded marginally hopeful. It would have been a shame to disappoint him.

'As a matter of fact,' I said, 'I took part in some trials only last year concerning swimfins.'

'Swimfins?' His voice took on a guarded, suspicious tone. 'What the devil are they?'

'A French invention. You place them over your feet. They help you balance and increase your speed. A friend of mine is thinking of manufacturing them. If you like, I could secure you a batch for a trial run.'

'We've got nothing like that here,' he said. 'French, you say?' He sniffed. 'I take it you've brought your swimming costume?'

'Just a spare shirt and uniform, I'm afraid. It hadn't occurred to me that I might have to swim. Silly, that.'

'We don't have any diving suits, you see. It's swimming trunks or nothing. Jolly unfair, I know, but it's amazing how quickly one gets used to it. Just like those chaps in the Serpentine.' He looked me up and down. 'You could have a go now, if you like, if you don't mind a spare pair of mine.'

He led me back through the docks, to a small quiet jetty on which stood a small hut, surrounded by a tangle of ropes. I stripped and put on his trunks, a ghastly shade of puce. Then he handed me a pair of gym shoes. The laces were stiff with salt. I went outside and walked up and down, trying them out for size.

'They fit all right,' I told him, 'but they seem strangely heavy.'

'That's the two pounds of lead in the sole,' he said. 'It helps you keep the right way up, when you trip the light fantastic.'

I nodded. Bailey popped back inside and came back with something looking like a school satchel with hose attached.

This,' he said, 'is the Davis Submerged Escape Apparatus. Very useful for escaping from submarines but quite unsuitable for operational diving. It's what you'll be using from now on. You breathe in through the mouthpiece via the oxygen canister, and breathe out into your CO_2 bag. If you feel yourself getting a bit short, just turn up the valve. If your mouth starts to twitch, it means you're giving yourself too much air and might pass out. It's best to come up sharpish if that happens. We can't afford another mishap. What's that?'

He pointed to the string around my neck. I lifted the jade and held it in my hand. For the most part I had forgotten about it by now. It was a part of me. Bailey regarded it with distaste.

'You might like to take it off, whatever it is. We don't want you strangling yourself on your first dive.'

'No can do, old boy. I'd rather go down without the life-saver than cast this aside.'

'Something Mummy gave you?'

'Something like that.'

He took me to the ladder. He tied a length of string to my wrist and handed me a pair of goggles.

'Just climb down and see how it feels,' he said. 'When it's time to come back up, I'll give you a tug.'

I went down four rungs' worth. I found the breathing hard and the goggles kept slipping off my face. I stopped there, looking out, seeing how the dancing greens of light hardened into a black-blue distance. I wondered what would be waiting below. I could sense something happening to me, something exciting, something a little frightening, like climbing the attic stairs in my cousin's house, into the room where the bats and the spiders and God knew what had been ready to leap out at me. My hands tightened, preparing for the final plunge. There was a sharp tug on my wrist. Surely I hadn't been down that long? I hauled myself back up. Bailey was looking anxiously over his shoulder.

'Got the hang of it? Good. Look. Bit of a flap on. I've got to go.' He bent down and cut the string loose. 'Try it out on your own if you like.'

He left me, and I descended again, this time all the way. I could feel the tide pull at my body. It felt strangely familiar. Funnily enough I'd had my first underwater adventure with Maitland, back home. We'd been out to the Marquis of Granby, quite a crowd of us. Maitland had hired a launch. We were coming back across the Thames, back teeth awash, and I managed to fall in. Now the Thames is a tricky stretch of water, everybody knows that, and if you fall in tight and at night, with the tide running fast, your chances are not good. The moment I hit the water and felt the cold and the current rush over me, I thought that this was it. Out in the running blackness I could hear them all shouting, racing up and down the deck looking for lifebelts and flares, but what struck me, apart from the fact that I was ruining my only suit and the taste of a good night's whisky, was that I could feel my legs putting up a rather good account of themselves, working slowly against the tide, so much so that I had both time and ability to keep one hand firmly on my hat, and make my way downstream to Maitland's boat. Now I was reminded of it, how at ease I had felt then, in this strange substance.

I held on to the ladder for a moment, then jumped down onto the soft sand. Clouds rose up, swirled up over my legs and body, obscuring my vision. I waved my arms in front of my face, to waft them aside, but they swirled about ever more frantically, as if I was trapped in a snowflake dome. Then I took a step forward and then another and I was free of them. I started to walk.

The first thing you are aware of, standing on the ocean floor, is the ceiling above your head. Like the sky above the earth, this ceiling is made of light, but it is also made of water, rolling this way and that, a constant visible barrier that separates you from the world you have known. You have walked through a magic mirror or somehow travelled in time. Your hands are not the same shape as before, they are flatter, and all the colour they once possessed has been erased. Bubbles float past you, beads of flawless air once trapped in the folds of your costume, each one bright and separate, rising up to an indefinable beyond that lies beyond your grasp. It is as if you are standing inside an enormous champagne glass, and as they rise up you realize that is what air is, God's champagne, intoxicating us with that maddening thing called life, but you realize too that you have left that world behind. You are in another universe now. You move forward. You can't see very far but you know that this goes on, along the bottom of the Atlantic Ocean and the Pacific, and if you wanted to you could walk the whole way round the world. It is yours, and yet you are not of it. You are a stranger, but you feel at home. Now you start noticing other things, the lush of green grass that washes in and out, the cluster of blooms that wave back and forth, and winding through them both the sandy track on which lobsters march in single file. A baby octopus brushes its tentacles against you. Fish cluster around your head. They gape at your goggles, their mouths opening and closing, opening and closing, like the valves of your heart. You start for a moment, but they mean you no harm. Suddenly they dart away, alarmed by a disturbance on the surface. You look up again, understanding, like the fish, that you must listen to its moods and explanations; everything you do beneath is connected to that surface. You ponder again its magical quality, how, though it can be parted by the hand of a child or by the bow of a battleship, in the moment of their passing, the water closes over, and the ceiling remains.

In those first few steps I believe I found my future. Alone, cut off, I was seeing the world as few had seen it before, a hidden world that I had glimpsed from hotel rooms and cliff tops and seaside donkeys without ever realizing the mystery that lay before me. For that's the heart of this world, isn't it, the mystery of it all? That afternoon I learnt that there were two worlds on this planet, and that the one we do not know is far greater than the one we do. Like the earth and the heavens beyond. Like the Lionel Crabb that Len and Pat and Mr K. knew, and the one sitting here in the sanatorium. Like knowledge itself. Sometimes I think we should move out of the land, leave it alone for a while, walk down into the water, grow some gills and learn to live there. Floating we take form and maybe floating we should live, and have no anchors at all.

Lot of rot, probably.

I climbed back up. Bailey was standing on the quayside looking at his watch.

'False alarm,' he said, 'though you were beginning to ring some bells. You've been down there a good five minutes.'

He fished out a packet of cigarettes, shook one out and stuck it in my mouth. Shielding the flame he struck a match. I pulled hard. It was damp but it was a smoke. Fresh air and a Senior Service. Nothing like it.

'How'd you find it?' he asked.

'Haven't had so much fun in my life,' I said. 'Fancy showing me the sights?'

'What,' he said, 'around the Rock?'

I took another deep drag, then rubbed it out between my fingers.

'No,' I said. 'Down there. Let's go for a spin.'

Six

A man in a white coat came in, clipboard at the ready, intestines draped round his neck. I never did like medicals at the best of times, and this was not one of them. He gave a small bow.

'I have come to examine you.' He spoke in English. It was a bit of a relief having someone who could speak the lingo. I was beginning to miss it.

'Feel free,' I acquiesced. 'I've nothing else on this morning.'

He hitched his coat up and sat down.

'Age?'

'Forty-seven.'

'Forty-seven?' He looked surprised.

'Born the winter of 1909. Unqualified bum-freezer, least that's what my mother told me. She was there at the time, I believe.'

Down it went.

'Cigarettes?'

'Don't mind if I do.'

He scowled.

'How many cigarettes do you smoke?'

'It depends. Thirty on a good day, as long as they're full strength. Heaven know how many if I'm reduced to filter tips, but they're not really cigarettes, are they? More like milk on a stick. And as for those Sobranies of yours. Absolute filth. Wouldn't tar the road with them.'

He scribbled some more. Couldn't make head nor tail of it. Just like doctors the world over.

'Drink?'

It would have been easy to make the same joke twice, but a man has his standards.

'I have been known.'

He looked to the door, frightened of going back empty-handed. It couldn't be easy having Crippen breathing down your neck. I gave it to him straight. It came to quite a list. The poor chap had never even heard of a pink gin.

'And now, if you please . . .'

Breathe in, breathe out; blood pressure, scales, press-ups, pulse rate, up and down a set of wooden steps tucked away in the corner. By the end I was panting like a dog at White City.

'Well, Doc, will I live?' He tapped the chart.

'You are overweight and your blood pressure is too high. You smoke too much and this—' He waved the beverage intake in the air. 'But yes, you will live.' And with that, he left.

Serov came in a few hours later. Same chart, but more squiggles on it. He sized me up and down.

'You are not a very fit man for Britain's top diver.'

'I've said it before, it's a state of mind,' I told him.

'Before? There has already been some doubt about your proficiency?'

'Not at all. It's what . . .' I stopped. 'Ah. Nearly had me there.'

He drew his mouth into a pale imitation of a smile.

'You can dive still?'

'I would have thought that was rather obvious.'

'From now on there will be no more smoking, no more drinking. What do you think of that?'

'Hoping I'll crack up under the strain, eh?'

'On the contrary, Commander. We want you stronger, more ready for the tasks ahead.'

'What tasks would they be?'

'Do you know,' said he, 'I'm not absolutely sure.'

*

Bailey left pretty soon after I arrived. I was put in charge of what became known as the Underwater Working Party and told to recruit more men. It was quite obvious from my own experience what should be the determining factor in judging someone's suitability: to wit, the size and shape of his hooter. If he had one remotely resembling mine, taking up a disproportional amount of space on the visage, then he was in. If he turned up with something snubbed or made for sniffing posies of violets, well, then he had to find some other way of endangering life and limb. There was of course the exception. Sydney.

He came bumping along the quayside one early morning on a borrowed bicycle. I was standing in the slug, preparing to cross the harbour. There was a cargo ship just in from Algiers I didn't like the look of.

'Lieutenant Crabb?'

'Yes?'

'I'm Stoker Knowles. I hear you're looking for men.'

I gave him a quick once over. His hair was plastered down with some pomade, and there were black coal rings around his eyes. Worse still, his nose reminded me of Myrna Loy. I was full up anyway.

'We've no bamboo shoots, I'm afraid,' I said. He looked puzzled. 'Your face, man. You look like a panda that's been in a punch-up.'

He rubbed the hollow of his eyes, to no apparent effect.

'Sorry, sir. I rushed it a bit, not wanting to miss my chance. I'm good for the stoking, sir, but I'm a swimmer in the main. My father wanted me to be a bugler in the army, but where's the swimming in that?'

'And where have you come from?'

He jerked his head, indicating one of the four warships in the harbour.

'Just off the destroyer *Lookout*, escorting convoys to Malta. You are looking for men, aren't you, sir?'

I cast off the rope and began to push off.

'If it's swimming you crave, Knowles, I suggest you stick to convoy duty. I'm sure the Germans will grant your wish sooner or later. We don't do a lot of swimming here. We dive.'

He took a step back and leaped on board. I opened my mouth to remonstrate, but he took no notice. 'Diving's my speciality,' he said.

'Back home, girls used to throw their mum's earrings in the local swimming pool just to watch me fetch 'em back up.'

'Well, you'll find no earrings at the bottom of this little lot.'

'That doesn't bother me, sir. There're no girls here either.'

Which wasn't strictly true.

We tootled over. The captain was very antsy about us coming alongside, let alone inspecting the state of his lower regions. There was nothing on his ship that he hadn't signed for in triplicate, and that included the barnacles. I undid my duffel coat and went down. I found it almost immediately, a torpedo, about three foot long, painted bright green and placed close to the engine room. It wasn't slung underneath, as I'd expected. It was clamped to the bilge keel by three rigid arms. Previously all I'd needed was a pair of wire-cutters and off they trotted to the deep. This was a much more serious proposition. I tied a rope around its belly and surfaced. The captain looked at me as if I had his propeller tucked into my swimming costume.

'Never seen one quite like this, sir,' I shouted up. 'Might take a bit of time to prise off. You'd better move your men forward, away from its influence.'

I chucked the rope to Knowles, who was staring down into the water, like a dog waiting for its ball to be thrown. 'Secure it to the stern,' I told him. 'When I've done we can tow it somewhere and take a good look at it.'

Knowles picked up the spare Davis set and waved it at me.

'Can I come down with you, sir?' he asked. 'It's awfully damp up here.' Another point against him. I was a stickler for the King's English.

'No. You may not,' I said, and went down again.

The mine had been fixed with a clockwork twist of the clamps. There was always a chance that unscrewing the blighters might set off a booby trap. That's what they loved doing, the Italians, inventing puzzles and conundrums that stretched our skills. It wasn't a war we were fighting, it was a battle of wits, two sides testing each other's ability to think clearly and to act cleanly and with aptitude. A cloudy moment and you could be strolling up the path to meet St Peter. Handling those mines was like biting into the wafer. You were close to the right hand, closer than you'd ever been in your life. God was inside that shell, resting on the feather of a spring.

Slowly I worked the first clamp loose. I could hear it groaning as it began to turn, but using both hands, it started to give. There was no booby trap. Once freed I began in on the second. If anything it was harder than the first. By the time I had it unfastened, my oxygen was running low and my arms had turned to straw. I surfaced and swam to the boat. Knowles was leaning over with a half bottle of rum in his hand.

'Stoker's rations, sir,' he said. 'I've got no fish.' I took a gulp and handed the bottle back.

'Fish?'

'Your hair, sir. You look like a guillemot.'

I suppressed a smile. As backchat went, it wasn't bad.

'The spare oxygen tank, Knowles, pass it over.'

He watched me intently as I refreshed my supply.

'Are you familiar with the Davis Submerged Escape Apparatus?' I asked.

'No, sir, but I can ride a bike without using the handlebars.'

I dived down again and set to on the third arm, but after a few turns it refused to budge. I stopped and put an ear to the beast. I could hear the mechanism inside, reciting its meticulous prayer. How long had it been down there. Twelve hours? Two? And how long to go? I paddled back a few feet and took a long look at it, as it changed its shape through the water's flow, one moment long and elegant like a racing car, the next fat and short and workmanlike, like a stubby pencil behind a chippy's ear. There was something illuminating in its immobility, its desire to transform. I took hold of it again and tried once more, but if anything it seemed more determined than ever to hold fast. They say horses can tell if a person is afraid of them, and I believe the same goes for mines. You have to look them in the eye with tranquillity in your heart. You have to show it that you are in control, and that morning I was doing the wrong thing. I was hurrying, becoming impatient. A couple more minutes and the mine would have won. Then there was a flurry above my head, and a body swam down, almost colliding into me in its eagerness. It paddled back, then saluted, quite prettily I thought, considering that apart from the Davis diving gear and the goggles it was wearing absolutely nothing at all. Something landed on my head, a piece of seaweed I assumed, until a paw reached out and put a pair of underpants back on. I looked through the creature's goggles and discovered the washed smudge of blackened eyes. Knowles. I shook my head. He'd have to go.

I pointed to the clamp and I mouthed the numbers out, one, two, three and mimed the turning and he nodded and we swam forward and gripped that clamp, hands over hand, like kids in the playground. I began counting out again and he joined in and on the unspoken fourth we brought everything to bear, the stoker who wanted to join and the lieutenant who wouldn't let him and the mine that lit the spark. When I saw the films of our Russian rockets rising from the plains north of the Caspian Sea, taking sputniks and dogs into space (for we uniformed men were allowed such glimpses of national glory), they reminded me of that morning, how slowly the clamp first turned, but how inexorable the movement and how unstoppable the force.

The clamp came loose and the torpedo fell away. We kicked our way to the top and dragged ourselves into the boat. Sydney stretched out a tattooed arm, took a small tobacco tin out of his trouser pocket and rolled out three cigarettes. He gave one to the chap at the wheel, one to me and planted the third in his mouth. He struck a match, lit the pilot's, then lit his. He paused and then reached for mine. It was a question that needed answering. I brushed his hand away quickly.

'Don't you know anything, Knowles,' I said. 'Never ever give a man the third light from a match. It is unspeakably unlucky. If you do it again, I'll pack you off back to the boilers.'

'The third light of a match, sir. A thing of the past.'

*

We made our home in Jumper's Bastion, an underground strong-point of thick stone, built to keep out earlier foes. It was a mite uncomfortable, but near to where we were needed. I snaffled more equipment, brought in a couple of cats for the rats and bagged a chief petty officer who worried at our heels like a terrier. When we had nothing better to do we'd sit outside stroking moggies and making up depth charges, shaving up the sharp edges of the can lids with a file dipped in water. We dived by day and we dived by night; under the sun, under the moon, in the wind, in the rain, it made no difference. Rum was all the protection we had. A diver with a full complement of ships to examine could polish off a full bottle before breakfast.

For all that, we didn't have it bad, not as bad as the Italians. Yes, our fingers bled and our unmentionables disappeared for the dura-tion, but the Italians had a river to cross; the tides, the nets, the depth charges, not to mention those infernal pigs of theirs, which carried them to their doom as often as to their glory.

The Italians; that I should meet them first here, as my silent enemy. Not a word exchanged between us, and yet it seemed as though their thoughts called me like the ringing of a sunken bell. In the early evening I often looked across to where I knew the villa lay, and thought of the men there, sitting down to a plate of something, shar-ing a joke and a bottle of wine, wondering too whether there was not another man like me, who had left his companions to wander down to the waters' edge, to pick at his thoughts and those of his unseen foe. When I had my flask with me I would raise it in the air and drink a toast to our strange compatibility.

That December the harbour got very full. The Allied forces' inva-sion of French North Africa had begun the previous month, and the navy was at full stretch. On the 5th I woke up to find the place burst-ing. In the inner harbour lay the battleship *Nelson*, to its starboard the two aircraft carriers *Furious* and *Formidable*, and any amount of ammunition ships and tankers. At the northern entrance lay four transport ships packed with American troops. I shook Sydney up and together we walked down onto the North Mole. It was an hour past dawn, and the light came low across the water, reaching into the depths of Algeçiras Bay. I raised my binoculars and took a good long look. There was the villa, with its red-tiled roof and that window facing the water, but behind the glass there was now a parrot in a cage, surrounded by hanging greenery. It looked a nice place for a honeymoon. A young woman came to the window, her dark hair tied back and a towel over her shoulder. She poked her finger into the cage and began to stroke the bird's throat. A dangerous thing to do with a parrot, I thought, given their propensity for tantrums. A man appeared, wearing little more than a string vest, and began a similar action on the back of the woman's neck.

'The lovebirds are up,' said I, handing Sydney the glasses. It took him a minute to adjust the viewfinder.

'They never stop, do they, the Eyeties,' he said, 'though to be fair . . .' He stopped. 'They've got a visitor, sir. Do you think they've taken a lodger? Or perhaps she's worn hubby out. She looks a bit of a goer.'

I snatched the glasses back. I never did like that sort of talk, even from the ranks.

The newcomer was taller than the other man, and from the way they stood back and let him take the centre stage, a bigger fish than they. His hair was sleek, swept back on a high forehead, whereas his compatriot looked like he'd just crawled out of bed, a clean white shirt slung over his bare shoulder. He had a swimmer's build, a swimmer's arms and a swimmer's chest. He looked clean and young and fresh, and for a mad moment I wanted to call him over, so that we could stop all this nonsense and swim the ocean together. The woman held his shirt open while he eased his arms into the sleeves. He gazed steadily out to sea, to where the supply ships were strung out. He appeared like a man as you might find standing on Victoria Station waiting to board the Orient Express. There was voyage and adventure in his bearing. He was looking at the unknown and it thrilled him.

'He must be feeling what Drake felt, when he put his eye on Cadiz,' I said.

The man shifted his stance slightly and looked over to where Sydney and I stood and the inner harbour beyond. The young woman returned and handed him a white cup on a white saucer. He took it without acknowledgement and stirred it with a tiny spoon, staring out to sea all the while. He lifted the cup to his mouth, sniffing it once before gently sipping. He began talking I could not see to whom, though the parrot was watching him. He moved the spoon expansively in the air, as if he was Toscanini at the Proms.

'He's counting them,' I shouted, louder than I should have. 'Well, drop in, why don't you? Bring your friends. We'll have a proper party.'

I was angry, angry at the ease by which he could make his choice, angry at the presumption of his success. Then he did something that changed all that. He dropped the spoon back onto the saucer and put his fingers to his lips and drew out a kiss, held it tenderly in his cupped palm as his hand flew east, in the direction of his homeland. Then he let it go, and I saw it flap its wings and rise up, out along the coast and over the Rock, to disappear out of sight. It was a homing pigeon, that kiss. It would get there, whatever the obstacle.

'Tonight,' I told Sydney. 'I'd bet your right lung on it.'

We mounted our cannons, out on the moles by the north and south entrances. In reality they were nothing more than boiler tubing with the firing mechanism of an ordinary rifle bolted onto the back end. You dropped the depth charge in, pulled on the lanyard and off she popped. Not the most accurate of weapons, but they looked effective from a distance, what with the bang and the water bursting up.

Night came quicker than most. I had everyone up and ready, out in the boats, up on the walls, manning searchlights on the nets. The moon was full, the ships cut-outs against a starry December night. I remember thinking that in England there'd be the blackout and frost on the windows. Sydney and I spent the night touring the harbour, inspecting as many as we could. We didn't do it in any particular order. We had a sense of what they'd go for, the ones that required a bit of daring, the ones that would make the world sit up. An easy tanker out in the sticks wasn't what they were after. They were

Davids, and there were half a dozen Goliaths ready to be felled. Hour upon hour we jumped, hauling ourselves along one bilge keel after another, half expecting to bump into someone Roman coming the other way. By two o'clock we had about as much strength left as a wet dishcloth. We sat in the back of the slug, and rested.

'Smoke, sir,' Sydney offered.

'Damn right, Knowles,' I gave back and we sat there, saying not much.

'What are you going to do, sir, when it's all over?' he asked, after a long silence.

'Buy you a couple of pints at my favourite local,' I replied. 'After that, I'm not sure. Something not as daft as this, I hope.'

We sat there some more, saying even less. We knew it couldn't last.

'Bathing-pool attendant, that's where I'll end up,' he muttered, flicking his fag end away, 'fishing little boys' whatsits out the water.'

A shout went up. A searchlight had picked up a silhouette outside the south entrance. We charged over, but there was nothing, save a hint of diesel in the air. I ploughed back and forth, while Sydney chucked in a few bangers of our own.

'Hear that?' he said.

I cut the engine. All I could hear was the ringing in my ears. Then a call, quite loud, defiant.

There were two of them, clinging to a buoy not twenty foot away. We dragged them into the boat while we raked the water with our lights. They had come within fifty yards of the *Furious*. I stood them up and shone my torch on them. They looked like a comedy act, one short, one tall, the taller younger than the shorter. They were dressed in dungarees and were shivering like a couple of dogs. I threw them an old overcoat and a blanket.

'Want a lift home?' I said.

They looked nonplussed. I pointed out to where that blessed villa lay.

'The Villa Carmela,' I said. 'The lovely señorita.' They looked askance. 'Conchita. The bloody parrot, boys.' I flapped my arms.

The older one shook his head and pointed down.

'Submarine,' he said carefully. 'Italy.' He opened up an imaginary hatch and made a swimming motion.

'Yes, you and Mussolini,' I said. The younger one's teeth started chattering. His lips were Prussian blue. I handed him the bottle of rum. He held it, hesitating.

'Go on, drink it,' I said, miming an action of my own. 'I know what it's like.'

The older one nodded his assent. The lad took a deep gulp, his Adam's apple gliding up and down like a bubble in a spirit level.

'*Bene*,' he said. It was the first time I'd ever heard Italian spoken. I liked it.

'*Bene*,' I said, and set the boat in motion. The elder took the bottle, looking back to a distant spot in the water. Somewhere down there was their chariot and their torpedo. They hadn't got through. I could see it in his face. Yet, as he lifted the bottle and let the liquid run into his mouth, there was something else playing on his lips; a toast perhaps, a silent prayer, to the others who were out there.

We didn't get any more out of them. I didn't expect to. We took them in for the official interrogation, but those boys wouldn't do any better with them. Sydney and I went back out on the moles and set to work with the boiler tubes. No pattern, that was the trick; one a minute for the first six minutes, then a gap, of say four. For a time we let them fly on the flip of a coin; three heads in a row and off one went. We hurled the bombs into the air and waited. The sea was a ghost, changing shape, making us believe in the power of the spirit. We were helpless, determined. Our eyes were open but we might as well have been blindfolded. We listened to the water and it told us nothing. Two hours we played this game, then I'd had enough. Sydney was about to drop in another when I walked over and hung my cap over the barrel.

'Hold up, Knowles. Let's wait a while. Make it impossible for them not to accept our invitation. Fifteen minutes should do it. And just in case they're out there casing the joint, act as if you can't get the ruddy thing to work again.'

'They won't be able to see much at that distance, sir.'

'No, but they might feel it though. You can curse if you want to, only be civil about it. I don't want to hear any of that stoker filth you were brought up on.'

Sydney started to bang away with a hammer, turning the black air blue with merchant navy epithets. I walked up and down, counting out the minutes. It was hard, to do nothing, to leave the door wide open to disaster. The night had turned absolute, the lights of Algeçiras sunk into an indeterminable grey mass. Even the villa on the hillside had vanished. Yet I knew it was there, and they'd be standing at that window, feasting on the same dry anxiety that I could taste in my own mouth. They wanted their countrymen to return, and strangely so did I. They'd be wondering about the suspension of activity, putting it down to either incompetence or ingenuity; either way making the decision to go. Their hearts would be running to the race, their goal just God's blessing away. Twelve minutes passed; thirteen, fourteen. Sydney removed my cap but I waved him back, using Nelson's words.

'Patience and perseverance, Knowles. They can do a great deal.'

I counted out another full three. They'd be moving now, under our water; their water too.

I gave the all clear. Sydney let loose with three in quick succession, his hands dancing in the air. The boom rose up, bouncing round the harbour walls. There was a clatter, like the beating of a thousand wings, and then in the hidden slosh of the black water and the slug banging up and down against the stanchion, came something else, the sound of a plug being pulled, a drain bringing up its lunch.

'What the hell was that?' said Sydney.

We peered in and out of the searchlights but could see nothing. Then it came, a cry, long and wounded, the sound a creature gives before it leaves this life for the next, and within it, a word, half formed: a woman's name I thought, or perhaps that of his patron saint. For though it was dark and I had only seen, never heard, him, I recognized his voice and knew that a clean white shirt was waiting, washed and folded, on his empty bed. Don't ask me how, but I did.

No ships were sunk that night. The convoys left; the harbour emptied. I sat it out, waiting. He'd come up eventually, and I wanted to be there when he did. They found him a couple of days later, pretty much mangled. I took myself over to the morgue. He was laid out on a rough stone slab, his number two alongside. He was dressed in a black rubber frogsuit, badly torn, though his name tag had survived. Visintini. Licio Visintini. Lieutenant. I looked at him, his sleek black hair and his pale skin, his high forehead and his steady stare, fixed upon the heavens. I envied him in a way, trying to blow up the greatest navy in the world. On his feet were what looked like a pair of swimfins.

'Well, I'm blowed,' I said. I coughed and addressed him. 'Would you mind very much if I had a go?'

I walked down to the quay and tried them on. I had to walk with my feet pointing outwards, otherwise I was in danger of tripping myself up.

'Very comical sir,' Sydney offered. 'Why don't you try for the Christmas panto.'

I undressed and lowered myself into the water. It was like one of those children's books, where you mix up different parts of people's bodies, a woman's head on a strongman's torso, the strongman's torso on ballerina's legs, the ballerina's legs on policeman's boots; that sort of thing. Suddenly I was possessed of a new lower half. I was stronger, quicker. I could turn and spin. I could hang in the water motionless. One careless flip and I upended and plummeted to the depths, like a gannet after his supper. No wonder they were giving us merry hell.

I went back to the morgue with the swimfins hanging in my hands. They had covered him up by that time. I pulled back the sheet and told him to his face.

'I hope you don't mind, old chap, but I'm going to keep these. I'll make it up to you the best I can.'

Officialdom was set on burying the two of them in the nearest piece of consecrated ground they could find, but I insisted: that wouldn't do. The next day I found a shopkeeper who sold me two

Italian flags and the day after that a willing priest to officiate at the service. We put their bodies onto the slug and took them out to sea and gave them a proper burial, with their flag wrapped around them and the right words said as we upped the plank. The service didn't make much sense to me, but I liked the sound of their Church better than I liked ours. I could feel a powerful faith following them down. They had found their place. They had probably never lost it. The sea had baptized me, but there was something missing. I stared down at the water, trying to see what lay within, but whatever was down there had vanished before my eyes.

Not long after I bought a phrase book and a parrot. I named the bird Vincent. I taught him everyday Italian words, *Pronto*, *Grazie*, *Bene*; especially *Bene*. He would sit in his cage, cracking peanuts and shouting out pleasantries to the passing trade. Now that I had heard their tongue, I longed for the moment when I could listen to their language flow back and forth, naturally, like the waters in which we lived and breathed.

*

At the beginning of April word came out that General Sikorski was stopping over on his way back to England. He'd been doing a grand tour, visiting Polish troops in the Middle East, Cairo, Beirut, Tehran. He flew in on a Saturday. I had hoped to call on the party that next morning to see if Eugene might be amongst them, but as usual with the Rock, nothing was as straightforward as it first appeared. The trouble this time was that his old sparring partner, Mr Maisky, the Russian Ambassador, was arriving in Gibraltar that very morning, on his way to Moscow, and by that time Russia had broken off all diplomatic relations with them. The Poles had asked the International Red Cross to investigate the site of the Katyn massacre, and the Russians were furious. So a certain amount of subterfuge was necessary. In the normal course of events Maisky's plane wouldn't have left until sometime in the afternoon, but it was arranged that he should take off for Algiers at around eleven in the morning, while General Sikorski and his entourage kept to their rooms. Maisky duly arrived at about three in the morning. We had been on full alert. It was normal practice when the top brass were flying in and out. After he landed we were stood down. I did a quick tour of the harbour and dropped into my bunk at around half four, thinking of my friend, and how like a war to keep us so closely apart.

I hadn't slept more than an hour or three when there was a loud banging on the Bastion door. I answered a mite groggy. Eugene stood there in full regalia, with a grin on his face, a stick or something tucked under his arm and a little briefcase in his right hand.

'What kept you?' I said. 'You've been here a good twelve hours. Come in and stroke the parrot.'

I led him inside, fighting the urge to scratch. One of our cats had fleas. Eugene looked around. It was a bizarre sight, I suppose, more like a zoo than a mess, what with the cats and the parrot and the rock lizards, who dealt with the flies. Still, we had hammocks and bits of tarred rope to show that we were bone fide navy.

'This,' he said, 'is very like you. Cocking a nose at everything.'

Vincent started squawking, '*Bene, bene, bene.*' I scratched myself after all.

'And how is the first-best man?' I asked. 'Not jealous that his rival is here too, I hope.'

'The General is in very good spirits. And this afternoon he will be coming here, to inspect you.'

'News to me, old boy.'

'They have had to make sudden arrangements, because of the . . . difficulties. This morning he meets Polish escapees. Then lunch. And in the afternoon, he visits the tunnels, the guns, and you. Then dinner, and afterwards, our plane to London.'

'Ah, London,' I said. 'Where is that, exactly?'

He laughed, but it was true. After waiting for Visintini to show, I'd hardly given London or the Cavendish or Maitland and the Nag's Head a moment's thought. It might not have existed, for all the sense I had of it. And yet I loved the place, or thought I did. There was only one reality where war was concerned, and that was where you were at any hour of any day. His laughter gave way to the same taut face I'd seen that first night.

'You remember what we were talking about? That time in your hotel?' He tapped his briefcase. 'There is much proof now, but because of the war, we are trying to surmount it. It is a very big time for us, you know, Lionel. Very big.'

He didn't say any more and I didn't ask him. Then he put down his case and pulled the stick out from under his arm.

'Forget your rum,' he said. 'This is much better. For you and your brave men. One hundred per cent.'

I had Sydney and the others clean out their bunks, and generally make the Bastion look less of a bomb site. The cats were temporarily rehoused with one of Knowles' willing Wrafs; only Vincent stayed. It's difficult to catch something criss-crossing the ceiling a foot above your head. *Bene, bene, bene.* By ten to three we were all lined up on the dockside in our best bib and tucker, our equipment and a few choice torpedoes laid out in front. I was nervous. I wanted to see how a man like that looked, someone who not only fought for his country, like every man jack of us, but who somehow *was* his country, like Churchill or the King or the great Auk. I'd seen any number of officials come and go, but not a hero, like him.

He walked down with his hands behind his back, like royalty, and when he drew opposite me I snapped to attention as best I could. Eugene stood a little ways behind. He was still carrying that little briefcase, but this time there was no vodka tucked under his arm.

'This is Lieutenant Crabb, General,' he said. 'You remember me telling you about him. He entertained us most royally in London.'

Sikorski took my hand. He had a strong determined face, not given to flights of fanciful things. His eyes were not hooded exactly, but narrowed, as if in a state of perpetual scrutiny.

'I am in your debt, sir. Yours is dangerous work, I hear.'

'In times like this, most work is, General.'

He nodded, then took in the Davis Escape Equipment, hanging round my neck. He squinted, as if he could not quite believe what he was seeing.

'It is a bit primitive,' I acknowledged. 'But needs must.'

'It is not the equipment that matters, Lieutenant, but the man behind it. A corrupt man will be destroyed, however modern his weapon. A nation is no different. We will triumph in the end, because we are right. God knows this, as do I.'

And I knew it too, then.

He stepped aside.

'May I introduce the rest of my little party. Lieutenant Kazhynski you know. This is my daughter, Madame Lesniowska.'

He spoke her name but I didn't hear it properly. She was dressed in battledress with a scarf tucked high under her chin and a little military cap stuck on a full head of hair. She was quite the loveliest creature I had ever seen in my life, young and tall and brimming with purpose. It had never happened to me with a woman before, but I could read her face like the morning paper. She was his daughter but she was also a Polish citizen, a fighter in her own right. You could see it in the steady glow of her eyes and the firm set of her mouth. She was there for her father and for the cause he led, but she was there for herself too and what she might bring to the world. For the first time I saw the future then, a good future, fuelled by things I believed in, nobility and sacrifice, knowing what is right, what is wrong, and your place in the grand firmament of it all. I thought of our own King and his own daughter who, God willing, one day would become my queen. I thought of the burden that would be laid on those royal shoulders and what a woman she must be, to carry it without complaint, as life and duty demanded, and saw the same resolve in this young woman's bearing. I thought of Maitland and his foul first-floor rutting and felt ashamed that he should take advantage of one of her own so. If she had been there, he would not have dared.

I heard a cough. I was conscious of them waiting, but did not know what to do. My hand half rose, then fell back. I wanted to grip her hand, feel the cool strength I knew would be there. I opened my mouth, and the words faltered on my tongue. She affected not to notice but held me with her eyes. It was as if she was shining a torch; she could see all the old rubbish floating inside, I was sure.

'We have heard a lot about you, Lieutenant. Everyone tells us that after the apes, we must come and see the crab. Is that not so, Father?'

It slipped out, and the General wasn't best pleased. But something had prompted that slip, and in that one heady moment I thought it might be me, not fully realizing what a ridiculous notion that was.

'Would you show me something of your operations?' she asked.

For the next twenty minutes I had poor Sydney and the others jumping in and out the water like performing seals. I explained the workings of the different mines, and gave them a guided tour of the green mine that Knowles had cut his teeth on.

'We even have one of their two-man torpedoes now, that we managed to dredge up. It's round the back, if you'd care to examine it.'

She acquiesced graciously, but as we set off, one of our ratters crossed her path. Sydney must have failed to catch them all.

'Better not that way,' I said. 'It's bad luck, you know, to cross the path of a black cat.'

She was amused.

'We have a pilot like you, Lieutenant. Whenever he flies, he never wears his Mae West. Always over the back seat he puts it. And when the plane takes off, instead of climbing up straight, he – ' she demonstrated with her hand, not knowing the words – 'flies like that, flat, before climbing again. Important people weigh more than others, he says.'

Eugene started looking at his watch. It was time to leave. I wanted to say something more but could only think of platitudes.

'I hope the war will treat you well, Lieutenant,' she said. 'Do you miss London?'

'Not very much. Only I wish I was going there now.'

I'd never said anything like that in my life, and from the way she pulled back, and blinked hard in the light, I could see that I had overstepped the mark.

'It will still be there,' she said, 'when this is over.'

'For all of us.'

She shook her head.

'When the war is over, I will be back in my country.'

'Of course.'

'Well, then.'

And with that she was gone.

That evening I sat at the water's edge, watching the stars, feeling cheated. I wanted to see her plane fly up and climb out of my life.

You always knew when an aircraft was going to take off from Gibraltar at night. They turned the searchlights off, so as to avoid the glare interfering with the pilot. By eleven it was pitch dark. I waited for fifteen minutes before I heard the roar of the engine and saw the Liberator loom up over the water, flying out towards the east. The plane rose momentarily, then levelled out, just as she had predicted. I sat there, waiting for it to start climbing again, but it didn't. It flew dead ahead, on a seemingly even keel. I jumped to my feet.

'Pull up, man, pull up!' I shouted.

She was up there, on the plane, not only her, but my future, my young queen and everything I held dear. And here was I, helpless below. All I could do was watch as the plane flew straight into the sea, hitting the water about three-quarters a mile from shore.

We got out there in fifteen minutes. There were four bodies on the water, Sikorski, two others I had never met, and what looked like the pilot. We got them all in the boat and ran back to shore. The General and the others were dead, but the pilot was still breathing. Brain matter was oozing out of the General from a gash in his head. It looked like dirty, frothy soap, the stuff that bubbles out of blocked drains. We made the pilot as comfortable as we could, cutting away his clothing to help his breathing, and as I did so I noticed something strange. He had his Mae West on, every strap, every fastening, securely in place. And I remembered what she had said.

We found four more bodies before we turned in. By daybreak we were back again, this time to dive. An Admiralty launch came out, instructing us to search for briefcases, with important documents inside, but I wasn't looking for them. I was looking for her, and my friend Eugene. They would both be dead, I knew that, but I wanted it to be me that brought them ashore all the same. The plane lay in about four fathoms of clear water, the sunlight streaming through, giving it a semblance of movement; the passenger section, which was low on the fuselage, had been torn away, and lay a considerable distance from the rest of the craft. As we approached I saw her, her body long and slender, caught on a wing, her arms waving in the current, beckoning me. I swam towards her, dreading what I would have to do next, take her in my grasp, embrace her, and bring her to the surface. As I drew closer she seemed to grow calm, her head shrouded by the coat she was wearing. For a moment I imagined her transformed, a mermaid, and that she and I could share a life under water, freed from the cares of the world above, no Poland, no Germany, no conflict between countries or men and women, only the freedom that limitless water can bring. Then I was next to her. I closed my eyes and wrapped my arms around her and discovered that it wasn't she at all. There wasn't even a body. There was just an overcoat, caught on one of the propellers, empty.

Inside the passenger section, personal items were strewn around; presents, too; boxes of Turkish Delight, cartons of cigarettes, a zip case with a dozen Leica cameras wrapped inside. Two suitcases of furs had spilled open, the coats somersaulting in the water like boys in a bathing pool. Eugene was in his shirt sleeves, still strapped in his seat, his right leg torn off at the hip, his hands folded carefully on his lap, the briefcase attached to his wrist by the length of chain. I did as I was told and brought the case up, then went back for his body. We searched the plane, front to back, bagging every scrap of paper we could find. Eighteen bodies we recovered, but not hers. All we found to indicate she had been there was a small jewel box with sliding doors, lying in the sand, some distance from the wreck. I wanted to keep it, but I knew it wouldn't be right. I wish I had now.

Later, when the plane had been raised, and the General's body flown out, the rumours started. It was sabotage. Churchill, some said, Stalin, said others. The pilot was in someone's pay, hence the Mae West. I don't know about that, but I know it's hard to crash a Liberator into the water at one hundred and fifty miles an hour and bank on surviving, whatever you're wearing. He was lucky either way. Stalin killed a lot of people, that's for sure. A planeload of Poles and a couple of Members of Parliament wouldn't have bothered him much, and certainly Maisky's plane had sat alongside Sikorski's for the best part of that morning. Perhaps it was plain misfortune. Whatever the cause, it left a bad taste in the mouth. I'd rather it was the work of dictators, Serov's hand in it. Rather that, than the hand of God, at such a time. But God doesn't give us a helping hand, not when we demand it.

*

Visintini, the General, Eugene; I was tired of pulling out bodies from the water, but I needed to find one more. During the following weeks I would take the launch out along the Rock's east coast, hoping to find her caught upon the rocks. Sydney offered to come with me, but I needed to look for her by myself. I never found her. No one did. I sometimes think that if I had, I would have been free of her, free to look upon others. Paola, Rose, Margaret, they were too much flesh, too much blood, when all I was seeking was something cold and drowned and eternal. Perhaps it was Sikorski's daughter who kept me in the sea over my allotted time, forever diving in the hope of one day finding her still, her hair tucked in, her beret set back on her head, her eyes fixed upon mine and the faults that lay behind. I think it must be so, for I thought no more of Gibraltar after that; only the leaving of it.

Seven

The first time I met Yurka he'd dropped one of his medals in the urinal. We were attending some sort of official parade, Lenin's birthday I think it was, and we'd both popped out for a five-minute breather. He was the guest of honour, the holder of the Hero of the Soviet Union, the nation's highest medal. He'd nearly finished and was shaking himself rather vigorously and it just slid off into the trough. There were just the two of us there and we both just stood there looking at it, sitting atop a number of soggy fag ends. I knew who he was, of course. Everybody did.

He scratched the back of his neck and swore vigorously, not knowing quite what to do. He was obviously a mite squeamish about getting it back, which amused me. The bravest of men can be proper little Miss Muffets sometimes.

'Allow me,' I said, and fished it out with the pointed end of the commemorative fountain pen we'd each been presented with that morning. I walked over to the large stone basin, held it under the tap for a minute or two, then dried it on the towel hanging below a poster urging officers to set an example as regards to personal hygiene. Gagarin hadn't said a word. He just stared at me, trying to gauge which direction this was going to take. Stalin might have been dead a few years, but a faux pas like that could still get you in an awful lot of trouble, however enlightened the times.

'Don't worry,' I assured him. 'Your secret's safe with me.' He clapped me on the back, pinned it back on his jacket and left, whistling.

Later, in the evening, he found me out, and we got talking. For all his fame, he wasn't best happy. They'd banned him from any more space missions in case he was killed, and he didn't like it. That struck a chord with me. He knew who I was by then, I think. People like him got told things, not simply because of their rank, what they had done. He was that type of chap, that's all, eager, baby-faced, a smile as big as the Urals. Everyone wanted to confide in him. He didn't refer to my past; he'd have been told that was against the rules, but there was an unspoken bond between us, the two of us wanting to serve our mother country the best way we could and so often being denied it. The look on his face, the way he gripped his glass, tipped the drink back down his throat, stirred some muddy waters.

Those years, the mid-sixties, I was stationed in Odessa. Gagarin had been given the run of one of the villas there. If he had nothing better to do, and when I had a few days' leave owing, he'd invite me over. It was a nice enough area, some miles out, but the house itself was a dark ugly sprawl of a thing, all stuck about with fir trees. You could have been in Siberia for all the view it had. To get to the sea we'd have to walk through the gloom for a good fifteen minutes. Once on the beach, though, he'd try to get me to swim.

'No can do, Yurka,' I'd insist. 'I've told you before. I don't believe in swimming for pleasure. Work and play, they're different concepts. You mix them at your peril. Opera singers don't sing in the bath, do they? Now run along while I have a smoke,' and he'd dash off into the briny while I'd sit there, keeping my distance. It wasn't as easy as it looked.

I remember once, he'd come back from one of his foreign trips, Canada, Mexico, Cuba. He'd invited me over to sample a box of Castro's finest. We'd been drinking all the afternoon, and my guard was down.

'What am I to do?' he complained. 'People see my picture in the paper and think, "That Gagarin, he's fallen on his feet! Pretty girls kissing him, the red-carpet treatment everywhere he goes." Look at me!' He patted his stomach. 'I do nothing but make speeches and eat. "Let me fly again," I plead, and they nod their heads and send me on another goodwill mission. I am running out of goodwill, Lev Lvovich. The next time I have to shake someone's hand I'll punch them in the mouth! You see if I don't! I want to go back, meet the universe face to face again. You have no idea how persuasive the earth is, floating out in space.'

I looked at him. He was short and stocky like me, with the kind of buoyant energy I'd once had, and when I saw him then, hunched over the table, with these uncalled-for weights dragging him down, it was as if I was looking at myself all those years ago. It wasn't Korablov who poured out the next drink, it was someone else. Someone I'd almost forgotten about.

'I wish I could take you up there,' he was saying, 'you would understand. Do you know I believe in flying saucers and visitors from other planets.'

'Oh, come on now!'

'No, really. And you know why? Because the earth is so beautiful. Anyone passing by would have to come and look, like you do the Pyramids or the Eiffel Tower or Buckingham Palace. You cannot believe how precious it looks, how it calls to you.'

There was a pause then. We were close to forbidden territory.

'Actually, Yurka, I do. Remember I've seen this earth from the inside. From what you've told me I think the ocean's very like your space. You can look at it, float in it, but you can't live in it, and by God, that's what you want to do the most, be a part of it. When I was your age I thought the day would come when I would take a deep breath, jump in the ocean and never come out. I would flip my feet and dive forever, down and down, gliding along the floor of a perfect tranquil sea. It would never end and neither would I. That's what you felt like up there, wasn't it, immortality tugging at your sleeves?'

He nodded.

'Immortality or death, one or the other. And now, Lev Lvovich. You have these feelings still?'

I swirled the brandy in my glass.

'No. I'm too old and this sea of yours is too cold, even for someone with a shell as thick as mine. My horizons have dropped now. I can barely see beyond the bottom of this brandy glass. But back then, diving in Gib with an unknown world before me, I thought if I could reach out, get close enough, I'd reach the promised land. But I stayed in the water too long, refused to let go, and when I did, found I was holding on to nothing. It just slipped through my fingers, as all water does. Don't do the same, Yurka. Be glad of what you saw and leave it at that. You've done something no one else has ever done; something no one else will ever do. There will be others following but Yuri Gagarin will always be the first man in space, the Columbus of the twentieth century.'

Yurka stubbed his cigar out and stared out the window at the tall dark trees. His voice came slowly, almost formal.

'I do not understand, Commander, Gibraltar? When was the Russian navy in Gibraltar?'

'No, not the Russian, the—' I stopped short.

He put his hand out, smiling.

'Do not worry, Lev Lvovich,' he said. 'Your secret is safe with me.'

★

Italy capitulated. It was only then we learnt how they'd done it, carried out their two-man torpedo operations under everyone's noses, without so much as a bus pass. Bloody clever they'd been, tidy too, with just a touch of flamboyance. That's what marks out greatness: the ability to thumb your nose and still get it right. It was all to do with that tanker that Bailey had shown me, my first day out, the *Olterra*, and those sulky sailor types, lounging round her decks, smoking cigarettes and exchanging jokes with the Spanish guards. Unbeknown to us all, the Spanish included, they'd managed to cut a great hole in the side, below *Olterra*'s waterline, and turned the ship into a secret launching base. They'd come and gone as they pleased, and no one had known a thing about it. And the man who first had run the show? My old friend Visintini. I might have guessed it. When they made a film about me (Oh yes, they made a film about those days, didn't I say?), they pretended I discovered what was going on and blew the ship up, but that's a load of horse manure. That's the trouble with writers and film-makers and the like. The real world is never enough for them; they have to fashion it to suit their own purpose. That's why I've never been much for reading. If you've come through a war, there's not much point to it. If you don't know what life's all about after that little lot, reading a book won't help you. War doesn't help you either, but at least you know that it doesn't. You know that that's it, this lot you have, and you better make the most of it. Everyone has a purpose; they're just not told what it is.

Gibraltar no longer needed our protection. Sydney and I were sent to Leghorn, on the coast of northern Italy, to help clear the port. As we lumbered down the runway and lifted into the air I took a last look at the waters below in which I had lived and fought. It filled the bay with a blue that came straight from a child's colouring pencil. It was hard to imagine that it was all over, that I'd never have anything more to do with my underwater foes. It left a yearning within me, a hollowness, to leave them with the scales so unbalanced. Despite all that had happened, I didn't want to leave at all. I got up off my haunches and bent my way forwards.

'How about a turn about the harbour,' I shouted to the pilot. 'For old times' sake.'

A gust of wind tipped the plane sideways. Suddenly I was sitting in his lap, feeling distinctly foolish.

'How about you removing yourself before I drop us all in the drink.' He was very polite.

The engine roared and the wind took hold of us again. There was a shriek from the back, as if the leading lady in some opera had been chucked over the balcony. I scrambled to my feet, poking the pilot in the unmentionables as I levered myself off and crawled back. Sydney was on his knees, covering the birdcage with my coat.

'I think it's best,' he explained. 'He doesn't like flying.'

Apart from Vincent, our clothes and our swimwear, we'd left everything else behind, even the mirror in which I'd trimmed my beard. By that time that had gone too. Later on, it was how everyone recognized me, clean shaven, with only two clumps of whiskers left high on the cheekbones to remind myself of my former incumbency, but up till that time I'd had what was known as the full set, beard, moustache, grown according to King's Regulations, which require that unless a man is completely clean shaven, the use of a razor is to be discontinued entirely. Abandon cut-throats all who climb aboard. I'd sacrificed mine so that I could use the Italian breathing apparatus. Over the months we had salvaged quite a selection of their gear. We'd had some British equipment sent out, but it was obvious to anyone with half a lung that the Italian stuff was far superior. The British tried to adapt it, and nearly killed us in the process. They ended up producing a one-piece suit with built-in reinforced feet. Entry was through the neck. You needed to be Houdini to get into it, and have his younger brother standing by to get you out again. It also leaked. An incontinent contortionist is what you felt like. On the other hand the Italian effort was a natty flexible two-piece. You slipped into it, folded the two parts over, snapped a rubber band over the join, and hey presto, were snuggled into an airtight seal. Their breathing apparatus was simpler too, less like having a small car attached to your face. Once I'd tried it all on I never wore anything else. People said it was unpatriotic, to paddle up and down in something so obviously unadorned with the stamp of the Empire, but to my mind what a man chooses to wear underwater is no different in principle from what he chooses to wear on dry land. When a fellow wants to walk down the Strand, twirling his cane, he buys accordingly, something Savile Row, something that's comfortable with the style and the setting. It's no different twenty foot down in the deep.

The man I had to thank for this new attire was a chap called Belloni, an unfortunate name for an English playground, but passable if you were keeping cave in Naples. It was he who had been the guiding light behind the Tenth Flotilla, who had devised their diving methods, their suits, their two-man torpedoes. Though we'd cursed his name roundly most of our waking hours, we all recognized him to be the true genius of our trade. We'd been given a picture of him, taken in Italy before the war, just in case he tried to take too close a look. Quite a lot of them did that, posed as traders and rode about the harbour in the Spanish bumboats, taking stock of our deployment. Trouble was we could never prove who they were. Had Belloni been given the luxury of more time and the blessing of fair fortune, the Tenth could have inflicted a damn sight more damage than they actually achieved. It made me think of what the General had said.

We took a roundabout route to Leghorn, flying first to Rome. Knowles was quite content to sit around drinking tea until it was time to take off again, but I was determined that we should see the sights. We stood on the Vatican steps, and I thought of the Pope and the power radiating from his hands; we climbed the Coliseum and I imagined the cries for blood rising up from that fearsome heathen bowl. All roads lead to Rome said the Romans, and they barely knew the half of it. City of God. City of Gods. I explained it all to Knowles as best I could. Back on the plane I asked him what he had thought of the place.

'They've got a smashing NAAFI, sir,' he said and rolled a cigarette.

We spent a month in Leghorn, hauling rubble out from the harbour. From there we were sent to Florence, where they'd made the mines we'd spent the best part of two years defusing. It was an awkward situation, after the Italians threw in the towel. Half of the Tenth Flotilla had taken to the hills under their commander, Borghese, to carry on the fascist fight. Others had joined the reds, the partisans. Those with any brains at all were keen to turn upon their former masters, but couldn't swallow communism at any price. Suspicion and intrigue abounded. We were told to join up with this American, one Lieutenant Marsloe, who'd had intelligence training and was very clued up vis-à-vis the lingo. *Bene, bene, bene.* The idea was to sniff out any remaining equipment and documents and try to glean what information we could. They gave us a map and a truck and told us to mind the holes in the roads. It was still a bit touch and go out there. Sydney was dead set on all the undercover stuff, but wasn't keen on being roped in with Uncle Sam.

'It doesn't make sense sir, a Yank from intelligence.'

'Oh,' I said. 'I didn't know you'd been to Windgap, Pennsylvania too.'

We drove over the dusty roads. It should have taken a day or two, but it lasted nearer eight, the countryside full of disaffected German units and vengeful partisans. On occasions nervous representatives of the British army would jump out of the undergrowth and question our sanity. Sometimes the front was only half an hour up the road. We'd get out, sit on the running board and have a smoke until the shooting subsided. Sydney had got hold of a couple of .38 revolvers and an old bushman's hat. He slung the guns low on his hip and tipped the hat over his eyes. He said it was to impress the Yank when we met him, but I think he was simply itching to get stuck in.

The roads became clearer. We ambled along as best we could, Sydney coaxing the engine, whistling some music-hall nonsense, while I watched the countryside rumble past, the clambering villages, the deserted squares, the folded fields growing I knew not what. We were in no hurry. Come noon we'd park the lorry, stick our legs out the windows and take a well-earned nap. At night we'd wrap ourselves in our duffel coats and sleep under the stars in some deserted grove, our stomachs swollen with requisitioned fruit. The days grew hotter; the country seemed baked into an eternity. You could hardly imagine why they had bothered to fight at all. Sometimes we'd come across a man coaxing his laden donkey up a narrow road or group of peasants working in the fields. Once we passed a family sitting round an enormous picnic lunch. How wonderful their life looked, the white cloth, mother's broad-rimmed hat, the old grandmother dressed in black, cutting up craggy loaves of golden bread. We drove past, longing to join in, and by the way the children stood and waved it was a hope they entertained too. Why we didn't I don't know. We were afraid, I think, afraid of such simple friendship.

But however long we took, it wasn't slow enough for that lorry. Every day it grew more sluggish, needed more water, drank more petrol. Five days out, climbing all morning, I was getting pretty fed up.

'We're not making much progress here, Knowles,' I told him. 'I could have walked that last hill in half the time.'

'Good idea, sir,' he said. 'Take Vincent with you next time. Every little helps.'

We had reached a plateau of rich pasture and forgotten apple orchard. The land enveloped us. It was hard to imagine being anywhere else. We drove for miles, shivers of heat rising before us, caught in a mirage. There was a silence to the air, an unspoken presence, though of farmhouses, people, any sign of human habitation, there was none. Any moment I half expected to find Sleeping Beauty's castle and a thicket of thorns barring our way. Around mid-morning we came to the far edge of the tableland and the hills began once more. Almost immediately the lorry started to falter, as if it could sense what lay ahead. Sydney put his foot down and took a run at them. Steam began to pour out the side vents. The lorry spat and choked and shuddered to a halt.

We jumped down and pushed her into the shade. Sydney prised up the bonnet and looked inside. The way his eyes moved from side to side, it dawned on me that he knew as much about engines as I did. Taking off his shirt, he wrapped it round his hand and unscrewed the radiator cap. Rusty water shot twenty foot into the trees. The engine hissed, the road ran red. We looked around. Not a babbling brook in sight.

'We could always stand on a bucket and pee in it,' Knowles suggested. 'Though I come from a long line of bad aimers.'

The sound of a single bell broke into the air. It was soft, like the colours that surrounded us, but sent shivers down my spine. I looked up. About a mile away I could see what looked like a ruined monastery, standing on the lip of a rocky hill, a wreath of smoke rolling up into the morning air.

'I'll take a look up there,' I said. 'You stay here and see no one makes off with anything.'

Sydney checked his pistols and propped himself up against the most comfortable-looking tree trunk. I went round the back and fished out my walking stick. By the time I returned he was fast asleep.

'Ride 'em, cowboy,' I said, and set off.

It took the best part of twenty minutes. The road must have taken us higher than I imagined, for I could feel my breath coming short, accompanied by a peculiar sense of anticipation. As I drew closer I saw that it wasn't a monastery at all, but a church, with an adjoining house, surrounded by moss and old walnut trees. The church was small, and yet possessed of a simple dignity as powerful as any Vatican; fine classical windows, neatly shaped buttresses and a simple bell tower ready to call to the flock below. Shafts of light streamed through the ruined transept. There was something for me here, I knew it. I had felt it on the path running up through the woods, seen it ripple in the leaves, and it hung now, motionless in the air. As I climbed up the last few feet of the path I could hear voices; a service I thought, but drawing nearer realized that there was not enough song or metre for that. I crossed the courtyard and standing by the chipped stone pillars peered in. Along one of the broken walls bent a row of stonemasons, chipping and chiselling at a line of stone blocks. They wore long white aprons over their clothes. The stones looked soft and yellow, like great slabs of warm butter. Leaning up against the wall stood a section of primitive scaffolding, one man balanced atop pressing fresh mortar in between the cracks. Flakes fell about the men's boots, their hair was white with dust; they looked aged, every one of them. There were colours too, in the soft blues of their trousers, the dark green of the wine bottles clustered upon the trestle table, the slash of scarlet wrapped around the plasterer's neck. I stood there, not making a sound. They did not see me, and in a way I find hard to explain I did not see them. I was witness to a scene that was taking place five hundred years before; it only lacked a Michelangelo to paint it.

One of the masons raised his head.

'*Buongiorno,*' he said. '*Come state?*' and went back to his hewing. He didn't seemed in the least surprised to see me. As I walked across he straightened up, laid his chisel on the uneven surface and brushed the front of his apron down. He looked pretty much made out of stone himself, with his arms covered in dust, and his face thickened with the chisel strokes of time. In a mixture of gesture and half-broken words he asked who I was and where I was heading to, and through a similar mixture I managed to tell him a rough approximation of the truth. I pantomimed the lorry and the steep hills, and when I puffed out the water in the radiator he laughed in recognition. I mimed the pouring of it and asked him for a can or a jugful, but he just smiled and put his hands over mine as if to slow me down, calling out to his companions. They laid aside their tools, and like him before, patted themselves down. He led me through a side door into the house and then out the opposite side, the men following in line like the seven dwarves. On a veranda overlooking the valley, presiding over a long wooden table, sat a priest in a black hat and a black habit. The table was laid on three sides, twelve places I counted. The fourth side, precariously near the edge, lay empty. After much explaining, far longer than I had needed myself, the priest rose up, and with his cloak billowing out, went to find an extra chair. We sat down. An older woman came out, with a huge plate of pasta. A younger woman followed, her daughter I assumed, carrying bowls of tomatoes and onions and green peppers. The priest said grace and we helped ourselves in turn.

It was in stretching over for the pitcher of water that I made sudden sense of the picture in which I was a participant. There was animated talk in the air, hands telling stories, food being chewed, wine being drunk. There was laughter and earnest conversation, and at the far end, the beginnings of an argument. I was sat in the middle, sandwiched between the priest and my other dusty host, breaking bread, staring out to the future. I was home amongst strangers again, part of a family, known and unknown.

A bird rose up, flapping its wings and squawking over the trees. I remembered that I had forgotten all about Sydney, asleep on the road below. I half rose in my seat, then sat back down. Sydney did not need this meal. When it was time I would take a bottle of wine for him, and a bite of food. Let him sit under his tree, I decided, dreaming of Wyatt Earp, while I sat up here, soaking up uncertain visions of myself, like a lizard in the sun. No, these men weren't my disciples, but this was my first supper if you like. I had found part of me in Gibraltar, but somewhere in this country lay the other half of me; my destiny, my salvation, perhaps the seeds of my own betrayal. I was gripped by sudden exhilaration and an unexpected fear.

When we arrived in Florence there was still fighting going on in the northern part of the city, where our hotel was situated. Sydney was shot at, and took great delight in reciprocating, sticking his pistols out of his window while I steered. It wasn't something I encouraged, but I felt it only fair to let him have his fun. By the time we arrived at the Excelsior he couldn't shove them back in his belt for the heat coming off the barrels. We got out of the lorry fast and scampered up the steps. I was carrying an upset Vincent. He wasn't used to gunplay, leastways not two foot from his cage. Sydney had his fiery pistols wrapped in his hat. The lobby was long and cool and quite empty. I rang the bell, and nothing happened. It was lovely to be back in hotel land. Walking through, a man was sprawled out in the lounge. I knew he must be American. The whole of Florence to look at and he was reading a magazine. There was a nice-looking bar, though, with the right sort of man polishing the right sort of glasses. I could see his point. He raised his hand in greeting. How he knew who we were, I had no idea. He was a good-looking fellow, with that American way of acting casual, as if nothing mattered much. He dropped the journal to the ground and ambled over in youthful ease.

'Commander Crabb, Tony Marsloe. It's a real pleasure. I've been sat here for days. You're very nearly as famous as your namesake.'

I bridled, though I knew exactly who he meant. They'd ragged me enough at bomb school about it. *King of the Jungle, King of Gamblers, Wanderer of the Wasteland.* Yes, I had a namesake, still have I suppose, an American actor, Clarence Lindon, nicknamed Buster, who spells his surname with an 'E' at the end, an olde-worlde crabbe learning to crawl in the new country. He played Tarzan once, *Tarzan the Fearless* in 1933, though in the main he lost out to Johnny Weissmuller. Personally I always thought that Buster had better swing to his body, less of a stuffed shirt when it came to yodelling. However, I didn't like to let on, not with Sydney standing behind me. He'd never mentioned Buster Crabbe, not once in three years. I ignored the observation.

'May I introduce my Number Two,' I said stiffly. 'Sydney Knowles.'

Marsloe held out his hand, then withdrew it.

'Your hat seems to be alight, soldier.'

We looked down. Smoke was pouring out of the vents. Knowles said nothing and tucked it under his arm.

'Actually sir, I'm part of the Royal Naval Volunteer Reserve. They don't countenance soldiers.'

Marsloe nodded and looked back at me.

'Is that bird ill, Commander?'

The parrot was lying on his side, one wing over his head.

'Temporarily deafened, I fear. His name is Vincent. He's teaching me Italian.' I coughed. The smoke from Sydney's boater was beginning to irritate. 'Knowles, would you care to go to the bar and avail yourself of a spare soda siphon.'

'As you wish, sir. Lieutenant Marsloe. If you'll excuse me.' He pronounced it the British way. *Lef*tenant. We both looked at the departing Knowles. The smoke rose up behind him, like a steam train coming into Euston.

'We pronounce it Lew, Commander,' Marsloe said. '*Lew*tenant Marsloe.'

'Don't you think he knows that?'

There was a slight scuffle with the barman, as Knowles reached over the counter.

'Actually Knowles is the very best,' I said.

Marsloe turned to me.

'Don't you think I don't know that,' he said and smiled. And I smiled too.

*

Like me, Marsloe had been following the mysteries of the Tenth, particularly after discovering that Borghese had been working on a plan to enter New York harbour and blow up chunks of his neighbourhood. Marsloe had a lawyer's knack for winkling things out. I was the nuts-and-bolts man. Thanks to some switching of sides, we broke the back of Borghese's fifth column. We learnt about new delayed-action limpet mines and Borghese's plan to aid the German submarines by infiltrating our newly taken ports. As our information gathered, I was appointed in command of all anti-sabotage diving operations for the whole of northern Italy. My knowledge was becoming positively embarrassing. Back and forth we went, Leghorn, Florence and in time, La Spezia, the Tenth's spiritual home. As we moved from one place to another, I began to gather up a small band of my former foes around me. They'd come in one by one, introduce themselves. We'd shake hands, have a glass of something and before they knew it I'd asked them to work with me, to make their Italy safe again. Venturini, Girai, Notari, their faces loom up at me even now, undamaged by time or disappointment. We were all young then, even the older ones. I can taste it still.

Yet, despite my promotion and our success, I began to feel out of sorts. Sydney tried his best to cheer me up, but it was no good. I became cross and irritable and, I confess, bomb-happy. They hadn't blown me up yet, and I told myself that they weren't likely to. In truth I didn't care one way or the other. Suddenly everything seemed wrong. I couldn't sleep. The food tasted terrible. I knew what it was, a bad case of Orkneyitis, that mysterious ailment to which those serving for long periods in Scapa Flow are said to be prone, its symptoms being increasing bad temper and a craving for an appointment elsewhere. Knowles, Vincent, the new-fangled mines, I couldn't stand the sight of any of them, especially the mines. If I couldn't get the bolts off easily I'd start banging them loose with a five-pound club hammer. Sydney would hide behind the sandbags with his hands over his ears. Even the cognac we'd drink before we called it a day began to turn against me. We were sat in the Excelsior's lounge one evening and Sydney ordered a glass for me and one for himself. I took one sip and spat it out on the flagstones.

'Knowles,' I shouted, 'I forbid you to drink that. It's absolute bootleg. Touch another drop and I'll clap you in irons.'

'As you wish, sir.'

He went to his little cubbyhole at the back.

I poured the rest of the muck into one of the decorative urns. It went on like that for weeks. Knowles started acting up as well. On his time off he'd take himself to his lair and stay there for hours on end. Whenever I went up and asked him what the devil he was doing, he'd hide whatever it was beneath the bedclothes.

'You writing love letters?' I would demand, looking at the suspicious bulge under his blanket.

'Something like that, sir,' he'd reply, his face bright red, and I'd nod away, even though I didn't believe a word. Knowles wasn't the type to write love letters. He wasn't the type to write anything at all, unless it was to forge a NAAFI requisition slip.

A couple of days after our last such confrontation, I was sitting out in the courtyard feeling particularly fractious, when he came over and handed me a glass of red wine. I took one sip. Exactly the same thing. Vintage bilge water. I hurled the lot to the ground.

'Are you trying to poison me, Knowles? I could have you up on the mat for this.'

He took my arm and led me to the nearest mirror. It was completely off beam. My face was thin, with lines like a pencil drawing and of a most peculiar colour.

'You've been mucking about with this glass,' I shouted. 'I won't have it, do you hear.' I turned round to face him and felt myself falling, as if from a great height, the air around me suddenly thickening, slowing me down. And then Knowles put his arms out and I remember feeling thankful, and strangely at peace and after that I don't remember anything at all.

I awoke in hospital. Jaundice. I was ill for two months. They tried to get me to go back to England but I wasn't having any of it. I was in Italy now, and I wanted to stay there. I asked Sydney to bring Vincent over for company, but the matron wouldn't allow it. Nasty diseased things, she said. Instead I put up some Picasso prints I'd bought.

'No pin-ups, Commander,' she declared. 'It offends.'

'They're not pin-ups,' I told her. 'They're pictures by a great artist.'

'If they've got naked bosoms and men spend hours looking at them, they're pin-ups,' she declared, and tore them down.

In a way she was right. I did spend hours looking at them, though

I can't say I'm an authority on bosoms. Frankly I find the whole business somewhat intimidating, the demands they make. They're easier to handle in an oil painting, though; on a couch, in a glade, flying low out of the clouds at thirty miles an hour, I can take any number of them. Picasso's are of a different order altogether. They come at you without warning, from all angles, magnificent but moderately menacing. They're the genuine article, like the ones that pop up in real life.

I kept the offending articles in my locker, for future reference.

Sydney would come and visit me once a week. He'd sit on the edge of the bed and try to make conversation. It wasn't easy for either of us, after he'd enquired about me and I'd enquired about Vincent. Word had got out that I was to be posted to Venice, to help clear the canals of the mines. Sydney wouldn't be coming with me. The war was over for him. We didn't know what to say to each other. I'd always thought that we'd end it together, or die in the attempt. Now, we were to be rent apart. One of the products of war is unlikely friendship, and the stronger it gets, the harder it is to acknowledge it. One day, he came in, with this book under his arm. In the pauses between looking out the window and winking at the nurses he would rub his fingers over the spine. As was often the case I fell asleep and when I opened my eyes, there he was, the book opened, his fingers following the lines, his lips mouthing the words.

'Not like you, ' I said, 'reading out of school.'

He blushed, like I'd caught him writing on a Valentine card.

'I've been thinking, sir, about what we do, diving, searching for things. Mostly it's mines and torpedoes, sometimes it's other things, briefcases and secrets, things that come from another time. Like the Red Cross investigating that massacre, sir, the one that Polish officer friend of yours was on about.'

'Russia, Germany, whoever, it was a vile piece of work,' I said. 'Would we do that? Could any God-fearing country? That's the point, Knowles, Germany, Russia, they've abandoned God and worship the idol that is man. Only Godless men could commit such bestialities.'

'Spain?' Knowles said. 'They've done some pretty rotten things, haven't they. And they're Catholics.'

I came back at him quickly.

'They've done away with the monarchy. It's the same thing. Overthrowing the order. It may not be perfect, but it's order that keeps us all in line, and we need keeping in line, the human race, that's my way of thinking. We don't have everything we want and never will. Some of us are dustmen, born to sweep the streets. Some of us are kings, born to rule. Breeding, Knowles, you can't get away from it. I mean Jesus came from a pretty special stock, didn't he? Likewise the monarchy. They see the world differently from someone trying to make a living selling swimfins or motorcars. They serve an ideal. As soon as we think we deserve better, order goes out the window.'

'I'm not trying to get above my station, but there must be a chance too for a man to better himself. There's nothing wrong with that, is there?'

I had to agree with him, though for some reason it sat uneasily. Is that what a man's aim in life should be, to better himself? I wasn't so sure.

'Do you know much history, sir?'

'Not much. A few dates. Christopher Columbus, Nelson, Strachan's victory off Ferrol, that sort of thing.'

'Those times when I took myself off.' He tapped his book. 'I've been reading about the Spanish Armada. Do you know much about that, sir?'

I knew quite a lot, in fact, but I let him talk on.

'When they cut and run, the Spaniards, they ran right into the teeth of this storm. It wasn't Drake that destroyed them, it was the weather, driving them onto the coast of Scotland. That's where they ended up, on the rocks, not only the soldiers and their guns and cannon, but gold and coins and all sorts, Spanish gold, Spanish coins, in chests and holds.' He clasped the book tightly, as if all that was precious to him, lay within it. 'You know when we dive down, how they loom up out at you, the mines, as if they've been expecting you.

That's how I feel about these coins, sir. When I'm trying to get to sleep, I can see them in my mind's eye, lying all motley green, untouched for hundreds of years, waiting for the war to end and me to come and rescue them. If we can dive for Italian mines and Italian torpedoes in Gibraltar, why couldn't we dive for Spanish doubloons off Scotland, and make our fortune? Make our fortune and spend the rest of our days on some island in the South Seas, with palm trees and coral reefs and all those birds of paradise.'

Poor Sydney, I could have told him why. I could have told him that you do not find dreams stamped upon motley coins. You do not find your dreams stamped anywhere.

We took our leave of each other a couple of days later. We hadn't done anything special the night before – you didn't do that sort of thing in those days. Life was just meant to be got on with. That morning I walked him out of the hotel to the waiting transport.

'We'll meet up, sir, after it's all over.' There was a hesitant, questioning look on his face. 'You are coming back, aren't you?'

'Whatever can you mean, Knowles? Course I'm coming back. I'm buying you that drink at the Nag's Head, like I told you.'

As I said it I knew it would never happen. We'd meet up all right, I was sure of that, but he didn't belong in Len's little snug, and never would. He knew it too. We'd have to find some other venue, a new meeting place for the new order. I could almost hear him thinking the same, but saying nothing. He nodded, then looked around him. I followed his gaze. There was a fountain playing. To the back of us an old man wheeled his bicycle across the courtyard, pigeons rising and falling to the squeak of his wheels. Across the way a woman opened up a first-floor shutter and began shaking a rug out the window. From deep within the room a radio was playing. *Catari, Catari.* It could have been Gigli, for all I know, for I knew nothing of him then.

'It's just – ' he waved his arms around the buildings – 'you have eyes for this, I can tell. You've had eyes for this ever since we broke down that morning. Came down that mountainside like a man in a dream. It's like when you light upon your other half for the first time, knowing, whether you like it or not, that you've found the rest of your life. Hypnotized, that's what you've been.'

'You do talk the most awful rot, Knowles,' I told him.

'What's your favourite food?' he asked.

'Gnocchi,' said I, a little too quickly.

'A pint of Wards or a bottle of red, which would you choose?'

'With gnocchi, are you mad?'

'See what I mean?' He brushed his trousers down. 'I'd better be off, then.'

'Yes, I think you'd better, before you put your other foot in it.'

'Look after yourself, sir, and don't you go missing it.'

'Missing it?'

'The opportunity, sir. What you find here, where it might lead you, don't you be frightened of it. It doesn't do to stick your heels in, to turn your back on this world. It wouldn't matter, you know, if you didn't come back. We'd get by.'

'Your country doesn't need you. Is that what you're trying to tell me?'

'Pretty soon the country won't need any of us. The trouble is, we need her, most of us, that is.'

I watched him walk towards the waiting vehicle with that lop-sided lumber of his, like he was still carrying his stoker's shovel. I wanted to call him back, to wrap him around me, to keep what we had. Once he'd gone, there'd be a hole in the defences. Corrosion would seep in, the edifice would begin to crumble. The war was coming to an end and Sydney was right. I was uneasy.

Sydney Knowles. Sydney Knowles. What's he doing now, I wonder? Something that belongs to him, I hope, digging up new potatoes on an allotment or running a couple of whippets, with a brood left home and a mantelpiece propped full of memories. Why, I might be looking down on him at this very moment, as he warms his stockinged toes and swigs his beer. He never believed that tale about finding my corpse in Chichester harbour either, a year after the Soviets reeled me in. With no head and no hands to identify me, who could, but then the Service always did like to stare improbability in the face. But the feet! No matter what the experts said about the length of immersion and the softening of bones and the little fishes nibbling at this little piggy and that, they couldn't disguise the fact that they were not the feet that Sydney used to tread on, or that Pat had oiled not a week before, to work the chilblains out. No matter. The navy had caught their Crabb and weren't going to let him go. So they packed me up and drove me out to the nearest grave they could find, with just a dog collar and my old mother in attendance. No Pat, no Sydney, no Len, no Maitland, and no Smithy; definitely no Smithy. I was glad of that.

Sydney found it hard to keep a job for long. I understood why. He'd stood on the ocean floor, seen the immensity of it; the idea of clocking in and banging out flanges – well, it can't be done. But he deserved better. He should have found those Spanish doubloons and bought himself a chariot with wings. Never looked at a painting in his life, never hid his eyes from the beauty of a Venetian dawn, never wept at the calling of a cathedral choir, but he was the man who helped save it all for the rest of us, the top of his head headed deep into the cold, the soles of his feet facing Titian's blazing heaven. No, I didn't believe in dreams. But when I got to Venice I found them everywhere, in every inch of reeking mud.

Eight

I had two attendants. Gert and Daisy I called them, both as ugly as each other. Quite which one was which didn't matter. They sat on two chairs playing with their fingernails, just to show no one gave a fig about me. The next time I saw Serov, he had a copy of *The Times* laid out before him, the date only partially obscured. The white file was nowhere to be seen. Same old glass of water. He pushed the paper over towards me. Monday, April 23rd. St George's Day. I'd been here five days. I thought of that picture of the old boy spiking the dragon with his long lance, the skulls of the beast's victims lying in the crook of his tail. I looked across at Crippen and saw those pursed lips, vengeful, pitiless fire in his mouth. Was that what I'd come to do? Lay him out before the citadel on the hill? Convert the Gentiles? Then it struck me. I'd missed the Queen's birthday. I took the glass and stood up.

'Many happy returns, Ma'am,' I declared, and tossed it back. Serov looked at me as if I'd gone off the rails. Gert and Daisy took a step forward, ready to grab me. I sat down again.

'You wouldn't understand. You lot murdered your Royal Family. Filthy thing to do. I hope Mr Khrushchev remembered to send a card.'

Serov waved the guards back.

'It is her unofficial birthday, I understand. How instructive it is to learn that your Queen should demand two birthdays while every-body else has the one. So we have given the whole family gifts, even though such privileged treatment is not something we normally condone: horses for the Duke of Edinburgh and Prince Charles and a small brown bear for Princess Anne. Nikki is his name. The horses are both pedigree prize-winners. It is something you are very keen on here, lineage.'

'You know the saying. "Breeding will out". On second thoughts, perhaps you don't.'

Serov drew the paper back, turned over the front page.

'Last Saturday the First Secretary travelled to Oxford, home of your University and the famous Oxford Debating Union. You lay great store in this society. Many of its chairmen—'

'Presidents,' I corrected him.

'Many of its presidents have become Prime Ministers or members of the government. Am I not correct?'

'Naturally. It's the perfect starting point, honing their skills for the Mother of all Parliaments. Democracy in action, when they're still wet behind the ears.'

'But all coming from one place? Where is the democracy in that? A ruling class, bred in grand houses, born with silver spoons and dressed in red hunting coats. You stand in foxholes while workers beat the fields for their enjoyment. We had this once. Now? Now we come from all walks of life. It is the land we love, the soil of Russia, not the owners of it. It is under our fingernails. We smell it in our sleep. The First Secretary comes from a black hovel in the Ukraine, the village not even a smudge on the map. His grandfather could not read. He himself went barefoot. Is that not admirable, that men of such lowly rank can rise to such heights? Did Anthony Eden ever go barefoot? Did Mr Duncan Sandys ever sleep with his father's pigs?'

'I don't think his father kept pigs.'

'Your rulers, the men who govern you, come from one class only. In the Soviet Union, it is open to anyone.'

'Anyone who's a party member. Otherwise it's still oink, oink.'

'Of course. That is our ruling class.' He clapped his hands. 'You see, we are not so very far apart. The necessity is the same, only the means are different. Some are born to rule, some are not. Everyone has their place, do you not think?'

I felt a little uncomfortable. I didn't reply. He continued, tapping the offending article.

'But this visit. The students invited him to take part in a debate. Unfortunately his diary did not permit it.'

'Just as well. He might have got a bit of a mauling.'

Serov smiled.

'You say this of the First Secretary, who only two months ago stood before the Twentieth Congress of the Soviet Communist Party and denounced Stalin? It was well for the safety of your students that he had to decline. When he speaks he speaks with his gloves off. Four hours he spoke, cataloguing Stalin's errors and crimes, Molotov, Malenkov, Voroshilov, frozen-faced, Khrushchev landing blows right and left.'

'We would call that a rant, rather than a speech. The whole point about a debate is to let the other side have a chance. Fair play. Like cricket.'

He pounced.

'A game. Exactly! Table tennis, back and forth, heads going from side to side. And when it is over, everyone packs up and goes home. Nothing has changed. Ours are different. We are called to account. At any time history may sweep us off our feet. It is the price one pays, when a country's destiny is in one's hands.'

He folded the paper into quarters. The crossword lay tantalizingly near. My fingers itched for a pencil.

'Which brings me to you. I have been thinking about you, Commander. Your destiny. What was it that sent you here?'

'Need we go through this again. I came on my ownio, toot seul.' I pointed to the crossword. 'Now if you need help with that, I'd be only too happy to oblige. Do you have such a thing in the *Moscow Herald*?'

'You are not listening to me, Commander. Not who sent you. What sent you? The motive. The First Secretary's question is of course the correct one. What sort of man does this in broad daylight? Perhaps you did not come to spy. Perhaps you came for another, more deviant purpose. Are you a delinquent, sent out to sabotage the First Secretary's visit, expecting us to leave, outraged? If that was the case, then we would ask who, who would want such a thing? The British? What would be the point. The Americans? It is possible. From them, any-thing is possible. Someone from my own country?' He stared at me hard. 'Do you work for a disgruntled faction within the Kremlin, is that it? Molotov, perhaps. Nothing would please him more than to see the First Secretary lose his temper, bang his fist on the table, cause a diplomatic incident, the visit to end in ignominy. He thinks Khrushchev a blunderer when it comes to foreign affairs.' He waved the suggestion away. 'But this is too far-fetched, too elaborate, even for Molotov. Tell me, you are not an agent of the Soviet Republics.'

I laughed. Serov joined me, a hollow rattle of a thing, like a dried pea in a tin drum.

'You are right. It is too absurd. Let us agree, Commander, that you are not an agent for renegades of the Soviet Republics. I absolve you of that accusation. Indeed I absolve you of all such fanciful accu-sations. You are not an agent for anybody, I surmise. Merely a patriotic frogman, asked to do one more piece of dirty work on behalf of his country. And to take the blame upon himself and himself alone, should anything go wrong.'

I said nothing.

'Careful, Commander. Your silence admits much.' He fingered the print again. 'Does this paper contain predictions of astrology?'

'Are you serious? *The Times*?'

'Only I remember, on my last visit, many of your newspapers do contain such stories, astrologers, fortune-tellers, the configuration of constellations. I mention it because I have to tell you my prophecy has already come true. Representations have been made regarding your intrusion. A disturbance in the water, we have told our hosts, we are not sure what, early Thursday morning. A saboteur? A rene-gade fascist, crazed remnant of the last war? Your government has expressed its regret and puzzlement. Prime Minister Eden, Foreign Secretary Duncan Sandys naturally know nothing of this incident and through the good offices of the Admiralty shower us with assur-ances of their concern and our unimpeachable safety. I expected no less, though let me tell you, in Downing Street, in Leconfield House, home of MI5 and MI6, secret-service fur will be flying. Someone is in for a pickling, mark my words. When we are gone intelligence heads will be rolling down Whitehall, bumping up against the wreaths that we laid in memory of your dead. Last night, so I am informed, Anthony Eden's face was a treasure to behold. But the result will be much as I thought. Soon your friends will begin to ask, "But where is our dear friend, Lionel Kenneth? Why do we not see him anymore? Why is his flat empty, his post unopened, his bills unpaid?" In a few days Mr Eden will have no choice. He will declare Buster Crabb extinct, a dodo, his death an unfortunate accident no doubt, or if matters persist, the result of a lonely act of reckless folly. You have been written out of the history book, Commander. We might as well finish you off. Why, if he had the chance, Prime Minister Eden would probably shoot you himself.'

'I wouldn't blame him. Getting him into all this trouble. Tell you what. If you give me the gun, I'll save everyone the bother.'

'Ah, Commander. But we do not wish you dead. You have not harmed us, only wounded our friendly expectations. Your country asked of you and you obliged. I respect that. I do not expect you to offer up the secrets of your country, to roll on the floor and beg for mercy like a dog. I know your secrets, anyway. Teddington, Portland Bill, your diving establishment here across the water. We are beginning something similar ourselves, seeking men like you, patriots, to brave the water. Tell me, what sort of man is needed to do this lonely work? What are the qualities we should be looking for? In Italy, for instance, the men you worked with, the men you fought against, what sort of men were they?'

So I told him. Well, it passed the time.

*

I hitched a ride on a plane carrying blood. I nearly asked a pint or two for myself, I felt that tired. I'd been out of hospital for little under a week. The plane was noisy, with no room to stretch my legs. My feet began to hurt. They weren't used to laced boots at altitude. When we landed it was late afternoon and the air was laden with a dank and heavy mist, more like mid-November than early April. Marsloe was waiting for me with what looked like a wedge of fruit cake in his hand.

'Buster,' he said. 'You look terrible. Where's Vincent?'

'You're lovely too,' said I, nodding to the cage behind my luggage. I was pleased he'd remembered the bird. He bent down and pushed the offering through the bars.

'We've got him a very nice room,' he said. 'Quite a view.'

I'd heard people bang on about Venice, of course, it was one of the dangers of living in Knightsbridge, but I couldn't quite envisage what all the fuss was going to be about. Marsloe showed me to a launch and we cut through the cloy, thin black poles sticking up through the flattened water looking like markers for lost boatmen. I felt as if I was sailing through a forgotten graveyard. After a while we turned into what appeared to be a broad canal, tumbledown ware-houses, half-derelict dwellings and bits of rusty crane peering out of the gloom. We carried on this way for about ten minutes then turned into a broader stretch. Though I could hardly see anything, I could sense that we'd come up in the world. Marsloe ran his fingers through his hair and straightened up, as if he was about to be introduced to someone important.

'Is this it, then?' I asked him.

'This is it,' he said.

We chugged on. I peered about as best I could.

'I must say I prefer Brighton myself. Two piers, one pavilion and an hourly train service back to London. This,' I said, searching for the right word, 'this is distinctly morbid.'

Marsloe held his gaze.

'If you say so.'

We sloshed around. I wasn't used to this type of water, murky and lifeless, like a pot of cold tea. I hadn't expected quite so much of it either. They'd simply plonked the buildings straight into it. It was quite mad when you came to think of it.

'The hotel?' I asked. 'Is it very damp?'

'The Danieli? Not very.'

We seemed to go on like this for a long time, chugging along in the middle of this muffled waterway, its edges blurred and motley, everything touched by a clammy whiff of sulphur. I should have shown more interest but all I wanted was a bath and a bed. When we tied alongside a jetty, a chap in a peaked cap took my bags and led me across to the hotel. It had a reputation, the Danieli, but I was too far gone to notice if it lived up to it. I followed the flunkey like a blind man, into the lift, along the corridor, up to the bedroom door. I knew it was going to be OK for the key he used was approximately of the same dimensions as his feet. It was a decent enough size, the room, suitable for one of the minor European monarchs, with a marble washstand in the far corner and a couple of comfy thrones by the window. The shutters had already been closed. Recalling Marsloe's words, I sat on the edge of my bed and debated whether I should take off my boots first and then open the shutters, or open the shutters first and take off my boots afterwards. Twelve hours later I awoke to find I had done neither. Slats of fresh sunlight ran across my face. I walked over to the sink and saw someone in need of shave. Then I remembered. I hadn't seen anything yet. I crossed over and worked the latch free.

The mist had gone. The morning had come.

I rubbed my eyes and Venice rushed in.

How long did I stay there? One hour, three? It's hard to say. How many times did I rub my eyes? Once? Twice? A hundred? Every time I opened them again I expected it all to have vanished and the world to have come to its senses, but every time, it was still there, that dome suspended above the water, like something a deity might hold in his hands.

I put a hat and coat on and went outside. I had an appointment with Marsloe at ten, but I had other things on my mind. They say that a young woman stepping out of water is one of the most beautiful sights known to man, the light, the bloom on her skin, and that may well be, but seeing Venice uncover herself that morning invoked similar feelings. I could imagine embracing Venice, going to sleep alongside Venice, waking to the glorious knowledge that she was lying by my side. To think that such a creature had existed without me for so long. I felt consumed by a sudden surge of jealousy towards all those who knew her better than me. I crossed the Grand Canal and plunged into a myriad of waterways, half hidden like overgrown paths, littered with sounds and shadows without form. I could envisage murder committed over Venice, suicides taken in her abandoned name, a city of souls subjected to every crossed passion. Possession, that was the word.

When I got back Marsloe was waiting for me in the foyer, looking at his watch.

'Sorry about that,' I said. 'But it's pretty easy to get lost round here.'

Tony laughed.

'It's absolutely essential, Buster.'

I went up and changed into my working clobber. Marsloe had the day mapped out. After breakfast he took me across the water, past the Lido, to the little island of Le Vignole, where the Tenth Flotilla had made their headquarters. There was diving equipment, half-digested chariots, torpedo shells, everything you might need to create a little homespun havoc, lying about like last Sunday's confetti. Just a burly sergeant and a spotted dog guarding the lot. Marsloe threw a stick in the water and we watched as the hound jumped in.

'He says they hid quite a lot of stuff down there, so the partisans wouldn't get at it.'

I tapped my chest. 'I can take a look now if you wish. I'm all togged up.'

'Later,' Tony said. 'I want you to meet someone.'

I've been in a couple of police cells in my time, but never one with water lapping at the bars. There were two fellows in there. The younger was pacing up and down going nowhere, as the young are prone to do. The other was playing patience on a three-legged stool. His head was shaved and his body nothing but a bag of bones, but I recognized him all right.

'Blow me,' I exclaimed. 'If it isn't Belloni.'

'And he speaks English,' Marsloe said, 'quite good English too. That's his son,' he added. 'But he barely speaks anything at all.'

'Well, tell him he can go home. It's father we're after.'

The gaoler hauled the younger Mr B outside. Belloni went on with his card game, pretending he hadn't noticed. I opened the cell door and stepped in. He was dressed in a tatty pair of shorts, and on the sleeve of his shirt he still sported the badge of the Tenth Flotilla, a skull with a rose in its jaws, laid upon the figure X.

'Signor Belloni? May I introduce myself?'

He looked up and quickly shuffled the cards back into a pack. There was a good deal of skill in those fingers.

'Speak up,' he shouted. 'I am deaf.'

I took a deep breath. It's not easy upping the decibels in a six by eight fleapit. I did it, but crikey, it hurt.

'My name is Commander Crabb,' I yelled. 'You may have heard of me. It's time we worked together. We are going to save your city, you and I.'

I held out my hand. He drew back.

'I know you,' he bellowed. 'You bastard my suit. I make it one way and you bastard it another.'

I shook my head.

'Not me, old chap. Some idiot at Whitehall. Belloni suits, numero uno. Nothing better.' I unbuttoned my shirt. 'Look. I wear one myself.'

Belloni minor was sent home to mater. Belloni major and I had a very civil lunch while Marsloe sorted out the paperwork. Strictly speaking he was a prisoner of war, destined for one of the camps, but that would have been madness. We needed him here. Thanks to the partisans it wasn't safe for him to stay in Venice, so he agreed to move to Le Vignole, and bring some of his old comrades with him. As we climbed into the launch a rowing boat came alongside, with two young women at the oars. On seeing the three of us, the younger of the two clambered to her feet and started berating me at the top of her voice. She was a good-looking thing, with a mass of dark hair and a nose that emperors would have sacked a couple of cities for, but she left me cold. Too pushy. Marsloe, however, was rooted to the spot.

'Look at that bust,' he whispered. I affected not to hear. He liked doing that, introducing 'buster' or variants thereof, into the conversation. She had an eye-catching figure, I had to admit.

'Anything wrong?' I asked Belloni. He shrugged his shoulders.

'That is my youngest daughter, Minella,' he barked. 'She says you are a bastard and that you are going to shoot me.'

'Tell her I thought about it, but I'm a very bad shot.'

He tried to reassure her, but it wasn't enough. She lifted her oar out of the water and started jabbing it in my direction. She had a good sense of balance and pretty good muscle control too. Put a pair of swimfins on her and she could wrestle torpedoes with the best of us.

'Oh, Minella,' intoned Marsloe. 'I think I might have to marry you.'

Her voice grew louder, her movements more reckless, the oar scything the air with increasing vigour. Every once in a while I was obliged to lean back, to avoid being clocked on the noddle. Pretty soon one or both of us were going to end up in the drink. That was all right with me. Marsloe would come to her rescue. Then suddenly her companion reached up, and placing a hand on her arm, spoke to her, softly and gently. They were not many words but they filled the air like a bar of music, like something Bach might have written, something of quiet, unhurried, strength. I thought of Sydney's recent words and the bell we had heard that distant morning. The oar dropped and the woman sat down, her breath defiant, her body subdued.

'And the other one?' I said. 'Who's she? Her keeper?'

'That is Paola. My oldest. Three good husbands she has turned down.'

At the sound of her name she looked across, first at her father, and then at me. If I didn't know any better I would have said she was smiling.

'Paola,' I said, and nodded my head in her direction. *Bene, bene, bene.*

★

There is a word in Italian, *tavola*. It means table, and if there was one word that could sum up my time in Italy, apart from the canals and the bombs and the wonder of my new-found city, it would be *tavola*, from that first lunch with the nameless workmen to the final meal with Paola and her family and me working my way into the thickets they had so painstakingly laid out.

We were rivals in a way, Tony and me, the way he threw his cap at Minella, the way I tipped mine in Paola's direction. Only he got in first. It was always going to be like that. He was American after all, and holding back is not one of their habitual traits. Tony was a good-looking fellow, young, muscular, with that overwhelming self-confidence that marks so many of his compatriots. He wore his uniform as if he'd just stepped out of central casting. He fitted in more easily than me. His Italian was relaxed; he knew how to flatter the mother, joke with the brother, knew the words of honour he should employ in the father's presence. More importantly, as far as Minella was concerned, he knew how to flirt, how to court such a restless young woman. I remember once as we came in on the boat, Minella and Paola waiting by the dock, how he stood on the port side, looking out, pretending he hadn't seen them, knowing that she'd be summing him up, his profile, his stance, the way his eyes were hitched to the future. That was the attraction, his prospect, his confidence. And what did I have to offer? Precious little. Men like me don't have a future. There's something static about us. At some point in our lives we say, there, that's it. This is me earning a crust, this is me with my feet up. Take it or leave it.

We began working with Paola's father almost straight away. At any time during the day, wherever you might be on our little island, you could hear him shouting at the top of his voice, as if caught in a gale. 'Papa Angelo, begets beauties, bellows baloney,' that's how Marsloe described him. Baloney. I used to love that word, the way it conjured up Italian mealtimes, bread and wine and great plates of steaming baloney laid out for one and all. Belloni appeared unruffled by his circumstance, but the truth was, in the early days his life hung on a pretty thin thread. There were all manner of unsavoury characters around who would have liked to make him suffer for their politics. The family, glad of the protection we gave him, were nevertheless solicitous as to his safety, and every lunchtime would ferry over a meal, just in case we'd decided to save everyone the bother and do away with him ourselves. For the first week or so it was Minella alone who came. She took after her father, with her fierce looks and haughty gait, announcing her arrival with a quite unnecessary exhibition of theatrics, shouting at the top of her voice a couple of hundred yards out. Its one advantage was that it gave Marsloe plenty of time to get spruced up, and by the time her boat slid alongside the steps, he was down there with his tongue hanging out, ready for inspection. Smartness in a man is an essential quality, but there's a time and place for these things, and for my money lounging about waist-deep in the Venetian primeval wasn't one of them. To begin with I thought she must share my view. She'd throw him the rope and walk straight past.

'Cut out the subtleties,' I suggested. 'Just roll over, like the dog you are.'

Blow me, though, if it didn't begin to work; day five, a manicured hand held out as she stepped ashore; day six, a broken sentence, delivered with the merest flutter of eyelash. That Sunday she decided to let her father starve and didn't appear at all. Marsloe slunk around looking like he'd just eaten a bar of soap. But the following day she came in, a little later than usual, standing on the prow, smiling and waving and flashing a set of ivories that would have graced Liszt's best pianola. That was it. By the week's end they were moseying down to her father's quarters with her hand laid out on his arm, as if they'd been going steady for years. I'd never seen anything like it. Just shows you what perseverance and a pot of brilliantine can do.

We began to set our clock by her, wouldn't even think of lunch until the air was torn in half by her imprecations. That's why the first time Paola made the trip she was tying up their boat before anyone noticed her at all. Marsloe was quite put out, his greeting dead on his lips when he realized who it was. He didn't mean to be rude. Time was precious in those days, that's all. I rather pushed my way past.

I hadn't forgotten that look. Who could? It reminded me of one of those expressions you see in paintings, like the Mona Lisa. In your mind the figure is always smiling, whether you are there or not. The smile is present for all of time. It plays on the face of the subject and it plays upon the spirits of those who have seen it. No doubt Rosa knows of that smile, as do her kinfolk who hurry back and forth on these cold Karlovy Vary days. Pat, Smithy, even Sydney, know of it. It crosses time and space, it is a smile fit for Albert Einstein and his equations. And that is how I saw Paola's smile and that is how I have always seen it. At its essence it contains the secret of our universe.

Her hair was tied back with a ribbon of some sort. She hefted the basket onto her arm and made to alight. She was less confident than her younger sister, and I liked her for it.

'There's no need, you know,' I called down. I spoke slowly, as one might to a child. 'We will feed your father.'

She shook her head.

'He must my mother's food.' She gripped her forearm and rattled her flesh. She had kitchen arms. I could imagine her with a rolling pin, smacking out pastry. 'In the war he was busy. He did not eat. Now it is the same. He is too thin.' She looked up, hesitating. 'You do not wish me to come?'

Was that a ploy on her part? I could see Minella saying it, lowering her fiery eyes, dependent and defiant, but Paola? And yet I suppose it must have been, for without warning I found myself floundering.

'You misunderstand me. I didn't mean . . .'

I paused. She waited. I was glad of the language difference. It hid my awkwardness, at least that's what I told myself. It did nothing of the sort, most likely. They are used to these sorts of things, the other sex, seeing grown men reduced to blubber. I jumped down and helped her ashore. As I took the basket I could hear the clink of bottles underneath the white napkin, smell a waft of cheese. I was conscious of the others watching, Marsloe especially. I didn't want to, but I felt obliged to raise the subject.

'Your sister,' I said, pointing to the now empty boat. 'She is not angry again? She is pleased with how we are treating your father?'

'She is very pleased,' she said, humour in her voice. 'Every day she is learning American, she is so pleased.'

'She has a good teacher. You speak the lingo very well.'

'I speak English, not American.'

There was an unexpected tartness to that remark which I rather appreciated. Perhaps Marsloe wasn't every woman's dream as both he and I had imagined. She took the basket back. There were goose bumps on her arms and her face shone from the water's glare. It was warm up on the quayside, but there had been a chill out on the lagoon that morning. As she strode up the steps, she caught sight of Marsloe and began talking again. The topic hadn't gone away.

'She is mad, my sister,' she confided, 'first this way and then that. It gives my father many headaches. Now she spends her days dreaming, adventure, romance, romance, adventure. The war has crazied her. She wants more.'

'More war?'

'More adventure. More . . .' She waved her arms about. 'This is an old country. She wants a young one, a new world. And so she dreams.'

I wondered whether she was conscious of what she was saying, of Opus 95. It was one of the records we'd played on the boat to China. Suddenly I could picture her in that little cabin, curled up in one of the wicker chairs, listening to that music. I could see us taking such a journey, her and me. Company, that was the word. A new concept for me.

'And you,' I said. 'What do you dream of?'

'Me?' She raised her eyes and looked me full in the face. 'I do not dream. I go to church and pray. Prayers are better than dreams.'

'Pray? Pray for what?'

I don't know why I sounded so surprised. Of course she prayed. There was an unflagging faith written on that face, a belief in the power without and the power within. There was her family and her city, there was her nation and the infinite beyond. She was bounded by unbreakable bonds.

She opened her hands. 'For prayer itself. That we do not forgot the strength of it, wherever we are.'

She went to feed her father and I hovered by the quay, waving away my own lunch, so as not to miss her. I wasn't going to flunk this one. When she returned I waited until she was back on the boat before I said my piece.

'I would like to go to church,' I said, 'even though I would not understand the words. Perhaps one day, if it wouldn't be too much trouble, you could take me to yours.'

She looked at me for a long time, as if to judge the sincerity of my request, and I too was searching for the answer to that question. Was it the thought of kneeling to God or kneeling beside her that had captured me? I felt ashamed of myself, in front of her honest face. This was a city of so many seductions. She settled the oars into their stirrups.

'Perhaps,' she said, and began rowing away.

*

Soon the sisters started coming over together, and the food they brought was not simply sufficient for the family, but for the two interlopers as well. Trouble was, we had work to do all over the city, and our timetable would not always allow for a couple of hours off at midday. So, weather permitting, it evolved into a later ritual, Paola and Minella rowing out early evening, the light still lying on the water, while Belloni set the table and Tony and I made ourselves presentable. Tony had all manner of ointments at his disposal, eau de colognes, hair oils, stuff to dab on your face before the razor, stuff to dab on after. I'd never seen a man for such scented toiletry. A comb dipped in a glass of water had always been sufficient for me.

The seating was usually the same, Belloni at the head of the table and the rest of us ranged round in order of seniority; Paola and me to his immediate left and right, Marsloe and Minella the same configuration only one place down, sisters and officers diagonal, Romeo and Juliet a salt cellar apart. Their father directed the conversation, rolling subjects down the pitch of the cloth for us to bat back at him.

He spoke, in the main, of recent times, of the world under water, rather than the one above. He was a tough old boot and hankered after his days of glory. His head was still full of wild dreams. If we'd let him have his way we'd have all trotted off in one of his new mini-subs and given Tokyo a spot of bother. Up till Italy's capitulation he'd been working on a plan to do something similar to New York, but now we were all allies, he was quite prepared to change the name on the map. Like all true military men he was resolutely democratic when it came to his country's choice of enemies.

Minella said little on these occasions, her American didn't allow it, but she made up for it with the way her presence seemed to set the globe alight. She had a strange incandescent quality about her, like phosphorus on water, as if the elements, the sun, the moon, the stars, were simply there to make her sparkle.

'She should be in films,' I said one night to Marsloe, as we watched them row back, Minella singing some improbable song to the sky.

'That's what worries me,' he drawled. 'When I get her home, I'm going to have to keep the blinds drawn.'

He was so certain of success, not surprising really when you consider that half his work was already done for him. Skyscrapers, jazz clubs, gangsters, New York had it all. She would cup her head in her hands, her eyes opening like daffodils, as he boasted of the lights and the nights and the way the high and the low rubbed shoulders with each other. He was a good chap, Marsloe, but I found it all rather tiresome.

'You must have joints like that in London,' he once said, aware of my studied silence.

'Not that I'm a member of,' I said, unable to disguise my pettiness. 'Some pretty nice pubs, though, where a fellow can nurse a pint and keep himself to himself.'

Paola leant forward.

'What is this, keeping yourself to yourself?'

And for once I didn't.

'It's a kind of unwritten rule in my country, like the constitution,'

I explained. 'Don't interfere. Don't pry. Don't offer things up. Keep everything ticking over, with the minimum of fuss. It's an expression of contentment, really, of not wishing to be anything other than what we are. Even when we're out, we're in. No explanations, no discussion, no one poking his nose in, offering up opinions. Every man's home is his castle, that's our motto.'

Minella sniggered, Marsloe raised his eyebrows. They didn't understand. They might have the odd palace, but castles didn't belong much in Venice, nor in New York. They had squares and courtyards and apartment roofs, they had streets and cafes. They had *tavolas*, where people could spread their conversations out for all to hear. Keeping oneself to oneself did not apply. I didn't say any more that night.

Though it interested us two men, Belloni's constant talk of war tired his daughters, Paola especially. She tried her best not to show it, making light of his belligerence, fussing over him, telling him to stop talking and start eating. She disguised it as a consideration for his health, but it wasn't that. She wanted peace and calm. She wanted that smile of hers to rule the world again. The more he talked of his plans and inventions, the more my eyes fell on her. One evening, when he was at the other end of the table, demonstrating to Marsloe the weakness in New York's harbour defences, I managed to question her. Paola, it transpired, had worked for him.

'In the war?' I asked.

'In the war and before also. Taking notes, asking for money, writing letters, governments, ministers, the navy. There is only one thing for Papa, the water, his submarines, his men, how they must breathe, how long they stay under. On land he is blind. Only in water does he open his eyes.'

'But what wonderful things to see there. As you must know.'

She shook her head.

'He does not allow us. Is not for women, he say.'

'Why on earth not?'

She shrugged her shoulders.

'It is not important.'

'He must have a reason.'

'I cannot say.'

Colour flooded into her cheeks. She did not want to embarrass her father, but I was determined.

'Tell me,' I urged her. 'Maybe I could talk to him, one diver to another.'

She took a deep breath.

'The top half of a woman, he says, is too much to go down.'

She fiddled with her food. I cursed myself roundly. That I should force her to talk of such things.

'Well, as far as Venice is concerned you're not missing much,' I told her as cheerfully as I could muster. 'It looks lovely on the surface, but down below it's an absolute sewer.'

She straightened up, dabbing her mouth with a slice of bread. There was a look to her face, to her eyes, as if she was glad of what had been said. I was aware of her then, as a woman with a woman's body, its shapes and suggestions just a few feet away. I was sensitive too of her being conscious of my intimations. Her physical presence had been laid out on the table, amongst the bread and salads, and I lacked the knowledge to know how to deal with it. I'd never really given much thought to that sort of thing before. Don't get me wrong, I came into this world the right way up, but it had always seemed to me that the man–woman business often proved to be an unnecessary diversion from the decent things in life. Plumbing; matters of the bathroom; knowing more than was good for you; it all got in the way, made life a little bit sordid. Let's face it, given half the chance, man's a bit of a pig at heart, and Heaven knows, there's enough muck available for us all to drown in. And yet, here she was, this Paola, with her smile and her womanly attributes, plucking at my strings.

'And other places?' she asked.

I jumped in, eager to please.

'Some other places it's crystal clear, with shapes and colours such as you've never seen before. That's how I imagine Venice, you know; as an underwater city risen from the sea, all fresh and sparkling. Somewhere down there is a whole kingdom of Venices.

Perhaps one day I'll find it. And when I do I shall come and take you there, and you will sit on a seashell throne, with or without your father's permission.'

I swallowed hard. I had made love to her! Almost without knowing.

She was pleased, I could tell. She looked over, to where Belloni was still extolling his plans, Minella playing footsie under the table, her calf flexed straight out. She had strong, swimmer's legs.

'You asked me to take you to a church,' Paola said. 'In three days, this Sunday, if you wish. But before, there is someone you must meet.'

'A priest?'

'Not a priest.'

'Who?'

'I will not say. But you will come?'

Her eyes opened, like cool caverns, inviting me to dive in. I felt a wave break over my head, my sense of equilibrium knocked sideways.

'Of course.'

A shout went up, a roar delivered in jest. Minella ceased her little game. Belloni clinked his glass and kneaded Marsloe's shoulder. Paola reached across and gripped my hand quickly.

'Then speak no more of this,' she said. 'Until Sunday.'

*

For the first time in my life I grew impatient with my work. Those two days simply dragged by. She didn't appear once. Perhaps the conversation had unsettled her as much as it had me. Perhaps she was beginning to regret her promise. Come that day's dawn, I was hammering at Marsloe's door.

'I'm off to see Paola this morning,' I said.

'You've told me,' Tony said. 'You've told everyone.'

Had I? I didn't remember that at all. I thought I'd been the duke of discretion.

'The point is, Marsloe . . .' I flapped the corner of my duffel coat. 'I think I might pong a bit. It's all very well out here, amongst the sea urchins, but seated next to her, in a church? I was wondering if you might make me the beneficiary of your expertise in this matter, volunteer an unguent or two.'

'I thought you'd never ask,' he said, and hauled me inside.

Three hours later I was waiting by the Zattere in our launch in full plumage, the first time I had worn the twin-set and pearls since arriving. To my surprise she came along on the dot. I shouldn't have been, of course. She wasn't one to play games. I'd been wondering about the tone I should adopt. I was going to church, after all, not a music-hall matinee. Where did formality end, familiarity begin? What was I seeking, Catholicism or courtship? As she stepped into the boat she raised herself on her toes and placed her lips on my old skin. It felt like I'd kicked a heap of autumn leaves, a feathery gentleness fluttering all about me. Then she drew away, her hand to her mouth.

'Tony,' she said, waving it back and forth, 'in his bathroom. You have been with Tony.'

I couldn't deny it.

'Why, have I done something wrong? He told me to give it the works.'

She shook her head.

'It is good,' she said. 'The water is very bad this morning.'

If it was I didn't notice. We rounded the Accadèmia and chugged up midstream, passing the palace where Lord Byron used to take a dip. It struck me then that if you liked bathing the Grand Canal was probably the best swimming pool in the world: lots of places to get changed, a decent length for a spot of doggy paddle and with a bit of luck someone waiting on the steps with a towel and a large brandy when you were done.

A short distance from his old quarters, we came to a broken-down mansion, imposing enough in a blackened sort of way, but dead like a fallen tree trunk. The shutters looked all gnawed and nibbled; the long iron balcony that ran across its frontage had come loose from its moorings and hung down like a ripped thumbnail. Rotten to the core, that was the phrase that sprang to mind. Throw a line round one of the pillars at the front and you could have given Samson a run for his money.

Paola tied the launch to the landing stage. It looked pretty unsafe to me, but she jumped ashore, unperturbed. She'd been here before, obviously. I followed her up the steps. As she pushed open the great black door, a flurry of cold air rushed over us. It smelt old and neglected, but more than that, it smelt diseased. I turned and looked back across the water. I had seen Venice from many angles. I had looked down at it from bridges, I had seen it from its walkways, its palace roofs. I had travelled its length, probed its muddy foundations, drunk from its verandas, but never like this, with a front door open and its life blood lapping at my feet. That's when I understood. It was alive, this Venice. The sulphurous bubbles that rose up from the milky water were its breath, the soft mire from whence they came its spongy lungs. The city rose and fell, a living thing, possessing a beauty which man alone could never have accomplished. But for all its loveliness, Venice lay sick, like a beast on a bed of straw, its eyes clouded, its heart troubled.

I followed Paola into a marble hallway. The walls hung with worn tapestries, a faint glimmer of light falling upon the stone staircase that rose in a curve at the back. We walked towards it, our footsteps echoing the building's desolation. Paola turned and smiled, a smile different from any I had seen before, a smile of knowledge and concealment. A single man and woman do not mount strange stairs alone for many purposes and the thought came to me that she had brought me here for that reason, so secretive her demeanour, so beguiling her steps, and I hated myself for imagining such a thing. Her hand lingered on the balustrade, as if daring me to touch it, and in that dare give shameless impetus to our ascent. The first floor, the second floor, I dared not speak. A Venice I knew by reputation only was threatening to envelop me, the Venice of masks and guttering candles, the Venice of falseness and base pleasure. What sort of prelude was this to our visit to her church? Or was there to be no church? I was climbing but the weight of temptation was dragging me down.

Then we were on the second floor, the hall caverns below. I felt dizzy and starved of oxygen. We walked the length of a long and narrow corridor, towards a small black door. Then we were through, into shuttered room after shuttered room, past shrouded furniture and pictures draped with white sheets, as if they were ashamed of what was about to take place within their walls. Finally she drew back a pair of double doors. I found myself blinking in the sunlight, unable to focus, like that first morning in the Danieli. Standing in front of the window was a woman dressed in black, staring at the water below.

Paola called out.

'Maria, here is my promise. I have brought him to you. Commander, may I introduce Maria Visintini. You knew her husband, I believe.'

Nine

I do not have many possessions; my government Order of Honour, the picture of Pat and her little dog sitting by their swimming pool in the South of France that Serov saved to keep me warm in those early Baltic winters, a good-luck charm from Yurka. They sent a dog up before Yurka. Laika was her name. She looked a bit like Pat's. The British would never have done that, sent a dog up. There would have been an outcry. But the Russians were very proud that their country had taken the lead. If it required a dog to do it, then so be it. I hadn't been there for long, so I couldn't see things in quite the same light. I felt sorry for that dog. There are worse things that have happened, I know that, but it was the loneliness she must have felt that got to me, the first creature to sail above the earth and the first to die there too. I can't remember what killed her. Fright, most probably. Mother Russia should have rewarded her, she should have spent her days on terra firma, with the Legion of Honour tied round her collar. After all, they rewarded me, the winter of 1960. Could have nailed it on and I wouldn't have noticed, it was that cold. If me, why not her? When I was at my lowest, I used to think of that dog, strapped in, head held tight, unable to look left or right, nothing she knew to hold on to.

What else have I got left of my life? Not much. The silver-topped cane got left behind at Portsmouth, my favourite frogsuit was dropped into the Channel wrapped around my headless stand-in and as for the George Medal, who knows? Perhaps Pat has it, perhaps Sydney. Perhaps it's growing crusty in some Whitehall basement, under bureaucratic lock and key, like its owner. No matter; there's not much value in such symbols of loyalty any more. I have nothing from

Paola, that is how it should be. She had already given me all that she could. But I do have a Venetian memento, kept in my wallet alongside Pat's picture, though in truth, why I still keep it I do not know. More out of respect than for any other reason. It meant something to me once, for in those days I shared his sentiments. Now it simply serves as a reminder of what was and what no longer is.

It can be a bit awkward, being introduced to the widow of a man you've recently consigned to the Almighty. It tends to stifle conversation. I stood stock-still, half expecting some brother or other relative to rush out from behind the drapes and have at me with a rapier, but instead she stepped out of the light, tall and elegant, and held out a hand, long in the bone. She wore no make-up and her fair hair was tied back tight. Like the room in which she stood, her dress was stylish but worn. Hard times it looked to me. There was the wedding ring, of course.

'We were all most grateful for what you did for Licio when he died,' she said. 'His friends watched from the villa. When Paola told me who her father was working with, I asked her to arrange a meeting.'

'She never told me.' I was a little put out that Paola hadn't seen fit to take me into her confidence.

'That was my idea also. I was afraid you would not come.'

'What is it you want to know? I can't tell you much. He died very quickly. I can tell you that.'

'Not for me,' she said, 'for me his death is very slow. But Paola brings you here so that I may thank you, for the honour you showed him. You shared many things, I think.'

It was a nice little speech, prepared, but sincere.

'I saw him only the once, through binoculars the morning before the raid. I liked the look of him.'

'We all liked the look of him. Me above all others. I liked the look of him very, very much.'

I could feel myself blushing.

'And could he speak English as well as you?'

She shook her head.

'Only Italian. Italia, Italia. He lived for Italia. He loved his country.'

'As should any true man.' I took a deep breath. What did she expect me to do, wring my hands, ask her forgiveness? It was all very well, being corralled by these two women, but I had to say my piece. 'Look, this is difficult. I cannot say I am sorry for what happened, for I too love my country, and will defend it to the best of my abilities. If that means the death of those who oppose it, then so be it. I don't feel bad about it, but neither did I relish it. It was what was, that's all there is to it. There are men who were my enemies who are working with me now. They know this, I believe.'

She gestured to a group of stiff-looking chairs.

'Please. There is something else.' From a small table she picked up a bundle of papers. 'He wrote many letters to me from the Villa Carmela. I would like to read some of them to you.'

'If you so wish it, by all means.'

She cleared her throat and shuffled the papers once or twice. I could see the slanted handwriting delineated in clean black ink. 'Since I have been here, I have ceased to belong to you, for my work occupies my thoughts completely,' that's how she began, and I thought how affecting it was that she should start with a letter that had cut her loose. As she worked her way through them, I could almost feel him moving away from her, swimming towards me. She read in a clear voice, barely faltering, the three of us seated in a bare semicircle, the windows leading to the balcony, open. Sounds were coming from outside, bells and traffic on the water, a young boy calling out, his voice shrill and urgent, yet in there, it seemed as if the world had been suspended for a while, so that I might apprehend it more clearly. I could see his life laid out, clean and white, like that empty shirt of his, and it dawned on me then that perhaps I was destined to wear that shirt, to take on his mantle, and let Venice and Paola and this calm and graceful widow wrap their faith around me, convert me to their religion. I sat and listened, only half aware of what was being said, acutely conscious of my own unspoken thoughts. 'My great plan is ripe', that phrase held, for in my mind's eye that is how I saw my future, hanging like some ripe fruit, and Paola ready to gather it in her hand, to consume it, the juices of my life running out of her mouth. Most of his other words have long since faded. I remember better Maria Visintini's fingers running anxiously up and down the pages, as she searched the letters, choosing the passages she wished to read, swallowing the phrases of those she did not, her only sign of nervousness. What she saw in my face I do not know, but in all my time in Gibraltar I had never written such a letter, never had someone like Maria, restless to receive it, and I felt a numbness come over me, as you do when you are alone in the depths of darkened water, with only the bubbles of your breath there to remind you that you are alive.

Then she paused and took out another fold of paper, tucked into the pocket of her dress.

'This was written a few hours before he left. You saw him that day, you say?'

'Yes. Early morning, from the harbour. It was in a very good position, the villa. Caught us on the hop, on more than one occasion.'

'And how did he seem?'

'Seem? Determined. Calm. Courageous. He was drinking coffee.'

'That morning, the son I was carrying, he started to kick most violently, struggling, as if unhappy. I thought then . . .'

Her voice trailed off. Paola held out a sympathetic hand which she squeezed quickly before resuming her equilibrium. I attempted a diversion.

'A son, you say. You have a son?'

'We had a son. He is with his father now.'

She began to read again. He knew his time was up, that much was clear. 'Nothing can stop us now save death', that's what he wrote, and yet he seemed to want death as much as victory, the two of them coiled together like strands of a rope. Death *was* the victory. A life devoted to his country, his soul would be safely delivered to the realms of eternal peace. That was the difference between him and me. He looked to glory in the heavens. I just looked forward to a decent G and T.

She folded the letter in half.

'This is all. It seems his belongings, my letters to him, much has been lost. When we surrendered, they left in great haste, I think. I have nothing of his from that time.'

I coughed uncomfortably.

'I have a confession to make. When we found his body he was wearing swimfins.' I hesitated. 'I am ashamed to say I took them from him. They were very good swimfins. Are very good swimfins, I should say. If you like . . .'

She waved the suggestion away. 'What am I to do with these things? Put them on the wall? No, you keep them. And something else. I have a photograph of him, on the estate of Duke of Salviati, where first their plans were put together. See?'

She held the photograph out. There he was, squinting into the sun, that clean white shirt again and a body simply aching with pride.

'He was a good enemy,' she said, 'as were you. So take this picture, so that you may look upon him, as he now looks upon you, working on his behalf.'

After a plate of little cakes and some idle chatter about our work, we took our leave and went to Paola's church. On the way she told me of Maria Visintini's circumstances. She'd been a secretary in the years before the war, but now was practically destitute, living on handouts from families like Paola's.

'She needs work,' she said firmly.

'Well, don't look at me,' I told her. 'You know what your father thinks about lady divers.'

The walk took a hot fifteen minutes. When we got there I wondered whether it had been worth it. We'd passed some pretty impressive-looking buildings, but this looked distinctly dingy. She caught the look on my face.

'Many are grander,' she said. 'None more special.'

It was packed, so we squeezed in at the back. It was my first time in a Catholic church, attending a service in Italian, and to begin with I wished I hadn't come. I knew the rudiments of it, but after the initial formalities were over there was nothing I could do save open my mouth and mime piety. In the end I just kept to my seat and let it flood over me. Though I hadn't a clue as to the detail, I got the gist all right, the order, the solemnity, the acceptance of complete authority. They had a way of doing things that never varied. It reminded me of diving. You obeyed instructions, followed the rule book, did everything in the right order. Once you'd mastered the routine, it was safe to jump in. The Catholic Church is the same. When it comes to the big day, it makes damn sure you're well prepared.

After a while I started to take stock of my surroundings. There were paintings all around the walls, like a frieze telling a story. The three to my left were easy enough: St George slaying the dragon; St George showing the beast off to a variety of dignitaries; St George baptizing another bunch of worthies, Turks judging by the profusion of turbans. There were others, though, by the same artist, which evaded me; one had a flat-faced little girl and a basilisk baring its teeth; another had some fellow leading a lion into a monastery and causing all kinds of kerfuffle. Androcles, I presumed, but it didn't seem quite right. Lastly, there was this chap at his writing desk looking out the window. There was something familiar about him, something nautical. Take his skullcap off and he could be propping up the bar at HMS *Vernon*. In one of the pauses in the proceedings, when censers were being clanked around, I broached the question.

'Who's the bearded wonder?' I whispered, nodding to the picture. Paola frowned. She didn't approve of my frivolity.

'St Jerome.'

St Jerome. Something at school came back at me. I hadn't been far out. Like Androcles, St Jerome had also encountered a lion with a thorn in its paw, only hadn't any Roman games to worry about. Once healed the lion had grown so fond of him he'd followed him around for the rest of his life.

'I take it he's the fellow with the lion too.'

She nodded, and holding her head down, whispered back.

'And in the middle, his *funerale*.'

It seemed odd that they'd sandwich his death in between two slices of his life but I let it pass, and turned my attention back to the last picture. St Jerome had been writing, but something untoward outside had made him look up. A sudden light had poured into the study, and he was held, transfixed by whatever it was he saw. A apparition, I presumed. A little ways back a small dog, the kind old ladies carry about in wicker baskets, was watching him intently. I thought of Licio Visintini and the way he had looked out from the villa that morning, with that parrot and its head cocked and Visintini's eyes raised, his hand stretched out, his spirit spiralling out across the sea. He'd had a vision too, a vision of his death and had embraced it willingly. He had a wife and an unborn son, both of whom he'd given up gladly, knowing the son would carry his victorious name through the years. Yet his country had lost the war and his son had died with barely a breath drawn. Nothing he had desired had come to pass. And I thought what must be left for men such as Visintini if not faith, and what a world it would be if we had none and existed only in the here and now; nothing beyond it, save a pointless universe. How could that be? There is always a beyond, a mystery, and our grace is to be given glimpses into it, fleeting moments of illumination. The universe is like the ocean, the place from which we came, reachless in its depth, capricious in its laws, capable of murderous rage and beatific calm, but there it is, lapping at our feet, washing over our souls, ready to carry us on our journey as we gaze upon it.

'And the dog-lover?' I asked. 'Who's he?"

'Dog-lover?'

'Yes, the man with the brush. The artist. What's his name?'

'Vittore Carpaccio. He was born here.'

After the service I took a closer look. There were myths and legends in his pictures, but there was a Venice too, a Venice that I recognized. His paintings were architectural, but through him the bricks and mortar had become the stuff of dreams. They hovered between the possible and the impossible. Later I found other works of his, but I came back to St Jerome as often as I could, and that window of his in particular. Ten years later, when I was no longer in a position to revisit it, some know-all proved that it wasn't St Jerome at all, but St Augustine, startled by the vision of the old boy on his way to heaven, but it didn't make any difference to me. It's what was in his eyes that counted, what was in Visintini's. Oh, that I could have seen, just one time in my life, what they saw!

Encouraged by my enthusiasm, Paola started dragging me to every church available. There are over seventy in Venice, so she had her work cut out, although I was an eager pupil. It seemed extraordinary that they'd have all this priceless stuff hanging around any old how. Everywhere you turned you'd find another Titian stuck on the walls without so much as a length of rope to protect it. Paola knew them all, or so it seemed. She could look at a picture and tell you its story, clearly and without apology. She trusted them, the same way as she trusted the Bible. The stealing of St Mark's body, Abel mourned by his parents, Samson and Delilah, she believed every one of them, it was as straightforward as that. Standing alongside her, listening to her solemn recitals, her hands clasped, her head uplifted, a kind of wonder on her face, I felt too that I was in the presence of a vision. A young woman, yes, but like the Venice in those Carpaccios of mine, a woman of this world and yet with one foot already in another.

'You know so much,' I said once.

'I know so little,' she replied.

'You see so much.'

'So little. But there are things I would like to see.'

'What things?'

'Things I should not want to see,' she said and would not speak of it again. But there was something between us now, something more than wine and company to egg us on, something which I found hard to give voice to, but which I felt, like the shiver of a stirring tune. It doesn't come easy for a man with my temperament to put these things in words, but we all have a little bit of poetry inside us. It's getting it out that's the hard part. But she was trying to get me to produce a couple of stanzas, I had no doubt about that.

I found Maria Visintini a job, working for us. Mention any branch of the armed forces and one thinks of machines and guns and ranks of fighting men but in truth military life is regimented pen-pushing gone berserk, and we suffered from the affliction as much as any unit. We found her a little office on Le Vignole, and from there she kept bureaucracy at bay, always respectful, always polite, but with her eyes fixed somewhere else. I'd seen pictures of it now, in great gold frames, with clouds and puffing angels and bursts of light streaming through, and though they were not depicted themselves, her young family were there too, I had no doubt of it. At the end of every day she would place whatever papers required my signature on my desk, shake my hand and return to those barren rooms above the Grand Canal. I liked to think that with the little money she was earning, she could make those rooms a little more hospitable. It was a way of easing her back into life, and I was glad to do that.

One afternoon, sometime in September '45, I was in the office, fending off more forms, when she knocked at the door and put her head round.

'You have visitors,' she said. 'Two.'

'Do they have an appointment?' I didn't care either way myself, but Maria liked that sort of thing.

She frowned.

'He says he is a friend. English.'

'Does he have a name, this friend?' For a moment I thought it might be Knowles, and my heart leapt. Sydney would put me back on track, put pay to all these female diversions. The door was pushed wide open. Maitland Pendock stood before me, in a dark suit and a panama hat. He'd put on weight.

'Maitland, what the devil are you doing here?'

'Anthony brought me.'

Behind him stood the haughty-looking cove he'd dragged along that night of Rose's party.

'We've just come from Rome. Anthony had a spot of work on. When I told him you were here he insisted we pop over.'

Anthony stepped forward. While Maitland had added to his quota of flesh, Anthony most definitely favoured the minus sign. He was quite the thinnest man I'd ever seen, brought on, not by lack of food, I thought, but something else. Anxiety? A different sort of hunger, unsatisfied? Most men are easy to place, where they fit, what they are, what they want, but Anthony was different. He dwelt upon another landscape, indistinct, hidden. You couldn't tell what was on his mind at all. I had a picture on the wall, a nice little watercolour of the Arsenal I'd picked up. He stepped forward, took one look at it, then moved his foot about, as if he'd trodden in something unpleasant. His suit was in the most dreadful crush. I decided to be civil.

'Nice billet, Rome. What were you doing there?'

'This and that.'

'Not the pictures, then?'

'Not entirely.'

'What branch did you say you were in?'

He ignored my question completely.

'I understand from Pendock that you have been greatly instrumental in making Venice safe for us once more. If that is the case, we are greatly in your debt.'

His voice had dropped from one of haughtiness to one of frank sincerity. He turned and went outside. I could hear him talking to one of the youngsters I had working with me. He could speak the lingo well by the sounds of it. Maitland walked round and plopped himself on the only chair.

'That didn't take him long, then,' he said, looking round the room.

'How do you mean?'

Maitland indicated his head.

'Anthony and the boys. He can sniff them out, you know. The ones that suit.'

'My lads. Not a chance.'

'No.' Maitland looked amused. 'If you say so, Lionel.'

That was the second time he'd called me Lionel, and it grated. No one had called me Lionel for years.

'And you, Maitland? Are you still in the swimfin business? I could put you in touch with the man who knows all about them, as it happens.'

'Swimfins?' He spoke as if he'd never heard of them. 'I've other interests now. The lid's been kept on London for years. Once this is all over . . .'

'Oh, how happy we will be. Yes, I know.'

Anthony stood in the doorway, leaning up against the doorpost, folding a little piece of paper in his pocket.

'Shut up, Anthony,' Maitland said, and stood up. Anthony looked around the walls again.

'What's the time?' he said.

'Time? About eleven. Why?'

Anthony fingered the pockets of his jacket.

'The thing is, we're a bit parched.'

★

I took the boat out to Murano, and sat them on a little pontoon on the Angeli, just below the bridge. Could he drink, Anthony. They all could, Maitland's pals, Anthony, Smithy, Guy. So could mine, for that matter. The war did that to a whole generation, gave it a real appetite for drink, not just beer which swelled you up, but those smaller, sharper drinks that lifted you out onto a lighter dance floor. We started off with white wine and ended up with brandy. Anthony seemed unusually interested in me, what I'd done, the nature of underwater warfare. After that he moved the talk effortlessly to art, the paradox of it, how he wished it could be harnessed to a greater good, but how its true appreciation resided in only the subtlest of minds. Europe after the war, Titian, the art of the cocktail, he glided from one subject to another, mellifluous and witty, but without a hint of warmth. By the end of the afternoon he'd laid the world before us, glittering like cold crystal. We all knew what each other was thinking, what everybody was thinking; where would we be, when it was all over. The sun was going down, a blood orange, squeezing its juice over the water. You could almost taste it. It seemed to heighten the feeling; the end of it all.

'We're living on the cusp now, don't you think?' Anthony said, 'The world hanging in balance. One tip of the scales and . . .' He

124

ran his fingers through his hair, like a woman does, and laughed. 'One tip of the scales. These Italians of yours. Weren't half of them communists?'

'Fascists, mostly. They took to the hills. Most of the communists that stuck around found themselves on the wrong end of lampposts.'

'And they rode these torpedo things, is that right, shaped like a penis? Sat astride them, two men and this great thing belching between their legs.' He giggled.

I looked at Maitland for help.

'But you never caught them, how they did it, did you?' he asked. I shook my head and told them the story of the *Olterra*. Anthony rubbed his hands together.

'You mean, on the surface all would appear still and quiet, while underneath . . . Yes, I see. How marvellous! How thrilling it must have been for them, moving unseen amongst their enemy, sending the whole works sky high, and no one knowing how it was done.'

'Well, don't sound so pleased about it,' I protested. 'It was our chaps they were trying to blow up.'

'But don't you think secrets are the best thing in the world? Secret meetings, secret lovers, secret drinking.'

'There's nothing secret about your drinking.'

'No?' He looked at the array of bottles. 'You think I started with these?' he said, tipping up the contents of the second brandy bottle into his glass. 'This is merely afternoon tea,' and gulped it greedily.

'Anthony's looking after the King's pictures,' Maitland put in, as his friend examined the other bottles for any remaining alcohol. 'What's the word, Anthony?'

'Surveyor.'

'Quite an honour,' I said, appalled that this drunken wraith should be graced by Royalty. He had a certain bearing, though, even when three-quarters cut. And a brain. You could see it practically bursting out of his skull. I could imagine him bending his head deferentially, speaking in subdued but authoritative tones. I could picture him laughing at them behind their backs too.

'But thankless in many ways,' he drawled. 'The Windsors show little enthusiasm for what they possess. They never have. George the Fifth once attacked one of his Cézannes with a stick.'

I felt obliged to defend.

'If it was his Cézanne, I don't see the problem.'

Anthony regarded me coldly.

'Anthony is quite indispensable to them,' Maitland offered. 'He's flown to Frankfurt and the Netherlands on their behalf.'

'Pendock!' The voice was suddenly sharp. 'You really should not talk of these things.'

Maitland shrank in his chair. I saw it clearly then, how he trotted after Anthony like a lapdog, and I didn't like it.

'No, that's not it,' I said. '*You* should not talk of these things.'

Anthony emptied his glass.

'You are quite right. I talk too much.' He looked at his watch. 'Fortunately I must take your leave. One of your boys has promised to show me some delights of his own. Finiculi, fenicula.'

And with that he got up and left. Maitland and I did a tour of the glass-blowers, now beginning to work again. We watched them give shape to globes of colour and light. It's a wonderful thing, glass. It makes the world seem fresh and dazzling. It's like the sea that way.

'I'm going to buy something to bring back,' I told him.

'You are coming back, then?'

'Not you too! Of course I'm coming back,' I protested, but I wasn't so sure now, and Maitland guessed it.

★

By then it was safe for Belloni to return home. Venice was opening up. The harbour was cleared, the canals made safe; the sunken barges, the scuttled hulls, the hidden mines all removed. My time was coming to an end. Tony and Minella's courtship had moved on apace. Their future was already the talk of the town. While not officially engaged, they had made known their intentions. They'd marry and move to New York. The whole family approved. But Paola was the older daughter, and they looked to her to fulfil their wishes first. They were funny in that way, the mother, the father, patriotic to their bootstraps,

126

but quite happy to let their daughters be carried off by a couple of foreigners. We still took supper with them, but now it was in the family's apartment off the Zattere. They were very fond of polenta, the Bellonis, which was both filling and seemingly easy to prepare. Paola's mother would place a big cauldron of water over the fire, and as the water came to the boil, gradually sprinkle the powdered maize into the simmer until it reached the consistency of porridge. She'd let it bubble for a minute or two, then remove it from the fire and serve it at once, pouring the thick, steaming mixture all over a wooden board placed on the table, smoothing it out with the skill of a navvy. Then we'd sit down and tuck in on whatever piece lay opposite. Sometimes there'd be a gravy to go with it, made out of stock and wine, sometimes small pieces of meat, pigeon or rabbit. It became quite my favourite food. Eating it was a simple affair, but there were rules. Only part of the polenta was yours. You had to be careful not to encroach on your neighbours, or penetrate too deeply into the territory opposite.

After the meal Minella and Tony would wander off and do what lovers do on the sidewalks of Venice, while I would take a glass of brandy and sit outside under the tree in the little square with Paola, and listen to her speak of everything but the one subject that lay behind her every look. I could feel myself being carried along willy-nilly. I can't say I objected. It was rather like one of those novelty rides you find in funfairs, the prospect of which seems quite exciting, but wouldn't necessarily do under your own steam. You have to be cajoled into it. Hop on, why don't you, see your world tip up, rush by in a giddy blur.

One evening, unusually, all four of us walked down to the water's edge. It was late. The moon was up and the water was flat and warm. The rest of Venice had gone to sleep long ago. Not much was said at first. La Guidecca lay softly on the other side of the water, its shape illuminated by the shifting moonlight. I took a long smoke.

'When your war is over,' Paola said, 'what will you do?'

Her and Sydney. Her and Sydney both.

'I'm not sure. Bit like that island over there, my future, half formed, just out of reach. I'll probably stay in the navy.'

I could sense a slackening in her shoulders, a feeling of disappointment.

'Why not?' I continued. 'It's a good life. You get to see the world. Besides, what else am I fit for?'

'See the world!' She turned, dismissing the notion with a scornful snort. 'You are not a boy, Crabbie, with a toy boat. See the world! Haven't you seen enough?'

It was the first time I'd seen her angry.

'You misunderstand me,' I said. 'It's not that. Wandering's what I'm used to, that's all. I've never had a proper home. I'm not looking for sympathy, mind.'

Tony waded in. He had it all planned out, naturally.

'Paola's right, Buster,' he said. 'It's time to put your marker down. Come to New York. A smart man can make a killing there and have fun doing it. Bring Paola. Make a foursome of it.'

Paola shifted uncomfortably. Minella whispered into Tony's ear. They both laughed. I didn't care for that at all.

'Is that what the world is going to be from now on?' I said, spit in my voice. 'Fun?'

'Why the hell not? There hasn't been too much of it recently.'

Minella began jumping up and down. 'Is right!' she shouted. 'Fun today! Fun tomorrow! Fun tonight!' And with that she ran out onto the little floating pontoon moored alongside and jumped into the water. Marsloe followed suit. He didn't even bother to take off his shoes.

They squealed and splashed. Tony started to circle her, threatening all manner of ungentlemanly behaviour. Then their arms touched and then their faces, and then they were kissing, quite openly, Minella's dress floating up around her like a giant flower opening its petals. I looked away, trying not to see.

'I'm cold,' Paola said. I took off my coat and put it over her shoulders. The lovers swam away, laughing and shouting. Everything went quiet. I knew what she was thinking, for I was thinking the same thing myself. The ease between the two in the water, and the awkwardness between Paola and me. We couldn't have jumped in, even if we'd wanted to.

'They seem to be enjoying themselves,' I said.

'Why, do you want to join them?' It was said sharply, a little knife in my side.

'No, thanks. I've been doing that every night for three years now. It doesn't hold the same thrill for me.'

'Not even when – ' she was interrupted by a loud shriek – 'your companion is different.'

'My companion might be different but the water's the same, take my word for it.'

'That cannot be right,' she said. 'Imagine a tree. One day you sit under it with your mother, making salad. The next day you sit under it, with your . . . your betrothed, drinking wine. Both times you look up and see the tree. But each time it is a different tree.'

'It is the same tree,' I insisted, 'but seen with different eyes.'

'Then it must be a different tree, for we can only know things by how we see them.'

'That isn't true. You know God, but you don't see him.'

'You are wrong,' she said, 'not once, but twice. I do not know God, but I see him every day.'

Tony hauled himself out of the water. He'd lost his shoes. Minella followed, standing on the pontoon, her dress shining in the moonlight like the skin of a freshly caught fish, full and taut. She seemed proud of what she had done. There was something terrible to it, the way they looked at each other, like Adam and Eve, their thoughts exposed. Then they ran off, back to the apartment, and we were alone again.

'Well, tree or no tree, I don't see the point in midnight swimming,' I said. 'There's nothing to see. I don't see the point in swimming in daylight much either. It's not as if you're going anywhere. Diving, that's a different story.'

Paola turned on me.

'Oh, Crabbie. Must you be so firm, so, so stiff.'

'I don't know what you mean.'

'You speak as if you do not approve. There is nothing wrong with jumping in the water if you want to, jumping in the water, or dancing round the square. Why shouldn't you?'

'Dancing round the square? You don't want to dance around the square, do you?'

'No! Yes. Yes! That is what I want to do. Dance round the square.'

And she pulled me to the square and danced me round that tree, a sort of waltz I would say, with her humming something tuneless into my ear, danced me close and discreet, a different Paola from the church and the Carpaccios and I thought, yes, this is a roundabout I could step up to. This world didn't tip up. This world didn't rush by in a blur. We swayed in the still of the night like anemones floating on coral. At the end she said, 'There. Was that so very bad?'

'That was lovely.'

'The tree is always here. Your dancing partner too.'

And then she kissed me and I went home.

I didn't sleep one wink that night.

★

My orders came. A short stint in Haifa and then back to Blighty. A farewell meal was arranged a couple of days beforehand, just in case they brought the date forward. Everyone knew what was expected.

'I'm nervous, Tony.'

'Don't be. They're all rooting for you. She's just waiting for the moment. Can't you see that? She wants you to bust in there.'

'I wish you wouldn't say things like that.'

'Why, what's the problem?'

I couldn't say.

They were all there waiting when we arrived, Mama, Papa, Minella, young Julio, all spruced up in their Sunday best, all save Minella, whose dress had nothing to do with Sunday at all. Marsloe held his arms out, as if to warm his hands by them.

'You look swell,' he said, 'but where's Paola,' and as if on cue, there she was, standing in the door. She had put on this white blouse scattered with little mirrors and a midnight-blue skirt that twirled from side to side when she walked. I don't know what it was, but there was something in her manner that was looser, freer. She would never be as good-looking as her younger sister but her beauty was deeper. She'd hidden it, that was all. All of a sudden I understood Minella's past theatrics. She would have known about it all along.

The meal went off with a bang. I'd managed to get hold of a crate of something that, if not champagne, was passably fizzy. Papa got to his feet and made a nice little speech about Venice embracing me as I had embraced it. We sat down, first to bowls of thick soup and then, inevitably, polenta. The talk was loud and lively. Toasts were called for, pledges made, trips planned to New York and London. Mama gave me her recipe for my favourite dish. Papa handed out cigars. Minella tried to sing a song but Julio stuffed bread in her mouth. It was a typical Belloni evening, boisterous and noisy, the family nailing their colours to the mast. Paola looked wonderful, relaxed and happy, as if the question had already been asked and the answer given. We talked back and forth, about what I have no recollection. I was conscious only of her smile and how she held her fork to her mouth, as she chewed and nodded and leant across the table to me, as if no one else was there. The time had come, I knew.

'Not long now,' I said. 'Leaving this beautiful city, your brave father, you.'

'Stop! You make me sad.'

'I could make you happier, if you like.'

She inclined her head, laid her hands out on the table. She was so close. I carried on.

'I'm off to Israel for a month, then it's back home. I could get my discharge papers, tie up a few loose ends and be back before the winter sets in.'

She tried to look surprised.

'You wanted to travel.'

'Not any more. I've packed enough suitcases to last a lifetime. Venice could be my last port of call.'

'But, Crabbie, what would you do here?'

'In a city of canals? Come off it. Anyway, if that didn't work I could try my hand at painting.'

'You are making fun, like Minella and Tony.'

'Not at all. Nothing too ambitious, mind. Portraits, that's what I'd start with. Someone who could sit there and smile.'

'Only smile?'

'One good smile's enough. One good smile to keep on one good face. That I'd try for, that is if I could find someone to sit still long enough.'

'Yes, you would take a long time, I think.'

'Oh, a lifetime probably. She'd have to have extraordinary patience, extraordinary fortitude.'

'She?'

My heart was racing. I was leaning out of the boat, my hands grappling with something wondrous. I was a fisherman catching a mermaid.

'Yes, Paola, she.'

Suddenly I realized that everyone else had stopped talking. I looked around. The whole family was looking at me. Paola said something sharp, and her mother shook her head and pointed to the board. Paola looked down and burst out laughing. In my endeavours I'd done a Cadiz, and raided everyone's undefended territory. I coughed an apology. Paola scooped a slab onto her fork and stuffed it in my mouth. They all clapped. Papa came round one side and slapped me on the back. Mama came over on the other and gave me one of those kisses Labradors specialize in. Minella did something similar to Tony. Julio sneaked a drink from his sister's glass.

They got up and made a great play of clearing the table, ushering me and Paola out into the courtyard. Venice sleeps early, least it did then. There was no one about. We walked out, imagining the whispers arraigned behind the shutters. We sat under the tree and I took her hand. It seemed quite natural.

'Do you want to dance again?' she said, wriggling her toes. Her feet were poking out of a new pair of shoes. They were small and perfect and I thought of them against my ugly brutes, the contrast they would make.

'Not yet.'

'To talk, then?'

'Talk? Not exactly.'

'Here would be a good place to paint your picture,' she said.

'Quite good.'

'Not private enough, perhaps.'

'I don't want anyone looking over my shoulder, if that's what you mean.'

'No. It is not what I mean.'

There was a silence. I thought, she'd have to get used to silences. It's what Englishmen were brought up on.

'An artist needs to study his subject many times before he understands it,' she said, 'in all conditions; the light, the dark, inside, outside.'

And with that she leant back and opened her blouse. She wore no clothing underneath.

'I am yours,' she said, 'if you should wish.'

She took my hand and led it to where she had laid herself bare, never taking her eyes off me. I could feel the bone of her lungs on the edge of my hand, and in my palm, something stirring, above the heartbeat, the agitation of the flesh itself, like a small animal, unbearably soft. Her face fell in repose, a mock sleep, as if to say, there, I have guided you there, now do with me what you will. I saw her lips settle, half open and her limbs arrange themselves just so. Had I prompted this offering, or was she simply her sister's sister after all. Had she sat in front of the mirror and practised this manoeuvre, left her room half dressed, knowing what she intended to do? Had these been her thoughts, when we knelt together, when she taught me the ways of her faith, her piety covered by the flimsiest of cloths. Keats was wrong. Beauty could lie as well as anyone. I thought of the Church I was growing to love and the incantations and the closed eyes of the congregation. I thought of the altar and what lay upon it, the bread and the wine and the body of Christ. She breathed in deeply; her body rose up under my hold, monstrous and misshapen, a cold pallor upon it, as if drowned. I drew my hand back.

'Dear Crabbie. What is wrong?'

'Nothing.' She pulled her blouse together and shivered.

'What, then. Am I not to your liking?' Her eyes were filled with tears. I shook my head.

'I have done something wrong,' she said. 'I should be more like my sister perhaps.' She started to cry.

'No,' I protested. 'Not at all.'

'But she has Tony. And I, I thought . . .' She could say no more. I turned and fled. I went back to Le Vignole, put on my frogsuit and sank into the water, cold and sightless. I could have stayed there forever.

I didn't see her again until the hour I left. She asked and I couldn't refuse. She was waiting with her father on the quayside, the two of them subdued. I shook Belloni's hand as warmly as I could, thanked him for all the work he had done. He responded, but with sorrow on his face. Paola led me down alone. I stepped into the boat. Was I really leaving all this?

'Will you come back, Crabbie?'

'It's hard to say.'

I could hardly bear to look her in the face.

'Is it me,' she asked, 'that makes you so afraid?'

'Me rather, I think.'

She smiled, but knew it was true.

'I would have been good,' she said and pressed my hand.

I had no answer to that.

*

And so I left. I climbed aboard a plane and watched the city disappear from view. Perhaps that was the trouble, knowing that she would have been good. What lay at home? A room, a bare bed, and wintry prospects. While here a young woman, her young arms and all the family flesh in between them. How terrible the happy future can be, the demands it makes. Forever happy, forever in love, forever in

Italy, in this fairy-tale city. But I was Lionel Crabb, a loner with an irascible temper and flat English feet. How could he live the rest of his life there, however much he loved it. How could he lie in bed next to this woman, with her warmth and her olive skin and her strong womanly smells, and learn a new life, how could he? All the boats he would be burning, the navy, the Duchess, his seat in the Nag's Head usurped, no longer Crabb's but some impostor's, while he strolled over the Rialto to some backwater taverna, perhaps a better Crabb, a happier Crabb, exposed to the vagaries of life, but Lionel Crabb no longer.

Poor Paola.

Ten

There have been three Roses in my life, and all in a different state of bloom. Rose the owner of the Cavendish Hotel, Pat Rose, the Queen of my English Heart, and Rosa the dragon of the dorm, of whom I know little, except her name and the mole on her cheek, and the way her hands are twisted, as if her life has been wrung out of them, hard and dry. They must have been shapely when they were younger, just as I can imagine this mole, this dark flaw now so settled upon her skin, must have once set off the bloom in her young cheeks, a spot aching to be kissed. First time she told me her name I nearly fell out of my chair. All these strands and twists, they bind me up.

The other day she came up to me with an official-looking document in her hand, something about her husband seeking work in Russia. With typical efficiency the form they had sent him was in Russian, not Czech, and the two of them hadn't a clue what to do. I helped her fill it in. She drew up a chair, and by signs and mimes and a few broken words we worked our way through it. I was conscious of her warmth and her breath and the way her head hung close to mine. When it was over, and the coarse grey paper had been folded carefully back into her bag, she laid her hand upon mine and smiled, not the usual smile you get in these places, the smile the self-sufficient give to the helpless, but the smile of one human being to another, equals. I hadn't felt so useful, and so utterly useless, in years. After she'd put the chair back in its place she came over and bent down and for a moment I thought she was going to give me a kiss, brush my old whiskers with her cracked lips, and I shrank back, terrified, for I do not think I could have borne it, but no, she merely rearranged the rug over my knees, patted my head and left, her stout legs carrying her away. That she should go home, to a husband and son and cook the supper and bang the pots about, and have that warmth about her!

Home! Did I ever have one? Never go back they say, never go back. Well, this old salt wants to go back, for better or for worse. Couldn't I saunter into the Nag's Head just one more time and find Len standing behind the bar, a napkin wrapped around the head of the bottle? Serve up the Supplicants, I would say and the door would close and we'd have an afternoon of it, with all the old times and all the new ones rolled into one; the stories I could tell, the things they could tell me. If only I could get these legs going again. I had the legs for it once, but now they're thin folded things, fit only for a blanket and a little rubbing. Looking down on them, it's difficult for me to imagine the power and stamina they once possessed. All they want to do now is to step out upon the English shore, carry the rest of this old body whence it came. Bring me your paperwork, Rosa. Brings me forms to fill, letters to write, envelopes to open. I will learn to love bureaucracy, if you can help me swim in such waters again. I would cross the ocean floor if only they would let me, emerge below the white cliffs of Dover, in a frogsuit and swimfins, with a bunch of seaweed in my hand.

*

I was pleased to be back, but it didn't last long. What with the navy shrinking and only the vague promise of some haphazard work as and when, prospects were decidedly grim. A lot of people who came out of the services found the same thing. Those last few months in Haifa, working under that burnt sun, I'd been dreaming of the soft green in the London parks and me leaning on a bar, talking to strangers with the afternoon lying ahead of me like a stroll along an old familiar road. I walked out of Portsmouth demob centre with nothing more than a chalk-stripe flannel folded in a cardboard box and a ticker full of hope. Paola was a thing of the past. When I got there London was grey and unwelcoming. Those first few months all I managed in the way of a job were a couple of cap-in-hand ventures handed down by old acquaintances, running errands that were better suited to some eager beaver fresh out of school than a man the wrong side of thirty with a proper war behind him. As always, Maitland came to the rescue, finding me a job in a small publishing venture of his.

'We're thinking of bringing out a sports writer's handbook of advice,' he said. 'How to win the football pools, that sort of thing. Could you write a few lines on that, do you think, earn a few extra bob?'

'I could give it a go. How does it work, exactly?'

'Writing a book?'

'The pools.'

Maitland looked at me as if I'd asked him what a wheel was.

'Every week you have to predict which teams will win at home and which will win away.'

'You mean Partick Thistle one, Brighton Hove Albion two, that sort of thing.'

'That sort of thing, yes. But most importantly you have to predict draws.'

'Why?'

'Because the less there are, the more money you win.'

That didn't seem to make any sense at all. I looked down at the form. It was crammed with rows of horrid thin little columns and terribly small print.

'You mean people sit down and fill these things out? Voluntarily.'

'That's right.'

'Every week, you say?'

He nodded.

'Not just for the money, surely?

'What else would it be for? It's the working man's opiate, Crabbie. A better life without the struggle. Leave your class and your cares behind. All for a penny a week.'

What else would it be for? The reason evaded me.

I wasn't a great success.

The trouble was I wasn't a great success at anything else either.

Others seemed to adapt quite easily, but this new world I'd returned to didn't seem to click with me at all. On the face of it, it wasn't much different from the one we'd left behind those few years ago, but there were things going on underneath, subtle changes, how people talked or walked into a bar, treated the staff. There seemed more of them too, climbing over one another, in the great rush for I knew not what. Civility had gone out the window, people lighting up in non-smoking carriages, not tipping their hat to a lady, that sort of thing. When it came to rudery, we were all equals. When it came to anything else, it was every man for himself. Honest camaraderie had gone out the window, unless of course you were drunk, and then it wasn't honest at all. We'd won the war in Europe fair and square; the double-dealing started at home. Every time I sat myself down in front of some desk or counter, whether it was looking for suitable employment or finding somewhere decent to rent, even buying a dog, some upstart of a clerk would shove a form under my nose and expect me to justify myself; name, age, marital status, former occupation. 'Getting my feet wet', is what I usually put in that particular box, 'None of your damned business' in the one preceding. The Whitehall disease had spread from the military to civilian life, only with none of the concomitant fireworks to offset the pallor. I had landed up in a land of buff-coloured envelopes. As if bits of paper could restore what was being lost. The country, I thought, is signing its honour away, in triplicate.

Funds ran desperately low. Rose gave me my old room back at the Cavendish, but when I got there, there was a resident's form waiting for me at the porter's desk. I proffered my very worst handwriting. Maitland offered to help me out with a loan, but a chap has his pride. One week, two weeks, nothing: by the end of the month all I had left in my pocket was a handful of loose change. I knew what I had to do. There weren't any pawnshops in Knightsbridge but I knew of one just behind Waterloo Station that I'd nearly used years ago, coming back from China. That Tuesday I set out, the weather mostly foul. Everyone I passed knew where I was going, I was convinced of it.

It was cluttered and badly lit, like all pawnshops. It's how they get their prices down. Nothing looks much good under a forty-watt bulb. I rang the bell and laid the stick on the counter. The owner came through a curtain. He was not at all what I'd expected; young instead of old, upright instead of stooped, and instead of scrawn, a frame more akin to one of Sydney's navvies, but with a terrible burn seared into his face. Then I saw the tattoos on the knuckles of his hand. I hadn't been far out.

'Merchant navy?' I asked.

He nodded.

'Me too, once. Then the other lot grabbed me.'

'Lucky you.' He dabbed the corner of his eye, where the burn had seared into his skin. It was red and raw and couldn't stop weeping.

'You got that there then, I take it.'

'Arctic convoy. '43. Fuel for the Russians. Night-time torpedo. Whole effing ocean on fire.'

Whether it was true or not I have no idea, but suddenly the tables were turned. My bargaining power had just been put out to grass. He looked at the swordstick and sighed.

'That top silver?'

'It's not the cane.' I unhooked the twine from around my neck and handed it over. In all these years I'd never taken it off, not once.

'Oh,' he said, his voice dropping. 'Jade.'

'But it's a nice piece. If you hold it up, you can see the moon in it. Look.'

He held it to his suppurating eye, and the light played upon it. Maybe the stone would bring him luck.

'It is good,' he agreed, 'but people aren't interested in jade these days. Six months ago, straight after the war, when servicemen got their gratuities, they might have splashed out on a piece like this, for the fiancée back home or what-have-you, but now, jade, jade is, well, superfluous to their requirements.'

He tendered a sad little smile, and made to hand it back. I refused the offer.

'The trouble is,' I told him, 'in the present circumstances, it's rather superfluous to mine.'

He nodded.

'Superfluous to requirements is the watchword of the age. That's what they told me, when I got out, and that's what I thought I would be, when I came home. I hadn't been married but the three month. What woman would want to spend the rest of their lives hooked up to this, I said to myself. Know what she said? Good looks were superfluous to her requirements.'

'You're a fortunate man.'

'I am that.' He looked me straight in the eye. 'I'll give you seven pounds, seeing as you're military. No argy-bargy. Seven pounds, straight. You won't get better.'

He counted out the money and handed me the ticket. 'Don't worry if you lose it. I'll remember.' I shook my head.

'I won't be back. Money's changed hands. The spell's been broken.' I had an idea. 'But there's life in it yet, believe me. Take a leaf out of your own book, why don't you. Give it to your young lady wife. Let it work its magic for the two of you.'

I took the money and hopped on a bus. Two changes and I was in the Nag's Head, nursing my spirits. I was tired of pounding the streets, getting nowhere. Maitland was out of town, and I hadn't had the taste of decent company for weeks.

Then this woman came in, with the look of a drowned dog about her. I'd seen her out and about before the war any number of times, but for some reason we'd never spoken. She had her crowd, I had mine. But she'd caught my eye more than once. She was a serious piece of knitting.

She slapped her handbag down onto the counter and slumped into one of the bar stools like she'd just been fished out of Algeçiras Bay and wished they hadn't bothered. She was wearing a white blouse under a light-blue two-piece, flattering to the figure, but the woman who usually inhabited it had let it out to another tenant.

I beckoned Len over.

'The floater on the stool, Len. She looks in a bad way.'

Len hadn't noticed her. He'd been busy polishing his brass. He ran a tight ship, and though we paid for the privilege, we were only allowed there on his terms. Step out of line, say the wrong thing, wear the wrong kind of shirt on Sunday, and you were out. But when we needed it, he was there to look after us.

He tucked his duster in his back pocket.

'Pat? She *is* in a bad way. The boyfriend drowned not long ago, on a sailing holiday. They were getting married this year. He was just waiting for his divorce to come through. Peter Aitken. Did you know him?'

I shook my head. He leant in, hands on table.

'That's two she's lost to the water. Her husband was a pilot in Coastal Command. Got shot down in '45.'

The water. What would I do without it?

I looked over. She was trying to light a cigarette. The lighter looked sturdy enough but her hand was dancing with the saints. I'd seen men half drowned, hauled out the water, similarly afflicted. She might be on dry land, but she was sinking fast.

'Well, maybe I can make it third time lucky,' I said, pulling out the wallet. 'Throw her a glass of champagne and keep the bottle handy.'

Len did as he was told and popped the cork. He had those pretty glasses behind the counter with hollow stems and bowls shaped like a cupped hand; the Supplicants I called them. I'd brought a dozen of them back with me from Murano, made him a gift of the lot. There wasn't much call for champagne glasses in my one-room bolt-hole.

Len pushed the beaker out in her direction. She didn't bat an eyelid.

'What's this in aid of?' she asked.

'You,' he said.

She laughed, but they weren't telling jokes where it came from.

'You better rename this pub the Bankrupt Samaritan, Len, if this is how you intend to carry on.'

Len shook his head.

'It's nothing to do with me,' said he. 'You've got that crustacean over there in the corner to thank for this.'

She turned; swivelled I believe is the correct expression, and though I kept my eyes on hers, it wasn't easy, not with all that slip of movement, the nylon shining into the unknown like dappled light on dark water. I stood up and raised my glass.

'To the most beautiful girl in the world,' I said, 'who I have admired for years.'

Well, wouldn't you?

We went to Churchill's that night. I don't know why, but it was as if Len had popped the cork out of me too: the RNVR, the war, the shambles that was my civilian life, out it all came, even Italy, and why I couldn't go back. Halfway through I discovered what I was doing.

'Here's me gabbling away like a Grimsby fish-wife,' I said, 'while the whole point of the exercise was to cheer *you* up.'

She put her hand over mine.

'We both know what it's like to lose, Crabbie. Know what it's like to win a few too, wouldn't you say?'

Later, as the cab drew up to let her out, I kissed her. First time since I couldn't remember when. I wasn't afraid like I had been with Paola, for I knew Pat would kiss me back in the manner a man such as myself requires. Cheerily, breezing across the surface of the water like a toy boat on a pond. Nevertheless it took a bit of nerve, putting my salt-stained visage up against such perfume and satin, like spitting tobacco juice onto a bowl of strawberries, but she didn't seem to mind. In fact she kissed me back.

'Do you know, Crabbie,' she said, wiping a smudge of her lipstick from the corner of my mouth, 'I think our luck's about to change.'

In the morning, she woke to a dozen roses on her doorstep. You know why? Because I believed her.

And you know what? She was right. Our luck did change. Right then. Right there.

Eleven

The door was thrown open. His face was white with rage. I kept it nice and breezy.

'Morning, Crippen. Buried any more bodies lately?' He flung the paper in my face.

'They invite him to dinner, then shower him with insults. It was a trap, to humiliate him in public. I should have been there.'

'What would you have done, shot them? Who was this anyway?'

I scanned the paper. It appeared that our loyal Opposition, the bolshies in the Labour Party, had given Khrushchev a rather rough ride the night before. The soup had slipped down well enough, as had the meat and two veg, but by the time pudding came around, things were distinctly frosty. Gaitskell and that firebrand Brown had begun questioning Khrushchev's penchant for locking up half the population of Eastern Europe, demanding that he throw the gates open and set them all free. Even tried to give him a list. Bit of cheek, I know, asking a chap to dinner only to throw bread rolls at him, but I had to admit, they had a point. Ironic that it should be a bunch of socialists to bring him up short. I almost felt proud of them, me, a true blue, proud of the reds! Things were changing fast. Serov was still fuming.

'This is not the first time your country has shown its hostility. When I was here in London in March, I received the same treatment; demonstrations outside the embassy, articles in your newspapers, the air full of false accusations. This, at the very time when the First Secretary was making his stand, you spat the misunderstood past in our face, a country that had fought in two wars on the world's behalf, first the capitalist war, then the fascist war, twenty million Russian souls lost.'

I found such pleading nauseating. Washing one's clean linen in public, I think Shaw called it.

'No one's disputing your nation's bravery,' I said. 'Or its sacrifice. It's there for all to see, in the record books. But that doesn't excuse what you did in places like Katyn. If anything it make it ten times worse.'

Serov sat down and leant back on his chair.

'Do you know what I did last night, Commander, while you were locked in your cabin? I slipped out with a party that was to visit one of your ships. I wrapped myself in one of your British overcoats, that would not protect a man for thirty seconds where I come from, and slipped ashore. I walked through the docks, all along the harbour, even into a little ways into the town, the head of the KGB roaming at will on British soil! I stepped off the pavement for a mother and her child, I smiled. She smiled back. To me, the Butcher! I stood out-side one of your famous fish and chip shops. It smelt good! I passed a policeman. I raised my hat. I almost hoped that he would stop me, demand my name and address. "I am the Head of the KGB," I would have said. "Arrest me! I have tales to tell." I returned and looked at this ship, and thought, yes, today we come in good will, but one day, if you do not treat us with the respect that is our due, if you continue to raise your fist at us, to bellow at us across the safety of your water, one day, we may come in a different guise. You have much to thank us for, and a few years ago you recognized this. You named streets after our generals, flew our flags, celebrated our victories. We have been your ally, Commander, longer than you care to acknowledge. We can be your ally again. The reason I went ashore last night? Not to gloat at the incompetence of your security, or to stick my tongue out at the country that had behaved so rudely to me. I wanted to do what was once denied me here, what is so often denied me, even in my own country, to stand unnoticed as a man, to walk unnoticed as a man, to be allowed to be a man. For that is what I am, and what I have to do is not always what a man wants to do, but he does it, one hopes, for the good of his country. You want to talk of Katyn. Very well. I will talk of Katyn. And you will listen. The tides of nations,

Commander, can sometimes sweep over the most deserving of people.'

He had calmed down. I realized that Gert and Daisy weren't there. He pulled out a cigarette case and flicking the lid open offered me one. They smelt glorious, but I declined.

'Go on, they are English,' he said. 'I had them brought specially.'

So I took one, the first puff since waking Thursday morning. I felt quite faint. Serov brought the front legs of his chair back to earth.

'We belong in two different worlds, you and me. You want to know about the Polish officers, the reason for their deaths. You think it was arbitrary, that I did it out of savagery, that I sat in my Kremlin lair and gorged on a feast of death. You know nothing of my country, Commander, though soon you may understand the parameters by which we work. A good word, parameters. I am more educated than you think. Imagine what we had on our hands. Thousands of captured Polish officers, who in '39 had resisted the necessary action we had taken to protect our own borders. They were rounded up and sent to Kozielski, set in the grounds of a former Orthodox monastery, five miles from the Smolensk–Briansk line. It is a pretty place. Who knows, one day you might visit it. The monastery was gloomy, overgrown, but we tried to make it as habitable for them as possible. We desired nothing but their comfort and cooperation. Why ever should we not?'

He paused, gathering his thoughts.

'First we created conditions in the camp that would render them susceptible to our needs. The food improved. The accommodation, though cramped, was made bearable. They were free to associate amongst themselves. There was no harsh regime to contend with, no work camps; they were not beaten or degraded. We wanted them to feel at home. We even gave them access to the small library that some of the NKVD officers had brought with them. Do you know which was their most popular book?' He leant forward. 'Churchill's *The World Crisis.*' He tapped his cigarette case. 'That was not a good start.

'So, we began to interrogate them, to find out about their motivation, their thoughts, much as I am here to discover yours, though interrogation was the wrong word. There were no harsh lights or sleep deprivation, no mock executions or any of the other little tricks for which we have become so renowned. At first it was not easy, for in their simplicity they imagined that we were trying to get them to divulge secrets, as if they had any secrets to give up. They had only themselves, and of course one's self is the greatest secret of all. If they had understood that . . .

'Every prisoner was interviewed separately; not once but two or three times. They had to give an account of their lives, their families, their careers, their friends and pastimes. We would ask them about their political beliefs, what world view they sought. Much of the information would come from their fellow prisoners. Not that they were betraying their comrades, you understand, far from it. They told stories of one another as if to demonstrate each other's integrity, told them with pride and fond remembrance. Often, when interviewing a man for the first time, he would be astonished by what we already knew, the house where he lived, the number of his children, his passion for horse riding. We let them write letters home, as many as they wished, to wives, to mothers, fathers, whomever they desired, lovers even, all free and without censorship, for it is only in such an atmosphere that talk becomes as common a commodity as air, on everyone's lips. We photographed them too, from the left, from the right, from the back and from the front. By the end we knew more about them than their own families.'

He looked up, half in reverie.

'It was a golden time: a textbook evaluation. Nothing haphazard or arbitrary was permitted to interfere with our deliberations. We took down every single word, placed the reports in envelopes and sent them back to Moscow, where we could sift through them, one by one. Back at the prison camp the atmosphere remained calm, even though they did not know how long they would be held or, once released, where they would be going. Some insisted they would be handed over to the French or the British, to fight the Germans once again, though why they imagined that we should allow such a thing was a puzzle to me. We were not yet at war with Germany.

The more pessimistic among them believed that they would be sent to prison camps further north, to work in the fields or the salt mines. But optimist or pessimist they knew they were Polish officers and would be treated accordingly.'

He smiled. 'That should have given them a clue.

'Put yourself in our place. We had in our midst fifteen thousand patriotic Polish officers and intellectuals. What were we to make of them, these honest fellows, their country gone, its borders erased? They were part of Russia now. What were their feelings about their new homeland, where lay the future of the world? What were we do with them? Send them back into the hands of the Germans or the British where they might be turned against us? Or let them live freely on Russian soil? Political theory recognizes only two methods of dealing with such a problem. Either those captured must be per-suaded to work for the good of the Soviet Union, or else . . .' He shrugged his shoulders.

'We tried to point them in the right direction, believe me, how we tried. We covered the camp with posters, writings from Stalin, extracts from the Soviet constitution. My officers would tour the camps extolling the virtues of the new state. We gave out thousands of pamphlets and newsletters, loudspeakers broadcast the best of Moscow radio. And what response did they give us? What did we read in Moscow, away from prejudice and personality? That while they would welcome Russia as an ally against their German enemy, they would never countenance becoming part of Russia themselves. Never! After all our work, after all our discussions, do you know how many were deemed fit to be absorbed? Sixty-one. That was all. Sixty-one.

'What choice did we have? Fifteen thousand captives and every one a potential thorn in our side. We did not make it hard for them. We proceeded methodically, without rancour, case by case. Names would be rung through, up to thirty a day. Those called would be given a celebratory meal, as if they were going home, and while they ate their fellow officers would watch through the window, envy-ing their food and good fortune. Afterwards we would gather them in the courtyard and present each one of them with a food parcel for the long journey; bread, some sugar and three herrings wrapped up in new paper. New paper! Grey, but new! It was a nice touch. No one had seen new paper in years. They left with hope in their hearts.'

'To Katyn.'

'To Kosy Gory,' he corrected, 'a small forested hill inside Katyn. A health resort about twelve kilometres from Smolensk.'

'And the sight that greeted them?'

He rubbed his cigarette out between his fingers.

'The sight that met them, Commander, was the sight they had orchestrated for themselves. We buried everything with them,' he added. 'Their papers, their diaries; money, photographs, everything. They vanished from the face of the earth. And that would have been the end of it. Only Germany invaded, captured the land. Rumours started to seep out of the earth.'

He would say no more of it. I sat there, remembering Eugene and what he would think of me, sitting smoking this beast's cigarettes. Eugene, his bones long buried, and that young woman lying somewhere on the ocean bed. Which was better, to have a grave like Eugene's, a plot of land and a headstone, or like hers, floating about the seabed, finding her own resting place amidst the sand and barnacles? Serov spoke.

'So there you have it. Part of the truth. My truth. The trouble is, there are so many truths in this world, truths of complicity, truths of self-interest, Stalin's truth, the First Secretary's. What is your truth, Commander, the reason you are here? Do you have one at all?'

*

Pat seemed to galvanize me into action. Every day I'd wake up with a new scheme. Maitland's disease, she called it. I started to develop some ideas about underwater photography, helping salvage divers working on wrecks. Fishing fleets were interested in the possibility of studying the habits of fish shoals. A year later, with Maitland's encouragement, I'd had even started writing a script for a film, *The Wonders of the Deep*. He said he might be able to find me backers. It seemed that my old life in the navy and my new life in civvy street could meet each other halfway after all.

Come the evening, Pat and I would hit the town. Tony and Minella had been right. It was time to let one's hair down. We went everywhere – the Nag's Head, the Grove, a new place that had just opened, the Trojan, out Kensington way. There were good Italian chophouses too; Bertorelli's, Luigi's, Bianchi's. They knew their food, and thanks to Ma Belloni, so did I. The first time I took her to Bianchi's, to sample the best spaghetti in town, the sign stuck on the wall outside caught light, and I threw the water from the ice bucket at it and blacked out the whole street. We stood looking down at everyone running in and out of the buildings. The waitress appeared at the top of the stairs, with a clutch of candles in her hand.

'That's more like it,' I said. 'Carbonara by candlelight. Should taste pretty good.'

Pat squeezed my arm. 'Oh, Crabbie, you old rogue,' she said. 'Don't you know? Everything tastes better by candlelight.'

Though she couldn't see it, I blushed. Not my style, the double entendre.

But by and large it was easy with Pat, her being a woman, me being a man. At least that's what I thought at the time. We'd have a few days together and then I'd push off for a while. But the war still hung over me, what I had seen, what I had done. It had seeped into my blood, and sometimes I could feel the fever rise up again, like an attack of malaria. I'd wake up in the morning, the sweat and shiver upon me, and no amount of canasta or carbonara or Pat sitting up at the corner of the bar, blowing smoke-rings at me, could dampen it down. I could smell the morning fug of diesel oil, taste the warm salt of the air, feel that ache invade my bones. I was back on the Rock, hauling my way along the hull of a tanker, waltzing on the seabed with a hundred-and-fifty-pound torpedo: Darling, you're treading on my toes. I could hear the sirens wind up and feel the ships lifting out of the water, my feet running down to the jetty, jumping in the slug as we headed out to throw our lot into the unknown. That was the kernel of it, the source of all my trouble, the unknown. To be sure there was the comradeship and the daily spoonful of duty to swallow, keeping strong for the country you loved, but hovering above it all was the lure of trusting your hand and the spring of the detonator to the capricious hand of God. There was a world then, a tragic, broken world, but a world all the same. There was the green of the rock and the blue of the sky and the white of my old plimsolls drying in the sun. There was Sydney and Tony and all the other chumps. There was Visintini's widow, dressed in her black veil, with her long slender hands and her faltering voice and her husband's wreath floating on the chop of the water. And then there was Paola, always Paola, Paola in the prow of her father's boat, head up, ignoring my indifference, Paola waving down at me from her little balcony in the square off the Zattere, Paola sitting on the round bench under the plane tree, with that picture before, framed and suspended in time, that eternal offering, glowing like oil in the dark. It had been my time, whether I liked it or not. No wonder it still broke out in me.

But Pat wanted to forget about the war. It hadn't been kind to her, as it had been to me. Pat wanted us to join forces, two against the world. She wanted an ally ranged alongside. She wanted to get spliced. I resisted for a time. I had only just escaped. She had her place, a neat little bijou in a mews near the King's Road. I had mine, the same snug little room that I'd started out with, with a view of the rooftops and the Brompton Oratory only a prayer away. I said my piece there almost every single day. The thought of chucking my one bag onto her bedspread made me feel uncomfortable, the doors I'd have to open, the things we'd both have to see, the proximity of it all. There are some unknowns that should remain that way, and the great divide between men and women is one of them. Nowadays it seems there's an expedition setting out to explore that particular territory every other day of the week, but to my way of thinking we should leave it alone, like we do the Antarctic. We should be content to stand on its edges, marvel at its great expanse and the great mystery that lies in its ever-shifting heart.

So it was against my better judgement that I agreed; engagement, marriage, the whole caboodle. I should have known better. A man has his way of doing things and a woman has hers. That's the crux of it. Not simply matters of the boudoir, either, though that's enough. Men want their world divided into separate sections; the office, the club, the wife, the nights out with the boys: as far as we're concerned there's no reason for any of them to spill over into one another. We want our lives built like a submarine, with each compartment sealed off; watertight. It's when the bulkheads are breached that the trouble begins. But women are different. They want the world to be opened up, of a piece, all flowing in and out, rising and falling like the tide. Something to do with their physique, I suspect. That was the trouble. I liked my life. I liked moving from one compartment to another. I liked slamming each door behind me. Pat didn't understand. Pat wanted to take a tin opener to the whole bloody lot.

We found a little house in the country to rent. There was a church nearby with good stained-glass windows, and a vicar who wasn't afraid of the Latin. There was a pub and a cricket green and a railway station just a brisk walk away. Three shovelfuls of nutty slack and I could be back in the smoke whenever I felt the urge. On Sundays we'd tool down there and spend the day getting the place ready for when we finally locked the door from the inside. I could very nearly picture myself standing by the mantelpiece, pipe in hand. Very nearly.

We got engaged the same day I received the George Medal. Pat had me practising tying the bow all week. I stood before the mirror that morning and saw a proud man staring back; both my monarch and my wife-to-be honouring my life. A lot of chaps deserved the medal a good deal better than me, a lot of chaps deserved a woman like Pat a good deal better than me, but there they were, the medal laid out on a little crimson cushion, and Pat, decked out in the same colour, all primed with pearls and perfume, a queen in her own right. We drove past the Palace gates in a hired Bentley. A footman opened the door. Another escorted us up the steps. We were shown into this anteroom where a man with undertaker's hands told me what to do. Then we were shown in, a line of us, a slice of ordinary life. I was second from last and while he was working his way down, I kept fiddling with my bow tie, to make sure it was straight. Then I caught the undertaker's eye and saw the frown dance across his forehead and my hands dropped to my side, the shame rushing up from my boots. My name was spoken and the King stood before me, and I bent my head and let the weight of those years fall against my chest. He spoke to me, his voice soft, but clean and clear. Three times he spoke, three questions, and three times I answered, as simply and straight-forwardly as I could. Then he leant in closer and spoke once more, and before what he said had sunk in, had stepped away, leaving me staring at the empty space ahead. To this day I can remember every single word. When I am alone, I speak them to my dormitory walls, let my lungs blow life upon them. To think that once I was so close to all that I held dear.

Afterwards we held a reception back in the hotel. They were all there, Rose, Maitland Pendock, the Nag's Head regulars, Lofty Gordon, my old chum from HMS *Vernon*, and dear old Sydney in his demob suit, his outsize feet pointing at a quarter to three.

'How's it going, Knowles?'

'Fair to middling, sir.'

'That bad.'

'Pretty much.'

'Still thinking about those doubloons?'

'I can hear the clink of them, sir, even in my sleep.'

'Well, if it's a diver you want, to carry your fortune up from the seabed to your piggy bank, you know who to call.'

'I'll remember that, sir. And you likewise, if you should find a bomb under your bed.'

'I think my bed is about to become quite dangerous enough, Knowles, without you underneath it.'

'Glad to hear it, sir. The beds you make. It isn't always true what they say about them.'

Len raised a toast for Pat and me. He'd brought us together. It was only right he should give us away. Rose threw purple cloaks around our shoulders, sat us on great wooden chairs and crowned us King and Queen of the Cavendish. It was a wonderful day. Everything seemed to be going right with the world. Then Maitland broke through the crush and introduced me to this chap he'd brought along, a business associate he said. He was tall, thin like a stick of rhubarb; about as green too, by the look of him.

'Congratulations on the medal,' he said. 'Though you had to wait a bit, I understand. Forty-four, wasn't it?'

'Forty-three, actually,' I told him, 'though it's no skin off my nose. His Majesty has got more important things to do than to worry about the likes of me. I'd have waited another twenty years if necessary.'

He nodded into his glass, then lifted his head up straight. He had sharp eyes, narrow and quick.

'And did he say anything to you?'

Well, I wasn't about to tell this pipsqueak, chum of Maitland's or no. I wasn't about to tell anyone, not even Pat.

'That's between me and my maker,' said I. 'And I'm not one hundred per cent sure I'd tell Him, without the King's permission.'

He leant back on his heels and smiled.

'You're quite right, Commander. I should never have asked.' He slipped a hand in his pocket, fingered something inside. 'And how are you finding life on the outside? Pretty bloody, I expect.'

'Today makes up for a lot of things,' I said.

'If they were all like this, we'd get no work done at all. I hear they're doing some useful stuff down Teddington way.'

Teddington was where they had the Counter-Espionage Underwater Station. I finished my glass off, looked around for the waiter.

'I don't know who told you that,' said I, 'but if I were you I wouldn't believe a word they say. You can never trust a blabbermouth.'

He held his head to one side, those eyes dancing with mine.

'And if I told you what was said to you this morning, if I repeated that last sentence, word for word, would you call His Majesty a blabbermouth too?' And he leant forward and whispered it, word for word. I didn't know where to look.

He put his hand on my shoulder.

'We share his sentiments exactly, Commander,' he said. 'We are all grateful for what you have done for the country in the past. Our desire now is to find ways you might assist us in the future.'

He handed me a card.

'Take no notice of all that guff at the end,' he said. 'Call me Smithy. I'll be in touch.' And with that he glided out of the room.

★

I didn't have to wait long. I was still in the Cavendish. It had been four months since the do and things were bumping along nicely. I came downstairs for a late breakfast and found Smithy sitting at my table with a copy of *Country Life* in his hands. He waved me over.

'Thinking of upping sticks?' I said, and sat down.

'I was thinking of going for a drive. Nice day for it, don't you think?'

'If you have a car.'

'I've got mine outside. Fancy a spin?'

I shook my head. 'Pat's expecting me.' I tapped his magazine. 'Our stately home needs decorating.'

'You haven't moved in yet, then?'

Well, of course I hadn't moved in. If I'd moved in, he wouldn't be there, leafing through the property pages. It was a way of telling me, the tabs they were keeping.

'Could you put the paintbrush aside until tomorrow?' he asked. 'We would be so very grateful.'

There it was again, that 'we'. You couldn't fight it.

'You'll allow me to have breakfast first, I take it. I'm booked in for my monthly rasher of bacon.'

'You don't want to miss out on that,' said Smithy. 'You're looking thinner as it is. I'll go and check the radiator.'

The bacon failed to materialize. I was given a plate of fried tinned tomatoes instead. Train smash, Sydney used to call it. I downed a second cup of tea, then gave Pat a bell. She was none too pleased, but there it was.

We drove through London with the top down. The traffic was

light, and soon we were heading south-west, past Teddington and out along the A3.

'I hear you were pretty cheesed off, being given the elbow.'

'It's not what a fellow wants,' I said. 'Particularly . . .' I hesitated.

'Yes?'

'I feel like a fish out of water,' I said. 'It may be only an expression but in my case it's true. I *am* a fish out of water. I don't know what else to do. God knows I'm willing enough to try my hand, but at what? Someone suggested I went into the City. Lloyd's or something. Said they'd fix me up. Met this chappie in the boardroom. It was all very civilized; they gave me a glass of sherry and said what an asset I would be to the firm, a man like me, how I'd stand for integrity and trust, being a medal-winner and all, but I thought, that's what I would be, a figurehead, to be gawped at, of no real consequence at all. What do I know about stocks and shares? There's only one world I do know, Smithy, and it's all under water.'

He hummed and hawed and continued driving.

'Are we going anywhere in particular?' I asked. 'Only I know a nice pub in Guildford.'

'Thought we might pop into your old stamping ground,' he said. 'There are some folk I want you to meet, who could need your skills.'

'Use your skills' is what he meant I supposed, but I kept quiet. I hadn't been down at HMS *Vernon* since demob.

'I thought they'd washed their hands of me.'

'So they have, Commander.' And he pulled on his ear and stared ahead.

HMS *Vernon*, the premier torpedo and mining school of the navy, was stationed down at Portsmouth. Years back it had been a proper ship, but it had moved ashore in the early twenties. Apart from the instructional side, there were three experimental departments, Whitehead (torpedo design), Mining (mine design) and Electrical (searchlights, telephones, batteries). After my return I had hung around there for a while, hoping to talk my way into a permanent posting, but they wanted younger blood than mine. Always the suitor, never the groom, that's what they should have chiselled on my grave-stone, not that bland description that Gordon relayed back to me.

We arrived at the front gates. They barely examined his pass. As we drove in I waved at Ariadne, the old ship's figurehead still loom-ing over the entrance in her green gown. She almost smiled.

'Well, she's still carrying a fair amount of poundage,' I said. 'Despite the rationing.'

We drove past the wardroom gardens and the tennis courts out towards the jetty. At Vernon Creek we turned left and scooted along out to the pier. Half the buildings I'd known had gone, destroyed by incendiaries and other mischief. It had taken a good many knocks during the war. At the pier a couple of young cadets were standing by a picket boat. Smithy introduced me. Blow me if they didn't salute. I felt quite chuffed. No one had done that in a long time.

We rode out to Stoke's Bay. The sea was flat, not like a pond, but like a canal, moving sluggishly with the motion of the little craft and the midday heat rising off the water. We had a little canopy over our heads and in the distance came the hooting of some barge or other outside the harbour. I could have been back in Venice, on the way to prise away another example of German unpleasantness. A cry came across the water, like the notes of a Neapolitan song, like one of my boys singing his heart out to some blushing beauty, reluctantly hurrying out of his sight. I remember thinking then that if I'd stayed I would have been diving in those green waters still, cleaning up the arteries of the most wondrous city on God's earth. I could have chucked my cap and settled down near some back-street cafe, Signor Crabb, the crazy Inglese who loved their city better than his own. It would have been a life, a better one perhaps than the one I've been left with. But there would have been troubles too. Paola would have seen to that.

Sitting half out the water was a bulbous object that looked as if it had been squeezed out the backside of an elephant. I thought the pigs the Italians had ridden were bad enough, but at least you weren't sealed in like a corpse in a coffin. Smithy drew his hand over the unsightly brute.

'It takes four, you know. Three to navigate and steer and see to the ballast, and one . . .' He pointed to the aft hatch and the ladder running down the side. 'A man could hop in and out of that, don't you think, if he had a mind to?'

'A madman, perhaps. Or a submariner.'

'Submariners tend to want to stay inside, Commander. What we're looking for is someone who will accompany them and when the time comes, go off on his tod.'

'To do what?'

'To look at things, examine them, report back regarding their make-up. Enemy warships, for instance, or certain of their harbour defences; anything that might be of interest to HMG and her allies.'

The enemy. I hadn't heard that word used for four years.

'I thought the war was over.'

'We have a new one now. As you know perfectly well.'

I nodded. I'd known for longer than he had, probably, ever since that plane pitched down and I was sent out to rescue the General's briefcase.

He turned and pointed to a shed, with the door half open.

'If you'd like to get changed, we've arranged for a little excursion.'

I looked across. Lofty Gordon was standing in the doorway, his face broken in two by a stupid grin. Across the way a flying boat was circling, ready to land on Southampton Water.

'Ha ha, I don't think.' I turned to Smithy. 'This is all very lovely,' I told him, 'but I haven't brought my frogsuit and I absolutely refuse to wear the standard attire. It's against my principles, drowning.' Smithy pressed his hands together.

'That's why, while you were having breakfast, I took the liberty of . . .' He nodded his head and Lofty reached in, and brought the damn thing out, still hanging on the hotel hanger.

Twelve

Someone died in the sanatorium last night, one floor down. This morning the body wagon trundled up the drive, smoke pouring out its rear end, and skirted round the side to collect what was left. They don't try to pull the wool over your eyes here, dress it up as a laundry van or wait until the dead of night. Out through the front gate you go, off into the netherworld with the exhaust pipe blazing away like a ten-gun salute. I rather like that, seeing my fellow patients come and go, as we all must. There's a tidal movement to it that I find reassuring: on your way at last. What they do with the remains is another matter altogether. If they're anything like Mother Russia used to be, then hold onto your hat. You're in for a long wait.

The first time I had to deal with Soviet burial arrangements was when one of our maintenance wallahs, Ivan, got in the way of a burst boiler and was scalded to death. I had to organize the obsequies. It was November and there were no next of kin. I'd never given the disposal of the dead much thought up till then, though I'd watched a few of my new-found comrades being slid into the sea, listened to that majestic funeral march of theirs rolling over the ranks. I assumed they'd bury the poor fellow. I'd forgotten about Katyn.

After the service it was left to me to escort the body to his interment. No one else came, which I thought rather bad form. We drove from the base through the outskirts of town, me, the driver, and unlucky Ivan in a box in the back. There was a heater in the car, a foul-smelling contraption that made your eyes water, but at least it kept the blood from icing over. Outside everything was drained of colour.

After about twenty minutes, instead of the hallowed plot, the driver pulled up in front of a warehouse half the size of Wembley Stadium, and leant on his horn.

'What's going on?' I enquired.

'Paperwork,' he grunted.

The doors opened and we drove in. Two men in belted great-coats and fur hats stood in a little glass-fronted office to the side, stamping their feet. I climbed out and hurried in. If anything it was colder in than out.

'Good God, man,' I said, 'don't they give you any heating in here?'

They looked puzzled and pointed to the rows of pallets ranged the length of the interior. Stretched out on top of them, all tied up in grey canvas bags, lay row upon row of bodies, name tags tied round their shrouded feet. And then it struck me. You couldn't bury bodies in winter here. The ground was frozen solid. All over Russia stood warehouse upon warehouse full of Soviet stiffs. Mother, fathers, sons, daughters, aunts and uncles, brothers and sisters, lying in limbo, their faces set at the time of their death. It seemed to sum up the place for me, all natural life suspended under the cavernous roof of the State.

'How many have you got here?' I asked.

He shrugged his shoulders. 'Twelve hundred?'

'And by the end of the winter?

'Who knows?'

'And when spring comes?'

He grinned. 'We burn them. In job lots.'

They lifted Ivan out of his box and placed him on a wooden plank that lay upon the arms of a forklift truck. One man tied a name tag to him, while the other stamped his papers, and then the truck trundled off and slid him into place. I went back to base and had what passed for a brandy.

So today I watched as they drove the poor fellow away, out down the main road and off in the direction of the wooded hills. Rosa came by a little later, determined to cheer me up.

'Tell me,' I asked her firmly, 'when I die, where will I go?'

She looked at me nervously, as if I was trying to provoke her into saying something foolish. I patted myself up and down.

'My body, Rosa. What will they do with it? Burn it? Float it down the river on a coal barge? What?'

Colour rushed to her cheeks.

'It is too early for such talk, Commander.'

'I'm just interested, that's all.'

'It is not for me to say.' She began fussing furiously with my blankets. 'Your comrades, from the service, perhaps . . .'

Ah, Sydney, if only that could be true, Sydney sailing me out to the Solent, or putting me on a train to Tobermory and taking me down to lie among his lost doubloons. Or maybe he'd go the whole hog and tip me feet-first into Algeçiras Bay, where Licio Visintini and Madame Lesniowska wait for me still. We'd find each other in time, bumping along the sandy floor, the pal who I never knew, the suitor who never took a fairer hand. What times the three of us would have!

★

That was the beginning of it. I was back in, on an ad-hoc sort of basis, first a sort of guinea pig, stuffed into all manner of contraptions to see if I'd come out alive, and then going on little underwater excursions further afield, a civilian working unofficially for the navy. We started going to places I shouldn't really talk about. France, Norway, back to the Med; ships to look at, soundings to take, new equipment to try out. It was different from jumping in and doing a few lengths with recalcitrant metal. There was still the dark water, and still the urgency, but there was also the secrecy, which made the absence of light more appropriate. In Gib it had been just a bloody nuisance. Now it was an ally, part of the deal. Welcome to the world of nods and winks. Smithy used to turn up in the strangest of places. I'd be standing in line in Harrods or sitting in a barber's chair when he'd appear behind a newspaper, saying, 'Fancy meeting you here, got time for a beer?' So he'd brief me and a day or two later we'd pop to HMS *Vernon* or wherever, and get kitted out. The chaps there would look at me in my pork-pie hat and silver cane and say, 'Oh, it's you, Crabbie. Off on one of our little jaunts, are we?' And I'd frown and look nonplussed, but I liked it all the same, getting accepted, making new pals. If I needed to stop over for a couple of days, there was always Lofty's or a spare bed in the wardroom. Sometimes Smithy and me would meet in the Brompton Oratory, or in the little Italian restaurant opposite. It was funny that way, the Brompton Oratory. Whenever I went there, it was full of men like Smithy, wandering about the church in the middle of the day, listening to the young choir, taking confessional, bent in prayer. Sometimes I thought they all must be spies of one sort or another, taking strength from God before going up against the great God-less opponent we now faced.

The other thing I had to deal with was the fact that I was beginning to become just a mite well known, the face, the whiskers, the walk. The *Sunday Express* started it, writing articles about me in the war, but it didn't take long for others to catch on. I was a bit of a hero, and that's not a simple thing to be. It strips away the ordinariness of who you were, and turns it into something quite the opposite, something you begin to believe you had all along. Yurka and I used to talk about it, though he was much more of an idol than I ever became; street processions in his honour, dachas in the country, any woman he cared to tip his samovar at. He even had a smelting plant named after him. I was more of a schoolboy sort of hero, comic strips in the *Eagle*, life-and-death struggles in the *Sunday Pictorial*, the Gospel According to Beaverbrook, and though I knew better than anyone how they all wrote it up a bit, I began to believe in that hero and the England he fought for, the England he still wanted it to be; fair play at the stumps and winning because of the way you played it. And now, I'd been taken back, up against a new foe, with new friends and fresh honour.

I loved every minute.

Pat wasn't too happy about it, though, the way Smithy and his little set-tos messed things up. Every time we tried to make plans, water got in the way. There were places I had to go, wrecks I had to inspect, hush-hush diving I had to keep shtum about. Conversation became more difficult, there was so much I couldn't say. Pat wanted me to find a proper job, one that had, in her words, prospects. She wanted me to spend more time on the cottage too, more time preparing for our new life, whatever that was going to be. That was another thing. The more I saw of the cottage, the more I began to dislike it, the way it sat in its garden like a smug little gnome. I wasn't a country boy at heart. I wasn't one for lanes and milking parlours and hoary old Joes with their gnarled sticks and pints of scrumpy. I preferred pavements and gentleman's outfitters and a variety of lounge bars to prop up of an evening.

The crunch came soon enough. 1950 it was, just after the New Year. We'd intended to go down to the cottage for a week. We were to drive there on the Wednesday, January 11th. As usual she would stay in what was to be our bedroom while I put myself up in the pub across the road. Pat was quite prepared to take a more modern view about that sort of thing, but I was adamant. 'Not my style,' I said. 'I'm carrying you across the threshold a decent woman. You don't move into a new house with tarnished taps now, do you?'

The morning we were due to leave, Smithy called. There was a rush job on, Malta way. I'd have to take my gear with me and leave for HMS *Vernon* Friday morning. When I called for Pat and broke the news, she took it badly, turned her lighter up full volume and set fire to the end of her cigarette. For a minute or two she wouldn't even look at me. I tried to reason with her.

'Can't be helped, old girl,' I told her. 'Smithy says this is important.'

'Smithy says! Smithy says!' She tugged at the ring. 'Why don't you get married to Smithy, and cut out the middle woman. It's just an excuse, Crabbie. I'm sick to death of HMS *Vernon*, sick of the sea, sick of Smithy. It's time to cast off. Them or me.'

Her mood had brightened by the time we got there, but I still had some headway to make. Pat had bought all these Victorian earthenware storage jars, ugly brutes they were to my mind, with 'flour' and 'sugar' written on the side. Couldn't see the point of them myself, considering all that stuff came in perfectly adequately labelled packets in the first place, but there we are. There was no room for them in the pantry and in a rash moment I'd promised to put up a shelf for the beastly things in the kitchen. Now, I reasoned, was the time to redress the balance, throw some goodwill onto those heavily tipped scales. We got there about eleven in the morning. Conscious of the approaching opening hour, I spent an intensive fifty minutes poking about in the plaster, drilling and screwing, not to mention some judicious wielding of the nuptial hammer. By twelve fifteen I had all the jars and their respective contents on parade. Pat was surprised that I'd managed to do it at all and insisted on taking me over the road for a well-deserved freshener. Perfectly acceptable crowd, publican sufficiently relaxed about closing times. How could I refuse?

We got back a little later than planned. I went into the living room for a spot of shut eye, while Pat busied herself in the kitchen, to put some much-needed ballast in our holds. I'd just settled down when I heard this shout, and then she called to me, sharp, like a newly commissioned officer barking his first set of orders. I got to my feet and sauntered in. The jars were all smashed to bits on the floor, the flour and what-not billowing out across the linoleum. The shelf hadn't come off exactly, but the brackets had come loose under the combined weight, tipping it downwards. The jars had slid off, one by one, like seals on a sand bank, flopping into the water.

'Bang goes the wedding cake, then,' I said.

'Get out, Crabbie,' she shouted. 'Clear this mess up and go back to your blessed pub.' And with that she stalked off. Whoops! Wrong thing to say. That's the trouble with the fairer sex. One moment you're sailing along, happy as Larry, the next moment, boom! Sunk without a trace. What did I do? What did I say? You touched the live wire, that's all, chum, tripped the switch, trod on the pressure point, consigned yourself to temporary oblivion. English women, Italian women, wherever they're from, they should all have a sign hung around their necks. Danger – Unexploded Mines. Careless handling can cause injury and even death.

I didn't see her the rest of the day, and come the evening she didn't show at all. At closing time I went round to the cottage. It was cloaked in the dark. I walked round the back. A little light shone from the bedroom window. I threw a stone or two, and called out. Eventually the curtains were drawn and the sash thrown up. There were things on her head, like she was wired up for some scientific experiment.

'Hello, gorgeous,' said I. 'Is Mr Frankenstein in?'

'You're drunk.'

'I can still see straight.'

'Well, see if you can walk straight. Go home, Crabbie.'

'I thought this was home.'

'What, with me here and you parked up the road? We're engaged, Crabbie. But apart from the ring, I haven't seen much evidence of it.'

I stood on the lawn. It moved like the deck of a flat-bottomed trawler. I grabbed a passing cherry tree and shouted up, emboldened.

'I could show you some evidence now, if you want.'

'In that state? Let's see what tomorrow brings.'

'Tomorrow it is, my own. I'll surprise you. We'll have a wonderful day, a day to remember. Now tell me, do you need to be earthed for those things?'

I went back. You know the story. A bar likes a man with out-of-hours tales to tell. Overslept too. But I hadn't forgotten and seeing Pat at the window with all that equipment in her hair had given me an idea. If a woman was content going to bed looking like a deranged plumber, surely a man was entitled to redress the balance?

I gave Pat a tinkle. She sounded quite friendly. She was having a lie in, then going into the nearby town, first to replace certain missing essentials then to get her hair done. She'd be back late afternoon. At lunchtime I took the hair of the dog for a moderate walk and then popped over to the cottage with my stuff. The shelf was still hanging from the wall by its fingernails. I tore the thing loose, lumps of plaster falling on my brogues. Upstairs I changed into the frogsuit, fished out the morning paper and clambered into bed. Pat's perfume rose from the pillow: coupled with the smell of the suit and the tang of old salt water, it provided a singular aroma to the occasion. I sat there, half upright, waiting. So this is what I would wake to; the double bed, the dressing table, the built-in cupboard; her side, my side, the bathroom next door.

I was just nodding off when the front door opened. Pat came in.

'Crabbie?' she called out. I said nothing.

'Typical,' I heard her say, though why she said it I don't know. It wasn't as if I was late or anything. She dumped some stuff in the hall and started to move around, first in the living room, where she banged some cushions about, and then on to the kitchen, where evidence of the misdemeanour still remained. I could hear her picking up the pieces from the bucket, then chucking them back in.

'Typical,' she said again, and rattled the lot outside. When she came back she was singing the 'Marseillaise', words and all. For some reason I found that rather irritating. Then back into the living room she went, fussed around for another day and a half, before returning to the kitchen. What on earth was the woman doing?

Finally footsteps came up the stairs. She had her high heels on, I could tell. They often do that, going to the hairdresser's. I positioned myself, the *Times* held up at the ready, swimfins sticking out the end of the counterpane. But instead of coming straight in, she turned into the bathroom. Water started running, both taps; the boiler cleared its throat and began to gargle. More singing, followed by the clatter of shoes, then the sound of a hand swishing water about. She was running a bath! I hadn't thought of that. I was beginning to think that perhaps this was not such a good idea after all, when the door was flung open.

'Ah there you are,' I said. 'Fifteen down's a bit of a bugger,' and lowered the paper. She was in her underwear, pink I think they were, and unseasonably frilly. I can't remember much more, because she crossed her arms over her bosom and started screaming. She simply screamed and screamed and screamed, unable to move.

'It's me, Pat,' I cried, jumping up. 'Crabbie. Don't you recognize me?' and she screamed again, only louder and then stopped, her hand covering her mouth. I stood still, not knowing what to do. We waited a moment, while she regained her breath, her chest beating like an injured bird's.

'What the bloody hell are you playing at,' she gasped.

'I thought it might rain,' I said and with that she ran at me, head down like a goat, and sent me crashing into the built-in cupboard, before running downstairs. Everything went quiet. I clambered back out, hung her clothes back as best I could and got changed. It always takes longer to climb out of rubber when you're in a hurry. I followed her downstairs. She was in the drawing room, drinking a large whisky, her raincoat wrapped round her. She'd lit the fire some time before, and there were sprigs of holly by the window, and on the small table by the settee stood a couple of champagne glasses and a box of Turkish Delight. That's what she'd been doing. I stood in the doorway, contrite.

'Where is it?'

'Upstairs. It was only a joke, Pat.'

'I never want to see it in this house again. Do you understand?'

'I didn't mean to scare you, Pat.'

'What do you think I'd be? I walk into my bedroom half undressed and find that . . .'

'I didn't know you'd be half . . . whatever. I just thought it would be a bit of a wheeze, that's all.'

'It wouldn't have been so bad if you'd, if it had just been you, in bed.'

'What do you mean?'

'What do you think I mean?'

'It wasn't meant that way, Pat.'

'What way, then?'

'I told you. I thought it would amuse you.'

'What, the first time I see my fiancé in our bed, he's wearing a frogsuit, and swimfins? Bloody swimfins. I suppose everyone in the Nag's Head knows about this.'

'No one. I only thought of it last night. I thought it would make you laugh. You've always wondered what I look like in my working clothes.'

'I was about to take a bath. I could have walked in stark naked.'

'That was a risk I was prepared to take.'

She laughed, then remembered.

'The bath!'

I ran upstairs and turned the taps off. Her blouse and skirt lay in a heap on the floor. I picked them up and laid them on the wicker chair. Pat had been inside them, as I had been in my frogsuit; different uniforms; worlds apart.

'That was a near thing,' I said, coming down. 'Another minute and I'd have had to put up a new ceiling as well as a new shelf.'

She put her arms around me. She was close and unduly warm. My hands hung at my side.

'Oh, Crabbie. You are such a fool, you know.'

'I know that. Absolutely. Don't deserve you. Don't deserve anyone, most likely. Bloody stupid idea, dressing up like that. Never do it again. Frogsuit utterly banished from the homestead.' I put my hands on her shoulders, held her at arm's length. 'Tell you what, Pat. I'll skidaddle with the unmentionable. You go and ablute yourself for an hour or so and when you're ready, we'll drink the champagne, drive up to London and have a slap-up evening, no expense spared. What do you say?'

She drew her raincoat together and looked around her.

'If that's what you want, Crabbie.'

'What could a man want more than that, Pat?'

And she shook her head and smiled.

★

Back in town we drove to Kensington, Pat looking out of one window, holding on to my arm.

'Oh, Crabbie,' she said, 'if only it could be always like this, dark and safe and fun.'

'That's the trouble, Pat. There's something wrong with this country. It's not the same as it was.'

'What was it, then?'

'Search me. But it was fixed, you know, like a clock on a wall.

Sometimes it went a little fast, sometimes it went a little slow, but it always came back to the same place. Now it's like all the clocks have been smashed, and I don't know what time it is any more.'

'It's the cottage, isn't it, Crabbie. You just don't want to set up home there, that's the nub of it. Go on, tell me otherwise.'

'I have been thinking about that, Pat. Not that I can't wait to get stuck in and all that, but I have been wondering, that perhaps it is a bit far away from everything.'

'You think?' She turned her head. 'Maybe it's me that's too close, Crabbie.'

'Don't say that, old girl. I'm not used to it, that's all. It's all a bit of a rush for me.'

'For you? It's you that's been banging on about marriage.'

'Has it? I thought it had been you. Isn't it what you want?'

'Not to someone who's married already.'

'I don't get you.'

'The service, Crabbie. Smithy, HMS *Vernon*. I want us to be a proper couple, Crabbie, but all it is, is you and me. Can't you see that?'

'Course I can. I try my best, Pat, but things just fall apart in my hands.' I turned them over. 'Look at them. Look OK under water, but on dry land, they're useless. Just like their owner.'

She took a hand off the wheel and placed it over mine.

'You've shy hands. I like that.'

'Shy hands! What sort of rot is that.'

'They're respectful, never think the worse of you, not like some I've known.' She took one and put it to her lips. 'But sometimes, though, I want them to think of whatever they like.'

*

The Trojan was one of the few clubs outside the West End to have a late-night drinking licence. The chap who ran it, Greville Wynne, was a business associate of Pendock, though he was more in the export line. It was a well-organized little enterprise, with a small dance band, a well-mannered bevy of waitresses and a chef at the back who could rustle up something decent if you got a bit peckish after the third bottle. Wynne wasn't as big or as round as Pendock, but he had the same sort of restless jauntiness, the same sort of quick watchfulness in his eyes. He had one of those moustaches that made you think of insurance salesmen, and like insurance salesmen he spent a lot of time on the road, touting his wares, only not down the leafy lanes of suburbia, but over into Germany and Czechoslovakia, attending trade fairs and the like. There seemed to be hundreds of men like Wynne and Pendock in London at that time, starting up little businesses on Monday, folding them up on Friday. People say that nothing happened much in the fifties, that it was a slow time. I should cocoa. The England you know was made in the fifties, and the rest of the world too.

When he was there, Wynne was always pleased to see me, and insisted on the first round of drinks being on the house. He liked to show his appreciation to those who'd done something out of the ordinary in the war, that's what Pendock said, but as I pointed out, nearly everyone in the war had done something extraordinary. In war everyone's special. In peace, hardly anybody is.

It was a quarter to ten by the time we got there, the four-man combo going through their Cole Porter routine, the dance area awash with couples. I'm not one for the light fantastic, but that night I felt in the mood.

'Come on, Pat,' I said. 'I feel like treading on your toes.' We slipped into the current and shuffled around. One, two three, one two, three.

'Perhaps you should wear your swimfins after all,' Pat said. 'Then I could tread on yours.'

She pressed her head against mine, and I thought perhaps it was going to be all right after all, perhaps the cottage would be all right, as long as I could come and go every once in a while, so long as we could come up here. If Pat wanted me and her to spend the night under the same roof, perhaps we should. Another plunge into the deep. It would be all right with Pat. She wouldn't try to suffocate me with it, wouldn't make it anything more than what it was. Probably wouldn't mention it at all. I'd have to go to confession, of course. I thought of Paola and wondered what she might be doing, whether she might be looking out her window, staring down at that tree, or whether . . . Suddenly I saw Wynne, standing at the side, beckoning me over. His face had gone all white.

'You probably haven't heard, but we've a radio in the kitchen,' he said. 'There's been a collision in the Thames estuary. A submarine's gone down, the *Truculent*, about three hours ago. Seventy-nine men on board, most of them still trapped inside.'

I marched Pat back to the table and plonked her down.

'Crabbie, what is it?'

I didn't reply for a bit. I was thinking. The tide in the estuary was too strong for normal divers. They would have to hang around for slack water, when it was on the turn. But with his self-contained gear and his swimfins a frogman wouldn't have to wait. He could reach the sub right away and once down, swim alongside, unfettered by lines or heavy boots. If there were men still alive, speed was of the essence.

'Greville will tell you,' I said. 'I'm off to use his phone.'

I rang the duty commander at the Admiralty. By midnight my offer had been accepted and I was on the road to Sheerness, my spare gear being brought up from Teddington. I got out there at around three o'clock in the morning. She was lying in seven fathoms, with the tide running at a full three knots. They'd picked up about eight survivors and as many bodies. They'd got out all right but had either drowned or died of exposure. From the survivors' reports there were a good forty men still down there, gathered in the unflooded aft compartments. The distress-marker buoy had been found, but we couldn't use that as a mooring; the strain would have been too great and it would have snapped and then we'd have lost her position completely. The only way I could get down to her was to use our boat's anchor to foul the submarine's superstructure and then haul myself down, hand over hand. I'd never gone against such a strong current. I jumped in and thrashed my way to the cable. I had a sodium lamp with me; they're better than ordinary lights, which simply glare back at you, like car headlights in a fog. It was a treacherous journey down, the cable taut and slippery, my body pulled out, a pennant on a stick. Two foot down and it didn't feel like water at all. It was more like oil, thick and dirty, working against my every move. Suddenly I could go no further. It was as if I was standing on a cliff top in a force-eight gale. The water tore at me, prising my right hand from the line, trying to pluck me free. If I'd let go I wouldn't have been caught until Christmas. I closed my eyes and let it rush over me. Do your worst, I thought. This is Commander Crabb.

Water is like the wind; there are always pockets of calm to be found, if you know where to look for them. You have to lean into a current sometimes, run your hands over its muscle, learn how to slip in between the sinews of its strength. I waited, conscious of its twists and turns, and then, in its moment of fleeting weakness, turned and regained my hold. I hung there anchored for a full minute, getting my breath back. I wish Sydney was here, I thought, and pulled my way down.

Nearing the bed, the tide slackened off, almost completely. My legs swung down. I was falling, like a feather on the moon, coming to a hard, abrupt stop, my feet pressing on my heart. I was on the bridge, the glow of the lamp only serving to hide its long, bleak shape. I started to work my way along, towards the engine escape hatch, tapping all the while. There was no response. It was a black world down there, and every step I made stirred up the blackness further. I was standing on a metal coffin. A few feet away from me lay God knew how many men, dead the lot of them, piled together in the cold black air. What was the difference I thought, between them and me? A thin sheet of metal, a few bubbles of oxygen? They had eyes still, there was still blood in their veins, their hair was grow-ing. Suddenly I wanted to join them, to break in and embrace them. I didn't want the cottage and the bath running and Pat's perfume in every room. I wanted the cold and the dark, and these pale, beckon-ing men. I thought of Visintini and how his hair swept back from his proud, stiff face. I thought of Eugene and his hands calmly folded on his lap. And I thought of the empty overcoat and the woman's body I never found, was never meant to find. I walked the length of the broken boat, seeing nothing, hearing nothing. It was like I didn't exist. When the time came I could hardly bear to rise to the surface. There are times when I don't know why I did.

★

Pat called it a day a month after the accession of the Queen. Three months later she moved to France and married a chap called Rose. If she could do it, I thought, so could I. Bad idea I know, but there it was. Margaret was the woman's name. I forget the boy's. Biggest mistake of my life, but at the time it seemed to be the ideal thing. I was attaching myself to a ready-made family; a son past the mewling stage, a woman who already knew how to be a wife, knew what a man might require. We set up in a little caravan in West Leigh, just near the Under-Water Counter-Weapons Establishment. I liked the caravan, liked the way drawers turned into tables and the tables into beds. It was like moving under water. You had to plan your actions ahead and move slowly, otherwise you'd get ensnared.

But it was hard, three people in such a place, two of them strangers to one, one of them strangers to two. I started to drink too much. I was missing Pat, though we talked on occasions on the phone. I spent a lot of time away, trying to give us all room to breathe, but it didn't help. I'd come back to a banged-up silence. There's nothing worse in a confined space, no one talking, everyone walking around each other like cats.

One evening I came back and found the field empty. All that was left was my suitcase on the edge of the bare patch where the caravan had stood. I walked a couple of miles and took the first train up. Back at the Nag's Head, Len offered to put me up for a couple of days, until I found my feet. I walked over to the telephone and fed in the pennies. She answered almost immediately.

'Guess what I'm looking at?'

'Prison bars?'

'A suitcase. She's left me, Pat. I'm back in London, back in the land of the living.'

There was a pause.

'I'm sorry,' she said.

'Don't say that, Pat. Raise a glass and praise the Lord. How's Napoleon?'

'Not so enamoured with his Josephine as he might be.'

'And how's Josephine?'

'Eating too much cake.'

'That's Marie Antoinette, Pat. Do I take it the entente is not so cordiale, then?'

'Turned to vinegar, Crabbie. Funny you should mention suitcases. I've just been thinking if I should pack one myself.'

'I don't know how you can stick it there, anyhow. They chopped off their monarch's head, you know. They're a republic. No English woman should settle down in a republic, Pat.'

'Not even Italy?'

'Italy's different. Italy's got the Pope.'

Someone shouted out my name. Maitland was standing by the bar, waving his wallet.

'Don't think anything,' I said. 'Hop on a train and get the first ferry over. You'll be back tomorrow lunchtime, a drink in one hand and a forkful of Len's shepherd's pie in the other. In the afternoon we'll buy you a brand-new wardrobe. Then we'll paint the town, plan our future. I won't make such a hash of it this time.'

Her voice grew impatient, like it had when we split up.

'Crabbie, you're still living in a black-and-white world. It's not as straightforward as that. You can't go back, Crabbie.'

'That's what everyone tells me. I don't see it myself. Why not? Why can't you go back if you want to?'

I could hear her breathing at the other end, and then the click of the receiver as she put the phone down. I made myself a promise that I wouldn't ring again. I kept it, though there were times when I found myself in the phone box opposite my flat, sinking to the bottom of the world. I'd found a single room in Hans Place. One room, one bed, one standard lamp and a wardrobe with a damp frog-suit inside. A convenient spot, though, the Brompton Oratory a short prayer away, a decent pub, the George IV in Montpelier Square, and

Harrods Food Hall just across the road. I liked going to the Food Hall. I liked the look of their fish, laid out on the marble like royal courtiers, their silvery coats, a vanished light in their eyes, as if they belonged to a different deity from my own. I'd buy them whole; mullet, mackerel, sometimes something bigger, a sea trout, a young salmon, and carry it over in my arms. It was companionable, to have a whole fish to look at. Sometimes I'd eat it dressed in the frogsuit, made me part of something again. Once I bought a bass that was too big for the little table. Its tail hung over the edge. Four days I ate that fish, moving it along as I worked my way through. Four days and I wasn't bored for one of them.

Smithy began to work me hard, the Med, the North Sea, once back to dear old Gib. They even sent me to Suez, checking the canal's defences. When the balloon went up, everyone assumed that we wanted the canal to stay open, and so we did, but only if we had unfettered access. What would have happened if Uncle Nasser had handed the whole lot over to the Russians, what would we have wanted then? The Russians in control of a free-flowing stretch of water, or one clogged to Christendom? And that's all I'm going to say on the subject, apart from the fact it was hot, nasty work. I was there for two weeks. By the time I got back I had a tongue like a French lizard.

I walked in the Nag's Head, sat in the corner. Len came over and put a glass of beer in my hand.

'Anything to eat?' I said. 'Something good and British?'

'We got a three-day curry going,' said he.

'That's the fellow,' said I. 'Bring me a large bucket of it. I've been in the desert, up to my neck in water. I need heating up.'

I opened up the *Times* and started in on the crossword. Very much a B-team effort. Hardly worth getting one's pencil out for.

The street door opened.

There was a rustle of movement, a kind of unspoken murmur. My paper flapped in the unwanted breeze. I held it down, filled in eight across and looked up. Pat sat at the bar, eyeing the optics. She was sporting some sort of nautical two-piece, topped with one of those silly pill-box hats, the type you want to chuck overboard. She had a small bag at her feet and an unlit Du Maurier in her mouth. She took out her lighter and brought forth flame; steady as a rock. Len came out with my fodder.

'That woman at the bar,' I said, loud enough for all to hear. 'Are we quite safe? She looks a bit of a Lulu to me.'

He looked across.

'You got a point there, Crabbie,' he said. 'That is the human bombshell, just come back from France. Seems the monsieurs over there didn't know how to handle her properly.'

I worked the curry into the rice and took a mouthful. Like Vesuvius, only with a bit of a bang.

'They tried to dampen her down, I suspect,' said I. 'Not the right approach at all. A controlled explosion, that's what's needed here. Break out the Supplicants, Len, and a bottle of your best fizz. Then you'd best take cover.'

I picked up my plate and walked over. She was still staring ahead. Len eased the cork across the room. Her eyes darted onto mine. Only for a second, but I caught them just the same.

'What's that at your feet?' I said. 'A booby trap?'

'Man-trap,' she said. Len started to pour.

'Any man in particular? Or just the first unfortunate who trips over it.'

'Only a man with outsize feet could trip over that,' she said. 'That's a vanity case.'

'What, with a hat like that?' I took another forkful.

'Something wrong?' she said.

'Not from where I'm standing.'

'Only there are tears in your eyes.'

I tapped the plate.

'It's the disappointment. I've had hotter semolina than this.' I held out the fork handle.

'Care for a dip?'

She turned, no, she swivelled on her stool. My eyes didn't falter this time, and she saw it.

'It's very unhygienic, to accept a used fork from a complete stranger.'

I reached out and sloshed it around in my glass.

'There,' I said. 'It's sterilized.'

'Aren't we all?' she said, and took a mouthful. She looked me up and down, chewing.

'You haven't changed much,' she said.

'Neither have I,' I replied.

She stood up. 'Oh, Crabbie!' she cried and fell into my arms, and for once I didn't care what spectacle we made.

'Another bucket and another bottle,' I ordered. 'And put the closed sign out. We've an afternoon ahead.'

Thirteen

The file came out again. He had a little picture of me.

'A cutting,' he explained. 'This is the *Truculent*, yes, the submarine that went down.'

'Bad days,' I told him. He nodded.

'Indeed. To see your fellow submariners in such a plight. You had left the Service by then. Or rather the Service had left you. You took a small flat in Knightsbridge. You live there still. You like it?'

'It's all right. A bit poky.'

He nodded in agreement. 'I know. Communal living. The noise of next door, the smell of cooking, arguments on the stairs. I live in such an apartment block, Granovsky Square. Many members of the Central Committee do. Rudenko, the Public Prosecutor, lives on the same floor as me. We drop into each other's flats in the evening and together decide who should be rounded up and dealt with. I arrest people and he signs the death certificates. A very civilized way of conducting business. The First Secretary used to live there too, in the top flat. He has moved to grander pastures now, a new villa on the Lenin Hills. The view might be better, but he has Molotov for a neighbour.' He paused. 'For the moment at least.'

He looked back at the paper.

'Your flat. Hans Place. Behind Harrods.'

'You're very well informed.'

'When I was in London I visited it several times.'

'Really? I must have been out.'

'The First Secretary was asked if he wanted to go shopping there, but he said no, there is nothing there that I cannot get back home.

It was a political thing to say, but not strictly true. There are certain gaps. You will find this.'

'I will?'

'Yes. It is time to grasp the inevitable, Commander. You are alive, but the world believes you are dead. The sea or Sebastopol awaits you. Come to Russia, why don't you?'

'Whatever for?'

'To see for yourself, of course. What else.'

'And then?'

'And then, who knows. The future. Look to that. I know much about you. Your time in Gibraltar, your time in Italy, the loyalty you showed your former enemy. I find that of great interest. That you should form an alliance with those who you fought against. You had to argue on their behalf too, otherwise they would have been locked up.'

'Or worse.'

'My point exactly. And yet you insisted. Why was that?'

'It was the right thing to do. Venice needed saving.'

'One small town in the world with a few German mines buried in the mud and Commander Crabb settles his differences with his former enemies and risks his life for a city he has never known?'

'I might not have done it for Swansea.'

'Yes, you would. If there was water and danger, and comradeship, you would have jumped in, feet first. That's what drove you to Venice, Commander. That's what you crave to embrace again, the grip of honest friendship, held fast in a man's hands.'

'I thought I did it because I didn't want to go home.'

'And do you want to go home now? To your little one-room flat, and your coffee bars, and your diving suit gathering dust.'

I said nothing.

'We know that the British have all but discarded you. Crabb is too old, they say. Crabb drinks too much, is too difficult. Your age, your experience, the very attributes which single you out, are arraigned against you. But much of England is like that now, a place where age is regarded as an incurable disease. It is America, of course, that has started this, America with its obsession with film-star looks, America which abhors wrinkles, which tears down its buildings the moment cobwebs appear. It is a young country unable to look to the past. It believes in youth not age; it craves speed in all things, which is the prerogative of all youth, speed in love, speed in fortune, speed in their very movement. Britain is an old country, but I see it here, this obsession. You are part American now. Look at your old people, how you treat them, no use any more, chucked away, piled on top of each other in filthy homes, like those soldiers who you felt such pity for. Be off with you, say their sons and daughters. Out of our sight!

'It is time to grasp the inevitable, Commander. You are not walking on England's shore again, I can promise you that, but though I take one country away from you, I can offer you another in its place. Is that not a precious gift for a man to give? There is a sea that awaits you, but it needs a Russian uniform to sail upon it. It is a different sea from that which you are used to, but you can learn its ways. There is an officer's uniform waiting for you. There are orders to be given, tasks to accomplish, ranks to rise through, men waiting to return your salute. There is a port which you could call your home, a mess to afford you comradeship and respect. We will not ask you to betray your country. The day we are at war with Britain is the day you will be shot. But it will not come to that. The more powerful we grow, the more stable the world will become. You can help us, Commander. We have young boys who need to learn from you, who want for the hand of an older man. Show them your skills, your decency, your honesty. Be a father to them, and they will love you as only military men can, in their deeds rather than their words. Take their hands, lead them into the water. Baptize them. Convert them to your religion.'

He put his hands together, in prayer, as if to remind me of how one went about it.

'Don't you need a licence for that?' I said.

*

Pat and me. Me and Smithy. She accepted the balance now. She had to. I still didn't have a regular job, but it would come. Smithy promised me as much, maybe within the navy itself. We went down to Portsmouth to take part in the Coronation Review there. Pat and Smithy and me in the middle. It had been deliberate on my part. They needed to get along.

Ariadne had been given a new set of paint, white and gold in place of her former green. She'd seen plenty of VIPs in her time, the Shah of Persia, King Abdullah of Jordan, but had never taken part in the crowning of a queen before. Foreign dignitaries, diplomats, all manner of swells came down for the Review. Every important notice was translated into eleven languages. I showed Pat around the place, the diving bells and the workshops, the blast marks where the booby trap had gone off on a German magnetic that they'd been stripping down. I'd hoped she'd be impressed, arm in arm with a man in dress uniform who was returning salutes as often as giving them, and so she was, but there was another reason for taking her there: I wanted her to accept the fact that I was like Ariadne or the other two figureheads on the base; part of the fixtures and fittings.

We sat out on the raised benches, Pat squinting her eyes, wishing she'd brought some sunglasses. I'd never had that problem. Smithy tried to be chivalrous and offered to lend her his, but she waved the offer away. She still didn't trust him. We watched as the ships sailed past and the ratings on the deck and the guns fired and the hooters sounding. When the anthem came I could hardly see to stand, for the tears in my eyes. The young Queen, brought to such a time so early in her life. I knew then I would lay down my life for her, as easy as Pat might ask me to pass her the salt, without another thought to it. It was her country, this England, now, a young sort of country, with new hopes, but surely there could be places in it for old codgers like me. We could still help her long, and by God we wanted to. There's nothing more an old man likes more, than coming to the aid of some young woman. It makes them feel fresh again, like a blood transfusion. At the end of it I took out my handkerchief, and blew my nose.

'Crying again?' Pat observed. 'Curries, Coronations, what next?'

She started to make her way down from the stand. Smithy pulled me to one side.

'Tomorrow morning, Commander, you'll receive a letter from the navy, stating that on completion of your present service you will not be re-entered into the Royal Navy. I know you'll be thoroughly disheartened. But that's the way it is. Whitehall's instructions, cutting back on the older manpower. There's nothing I can do.'

And with that he elbowed his way past Pat and scuttled into the crowd.

'What's up with him?' she said. 'Caught short?'

I looked down at my uniform, the decorations on it, the way it shone in the air. In the last few years I'd come to believe that I'd never have to take it off.

'They've chucked me, Pat, chucked me, without so much as a by-your-leave; no job, no pension, not a boatswain's barnacle. You show a bit of aptitude, a willingness to serve your country, and then some faceless wonder tells you thanks very much but . . .' I laughed as the words came back to me, ' "You're surplus to requirements." Well, damn them, Pat. Damn the Royal Navy. Damn the fountain-pen brigade. And damn that Smithy, for doing it on this day of all days.'

'Amen to that,' said Pat, and we got the train back to London and together got thoroughly soused. And that's what I did for any number of weeks. Where I got the money from I don't know, but come noon I always seemed to have a glass in my hand. I was still a bit famous, see. People would buy me drinks. All I had to do was to spin a few yarns. Singing for one's supper, I believe it's called, though I don't remember much in the way of food. Liquid memories; all I needed was a pint or two, a decent size Scotch, a splash of soda and out they ran, all over the bar-room floor.

*

I didn't surface for months. Sydney must have heard, for he managed to get in touch. The doubloons were calling, he said. I had nothing better to do. I went up to Tobermory, on the Isle of Mull. A Spanish galleon lay out in the bay, beneath five fathoms of water and centuries of silt. I arrived early afternoon. Sydney was waiting for me on the quayside. We shook hands, looked at each other straight. Though his hand gripped strong, his face was pale, that old colour of the sea quite drained away. They had been a long time passing, these years after the war. I could see them in the corner of his eyes, the set of his mouth, the disappointments they had produced. I wondered how many he could see in mine. Neither of us had come through with flying colours.

'Good to see you again, sir,' he said. 'Smoke?'

'Not one of your infernal roll-ups, I hope?'

'I made it last week, specially, sir. So it would be nice and dry.'

'Very well. If needs must.'

We stood there in silence, looking out to sea.

'Fresh air and stale tobacco,' I said at last. 'Nothing like it.'

'And on such a fine summer's day, sir. Trouble is, you can never tell on this part of the coast how long the weather will hold. So if you don't mind disrobing, we'd best start right away,' and he pointed to a little hut at the back where a half bottle of rum stood by the door.

There were about eight of us. It should have been fun, meeting some of my old chums again, spending the day in the clear, fresh water with men who knew their business, spending the evenings in the little quayside bar, drinking the warm beer, singing songs, reminiscing about glories past. The weather was glorious too. Morning after morning we'd wake to a sparkling sea, a light south-westerly, and the smell of fried kippers for breakfast. We worked in shifts, sucking clay from the seabed with something like a giant vacuum cleaner, and we were good at what we did. But there was emptiness to the venture, to my mind, something vacant in our singing, something hollow in our well-worn tales, and though we were efficient in our diving we lacked heart. It should have been like *Boy's Own Story*, with maps and charts and the thrill of buried treasure, but it wasn't like that. We were joined not by an old camaraderie but by a new kind of impetus, robbing graves for rings on our fingers. By the beginning of October we'd sunk a deep shaft down close to the vessel, but were hindered by the size and quantity of large stones that lay on top of it. It was as if the souls of the dead sailors had rolled them over themselves, to protect their ship, their treasure, their very reason for life, just as the Egyptians had done in their pyramids, or that other stone, rolled over that cave in Palestine, to protect the most precious body of all. There were men on those ships, like the crew of the *Truculent*, and like that crew, they lay there still. Dead for a good while longer maybe, but honourable men nonetheless, who deserved better than our grubby fingers tearing at their bones. We came away empty-handed, and I for one was thankful that we did.

I returned to London out of spirits and out of pocket. I thought I'd been getting on with my life, when all I'd been doing was standing still. Seven years and nothing to show for it. An old snake in an old skin. Maitland took pity on me, and this time I did not refuse. He had a new furniture business by then, Elmbourne Ltd, and was branching into supplying coffee bars with do-it-yourself tables, espresso machines, et cetera. He offered me a job working Soho as a sales representative. Not my kind of people, the coffee-bar crowd, a bit too young, a bit too flash Harry, but it kept me out of trouble. At least that's what I thought at the time. The people behind the counters, however, were a different story altogether. Naples, Rome, they all hailed from somewhere in that beloved land. They were young men, most of them, like my flock had been, but come to London to seek their fortune. I found I could talk to them in the way their own kind did, with music and impatience in my voice. '*Buongiorno*,' I'd say as I walked in, '*Come state?*' and before we did anything we'd have a coffee and a chat about something back home. They'd take out pictures of their families, their mothers, their brothers and sisters and grandparents (fathers didn't seem to figure much), and tell me of their towns and cities, how they were picking up the pieces. They knew I'd understand, for that's what I'd done too, and to the most precious city of them all. Then I'd flip through the order book, suggesting new lines, better furniture, a new kind of machine, and they'd listen sympathetically, try and put a little business my way. I carried a little of the old country with me. *Bene, bene, bene.* Though I didn't like to admit it, for the first time in my life I was holding my own in a job on dry land. It should have satisfied me more than it did. My order book was getting fuller by the day, but its owner felt empty. I was a salesman, one among hundreds, cracking jokes, selling lines, chirpy in the face of inclement weather and obstinacy. I had fought the finest underwater enemy the world had to offer. I had been honoured by the King. I had dived on Her Majesty's Secret Service and had been a hero to many an impressionable schoolboy. I had stood for something. Now I was selling frothy coffee and serviettes and plastic-covered bar stools. Now I licked my pencil and tipped my hat and went from counter to counter in search of my transient pickings. I was a salesman. Nothing wrong with that, was there?

Maitland's offices were in Seymour Place, off the Edgware Road. I'd get there around ten, ten thirty if Pat and I had made a night of it. I was still obeying the Queensberry Rules as far as she was concerned. A skirmish every now and again in the back of a cab, or a couple of rounds in her front room with the curtains drawn, but nothing below the belt. It wasn't always easy, for she'd got the bit between her teeth since I'd left the Service. Whatever, come morning I'd be up those office stairs, bright and breezy, get my marching orders, and be out on the road by eleven at the latest. A routine, that's what I'd fallen into, running on a set of rails, clackety click, clackety click, and you know, it was nearly as bad as I'd imagined. So this is what we fought the war for. I couldn't see it changing either, at least not for the better, and when it came, I barely noticed. A rattle over a set of points, a slight shift, that was all it felt to me.

Maitland might have had an eye for business, but there was a very easy-come, easy-go atmosphere about the place, any number of people going in and out at all times of the day. Anthony started to come round a lot, though it was hard to see why. He never seemed to enjoy Maitland's company much, but early evening there he'd often be, his gaunt frame draped over the little settee Maitland had in the outer room, his eyes drooping as if half asleep, drinking something alcoholic out of one of Maitland's tin mugs.

That day Maitland asked me to pick up a book he'd left at Anthony's flat in Portman Square and take it round to this bookshop in the Strand. He wanted it evaluated. It wasn't exactly on my route, but the boss is the boss, friend or no. I showed up at around half twelve. The building seemed unoccupied. I rattled up in the tiny lift to the top floor and was greeted by Anthony, dressed in shirt sleeves and slippers and reeking of drink. I was quite content to be given the parcel there and then and tootle off, but he insisted I come in. I wiped my feet and did the honours. I'd expected the flat to be a place where comfort was somewhat of a priority, chock-a-block with antiques and bookcases, with good carpets on the floor, but what I found was more like a Spartan holiday camp than a home; bare and functional and without pity, as if the owner took no pleasure in his surroundings. He led me into the kitchen; a small white table, one solitary chair, with linoleum curling at the edges like yesterday's sandwiches.

'Would you like an aspirin?' he asked, going to the little cupboard, set in the wall. 'Only I'm having a couple myself.'

I declined and watched him while he washed them down with water.

'How about something a little more palatable. Say a splash of gin and tonic?'

I said I didn't mind if I did. He fussed about on the draining board and turned back with two tall tumblers, lurching slightly as he handed mine over. I took a taste. If there was any tonic in it, it was pretty reluctant in coming forward.

'Have I made them a trifle strong?' he asked, as he read my expression. His words, though not slurred, were spoken carefully. He was driving under the influence and trying not to show it.

'Not at all. Thirsty work, selling non-alcoholic beverages.'

He sloshed a little more gin into his glass.

'You must have pretty some good views from up here,' I ventured.

'It's a pleasing enough position, although I'm not entirely happy with the furnishings, as they stand. That chair, for instance. It's far too comfortable.'

'Get a monk in,' I suggested. 'He could advise you.'

Anthony sat down and put his hands together. I never saw a man's hands more built for praying. Michelangelo would have had a field day.

'I don't think I've had the pleasure of a monk on these premises.

186

Most orders in one form or another have partaken, tinkers, tailors, soldiers, et cetera, but never a monk. That's very good, Lionel. I'll invite one to my next gathering. You've never been to one of my little dos, have you?'

I shook my head, rather wishing I hadn't accepted his invitation after all.

'Not that I can remember.'

'Maitland's quite an aficionado,' he continued. 'I'm surprised he's never brought you along.'

'Perhaps he thought I wouldn't fit in.'

'That must be it, although I'm sure he is wrong about that. But then Maitland is wrong about a good many things, don't you think? He told me he voted Labour last time around.' There was a smirk on his face. Drunk or not, I didn't like it. A man's politics is in his own business.

'He's been very decent to me.'

'Yes, but being decent isn't everything, is it?' He dipped one of his tapered fingers into his drink and stirred it slowly. 'I've been drinking all morning, you know. It's not so very reprehensible, is it, to drink all morning, every once in a while.'

'It's a free country, though I wouldn't start rearranging any of Her Majesty's old masters. You wouldn't want to be carted off to the Bloody Tower.'

'No. I wouldn't want that.' He lowered his eyelids. He had hooded eyes, made you think he was half asleep. Then he lifted his head.

'Suez is a running sore, don't you think? Eden simply loathes the lot of them. It will all end in tears.'

I tried to read his expression, to see if he knew of my involvement. Maitland had a lot to answer for.

'He does seem to have put their noses out of joint,' I admitted, 'though I don't have any time for Nasser either. He's as bad as the Russians.'

'You think? That's a relief.' He paused. There was a picture on the wall behind him, of serpentine trees and feathery foliage, rather good. He caught me looking at it.

'One of your own?' I asked. 'Or on loan from the Big House?'

Anthony's spine straightened up with undisguised conceit.

'I bought that in a junk shop in my Cambridge days, for four and sixpence. It's a Corot.'

'An original?' I sounded surprised.

'More than likely. It certainly looks the part. Most forgeries are an insult to the viewer's intelligence, Corot's particularly. Of the seven hundred proven originals, eight thousand are to be found in America alone. Still, that's the United States for you. This, I believe to be genuine.'

I stepped forward.

'How can you tell? I can't see a signature.'

'How?' He took it off the wall, and brought it round. Suddenly the drink and the arrogance disappeared. He was animated, wanting to share his affection, his treasured knowledge with me. He held it out to me, as a mother might do her newly swaddled infant.

'It scores on a number of levels. It is an attractive drawing, certainly in the style of Corot. More importantly, it compares favourably with a number of other drawings known to be Corot's, though, and this is highly significant, it is in no way copied or adapted from them. It is most certainly on the right paper and it bears no false signature or sales mark, like so many of them do. Lastly, and perhaps most crucially, the lines betray none of the hesitation, or lack of spontaneity, that an imitation would possess. If it had come to me from a dealer I might have been more suspicious, but from a junk shop? Yes, I think it stands, for the moment at least.'

He put it back on the wall. So this is what he prays to every night.

'Forgive me,' I said, 'but I would have thought it was the other way round. Most people couldn't tell a Corot from a carrot. Anybody could pass a Corot off in a junk shop.'

'And what would be the advantage of that?' The tone of superiority had returned. 'Financial? Knowledge that he had duped an idiot? No, a forger would go to a dealer, an authority. He'd say, "I've found this little drawing in a little back alley in Paris. What do you think it might be? A Degas?" And the dealer would look at it, and consult his library and his vast knowledge and pronounce, "Not a Degas, but one might make a tentative association with Corot. Let me keep it a while," and he would keep it and look at it, and after a goodly time, he would decide one way or the other. Leading people by the nose, that's the name of the game. A master forger lets the expert decide. And why?' He leant into me, his frame unsteady above me. 'Because only experts are worth fooling, Lionel, and the greater the expert, the greater the forger's satisfaction.' He relaxed back into himself, and poured himself another shot. 'A game for sly rogues, the art world, don't you think. Anyway, do you like it?'

I spoke to it as best I could. I suspect what I said was pretty much worthless, but he clapped me on the back and told me I had an eye. How his manner had vacillated over the last few minutes. Now he was warm and interested, and I felt curiously close to him.

'Venice gave me that,' I confessed. 'There never was such a city, nor country, so in love with its own beauty.'

'And your former trade? You do a lot of work down in Portsmouth, Maitland tells me.'

'Correction. I did a lot of work. I'm retired now.'

'I've never been that far south. It must be an entertaining sort of place, with all those sailors.'

'I wouldn't know. I just went in and out.'

'Don't we all?' and he started to giggle, like a schoolgirl, before forcing himself to a stop. 'Do you miss it? Maitland said he thought you were pining for something. He thought it might be,' he hesitated, 'companionship.'

'You know Maitland. He talks too much.'

'Don't we all,' he said and giggled again, and this time could not stop. He was still giggling when he put the parcel in my hand and showed me to the door.

It had been a hot morning, with the promise of greater heat to come, and I decided to walk. London was stepping out, throwing off the drab post-war. It was the young Queen who was responsible, I was sure of it, and I cursed myself for not asking Anthony what she was like. Not that he had any right to tell me.

190 the Strand. I had to look for it. You don't get many second-hand bookshops down that neck of the woods; the rent's too high. It was at the back of this building not a hundred miles from the Savoy. The bell tinkled as I stepped in. Brand-new shelves lined the walls, and on them were oddly regimented rows of books. One expects something altogether more haphazard in a bookshop. Running down the right-hand side of the room was a long glass partition, from behind which came a furious clacking of typewriters. Through the gaps I could see a flock of secretaries working ten to the dozen, hair-dos bobbing like birds on a seed table. You could hardly hear yourself think, let alone read. Standing facing them was a broad, thickset man, holding one of those pocket-book classics, though he seemed more interested in the flashing fingernails behind the window than the volume in his hand.

'Mr Kroger?' I asked and he shook his head, indicating that he was a customer, like me.

'My apologies,' I said and he shrugged his shoulders and pre-tended to go back to his book. From behind a table at the back came a quite different-looking fellow, tall and middle-aged, but brimming with well-preserved youth. He had that blond wavy hair that seems to come in bottles. American, I surmised. Mr Kroger. I explained on whose behalf I had come and handed him the book.

'I've got something else that Mr Pendock might care to see, if you don't mind acting as my postman too. It would save me a couple of stamps, and in this game, every little counts.' He turned. 'And you, sir, is there anything else I can help you with?'

The squat fellow shook his head and slipping his hand into his pocket, left the shop.

'Hang on!' I cried. 'He's just run off with one of your books. Quick, let's grab him.'

He placed a restraining hand on my arm. 'There's no need to con-cern yourself. He's already paid for it. Now, if I can find that other volume.' He went back to his table and started wrestling with a sheet of brown paper.

'Mind if I have a browse?'

'No bookseller minds a browser, Mr Crabb.'

I took a look around. Apart from acres on American history, he seemed to specialize in books on crime and punishment. *Sixteen Years in Siberia, Bygone Punishments, The Hangman's Diary of Franz Schmidt.* Not titles you see every day.

'Do you get much call for this sort of thing?' I shouted out above the rattle. He waved a pair of scissors at me.

'Every country in Europe, as well as Canada and the States. Mail order, that's the way to run this business. Now, if you'd be so kind.'

I took his parcel and went back to my rounds. Maitland was promoting a new kind of coffee. Two Left Feet they called it, rather appropriate considering the state of my own. By four I was at Giulio's, round the corner from Wardour Street, to check if our latest machine was behaving itself. By the time I got there, the weight of my jacket was sticking to my back. Giulio, eager to demonstrate his skill, insisted that I pull up a stool and sample a brew. Ah, those proud Italian eyes: how hard it is to resist them.

'Fire away,' I said, 'and throw in a bun or two. I haven't had lunch yet.'

Giulio attended to his chrome, steam spluttering around his head like something out of Pompeii. He poured the result out into one those translucent cups that look like they've been fashioned out of seashells and set it down in front of me.

'It's pretty free with the froth, isn't it?' said I and blew a little too hard across the surface, the foam bowling along the counter like tumbleweed in a ghost town.

'You're not going to drink that?' a voice said, the kind of remark you expect in some Wild West saloon after a hard day's cattle rustling, not in a London coffee bar, just off Piccadilly Circus. I looked across. There sat the squat fellow I'd seen in the bookshop, nursing one of those small black coffees Italians ingest instead of food. He was good-looking, in a chunky un-English sort of way, decked out in a smart, but slightly common, blue suit. His hair was jet black and ran over his head in thick curly waves. Under his jacket I could see the marks of heavy perspiration soaked into his shirt.

'And why shouldn't I?' I asked.

'Cause you're a man, ' he said. 'That's for boys who still yearn for the milk from their mother's teat.'

Giulio blushed. Like most Italian young men, he yearned for his mother's teat practically every single day. The man on the stool stretched out his hand.

'Gordon,' he said. 'Gordon Lonsdale. Haven't we met before?'

It was the wrong way round of course, his introduction, but I put it down to his funny accent, not American, not English, not anything that I could lay my hands on.

'Crabb,' I said. 'Lionel. Kroger's bookshop. Not two hours ago.'

'Ah!' He patted his pocket. 'Dickens. I am crazy for him.'

Giulio pointed a stubby finger at me.

'This is Signor Buster Crabb,' he said. 'Is very famous.'

I scowled. He knew I hated to be called that. The man raised his eyebrows, thick, bushy things.

'The film star?'

I put my hand up.

'Hardly. He spells his surname with an E.'

'And wears strange clothing.'

You don't know the half of it, I thought.

'You're not from these parts,' I ventured, trying to move him off the subject.

'Vancouver,' he said. 'But there's better pickings here, for my line of work.'

I don't like to be nosy, but he was offering.

'Which is?' I asked.

He dabbed his mouth with the little paper napkin at his side.

'The entertainment business. Jukeboxes, one-arm bandits; I buy them up, I lease them on. It pays its way, but the trouble is some of my rivals . . .'

He ran a finger over his throat. I knew what he meant. Conmen and cut-throats, Soho was chock-a-block with them.

'So I'm branching out into bubblegum dispensers. Got a fellow making them for me down in Broadstairs. Ever been there?'

I shook my head. I kept away from that part of the country as far as possible. Margaret lived near there now. He fingered his cuffs.

'Today I'm getting rid of the last of my fruit machines. One more to go. It's a devil to move.' He screwed the paper napkin into a little ball and wedged it carefully into his cup. 'My office is round the corner. Care to give me a hand?'

I took off my jacket and we bundled the brute across the road. Once we'd got it into the corner, he fed it a handful of change, pulling levers and pressing buttons like he was a music-hall artist with a row of spinning plates. Then the spinning stopped, and he stood back.

'Now it's your turn,' he said. I shook my head

'I'm not a gambling man, save the Grand National. But that's like having fish on Fridays.'

He smiled.

'Everyone's a gambling man, Mr Crabb, whether they admit it or not,' he said. 'Some of us are more honest with ourselves, that's all.'

He was right, of course. Every dive I'd made in the war had been a gamble. Every trip I'd made with Smithy had been a gamble. Next time I asked Pat to marry me, what were the odds on me crossing that finishing line? Who'd have bet that I'd actually *want* to get married again?

'How much will it cost me?' I said.

He tilted his head to one side, pleased.

'A shilling should see you clear.'

'That's the best part of a pint of bitter,' I protested.

'You English and your beer! Forget tradition. Take the plunge.'

If he hadn't said that I don't know that I would have. But he did, so I dug a coin out of my pocket and slotted it in.

'Don't pull down too hard,' he told me. 'Squeeze it gently, like you would a woman's breast.'

'Steady on, old chap,' I remonstrated. 'It's a bit early on in the day for that sort of talk.'

'Then, if it makes you happier, like the trigger of a gun.'

You might think that a funny thing to say, but the war was only ten years gone. We all knew about triggers and guns and bushy-top trees. I eased the lever down, felt it lock into the cogs, pulled it gently through. A blur of oranges and apples and something approximating plums span before me. Gordon began to laugh, a lock of his black hair falling across his face. Then the tumblers clicked into place, and blow me if I wasn't looking at a line of cherries. The machine started to chunter out a clatter of coins. Five half-crowns, to be precise. Gordon came up behind me and clapped me on the back.

'Bravo, my friend,' he said. 'And just in time too.' He tapped his wristwatch, a big golden thing, as big as the moon. 'I know a club whose doors have just this minute opened. Your round, I believe.'

Jane's it was called. It had green-baize doors and someone who'd had a run-in with a razor standing by them. Inside there was a girl behind the empty bar, tall, big lips, chewing on a liquorice stick.

'Hello, Gordon,' she said. 'You never called.'

He tugged at his throat.

'Laryngitis,' he said.

'Break my heart, you do.'

'Ah, Natalie. I break everyone's heart.' He turned. 'And you, Lionel Crabb. You have a girl, whose heart you break.'

'I wouldn't put it quite like that.'

'You have more than one, yes!' He draped an arm over my shoulder. 'You see, my dear, it is the only thing to do in such a city as this. To do otherwise would be an act of a blind man. This city is like an orchard in summer. So much fruit to pick,' and he threw his head back and showed the white of his teeth

He was flash, Gordon, if you'll forgive the pun, with a laugh like the bark of a young dog, but despite his shortcomings, the way in which he always tried to bundle you along his path, his coarse humour, his penchant for loud jewellery, I found I was drawn to his company. Like a cold shower; you didn't want to be in it for too long, but you always came away feeling refreshed. He was an unashamed womanizer, fascinated by them. Usually I can't stand the type, but with Gordon it was different. He was like a puppy with a slipper, so happy at his play it was hard not to look at his overeager antics and not laugh. When I got to know him better I used to go round to his flat near Regent's Park for a spot of poker. Like mine it was situated at the top of the building, but in all other respects it was the penthouse to my basement; a neat little hall complete with umbrella stand and hunting prints, a lounge with a view across the park and a bedroom you could pitch a Bedouin tent in. He'd have any number of pictures of his conquests dotted around, Hilde, Toni, Carla; blondes, brunettes, red-heads; Italian, French, German, it didn't matter to Gordon as long as they were young and pretty and infected with his charm. He never seemed to tire talking of them. It was almost as if he'd never seen them before, and of course knowing what I know now, that wasn't far from the truth, for it was Western girls that he was fascinated by, Western girls with their Western looks and their Western grooming; Western girls, their piled up hair and their mascara; Western girls with their knee-length skirts and their high heels and lipstick that he blew kisses at every time they passed him in the street.

After that first drink we arranged to meet at Churchill's a week later. I took Pat along. I knew she'd like him. Characters, that's what made Pat's clock tick, people a bit out of the ordinary. Well, Gordon certainly fitted that bill. We spent an hour there, Gordon gaily commentating on every glamour-puss that fluttered by, before Pat made the mistake of telling him the waitresses at the Trojan were renowned for their looks. He insisted on going straight away.

'All the girls here are ugly,' he pronounced.

Pat wagged her finger at him. 'Gordon. That simply isn't true.'

He clapped his hands over his eyes. He had hairy, animal hands. 'Every one of them. I am the beast. I should have beauties. Take me to this Trojan immediately. I want to frighten some pretty girls.'

So off we went. I signed us all in and managed to get a table. As it happened, that night there were only men serving. Greville borrowed most of his staff from the airlines he used; stewards or stewardesses, one thing they all had at their fingertips was how to deal with the public, how to smile, how to serve a drink, how to make the most unprepossessing baldy feel like a lion's mane. Gordon didn't mind. The dance floor was full to overflowing, and every time a good-looking judy passed, he'd wink at her and hold up his glass, beckoning her to join our table. If I had done it they'd have caused no end of stink, but there was something about Gordon, the way his hands would frame that shameless, impious smile, that set them thinking. They'd grin and turn their heads, pretending not to see, or to fake indifference, but it was funny how quickly they came round again, how so many of them managed to turn and twirl themselves directly in front of him. He was a predator, but an attractive one, in a brutal, uncomplicated sort of way, and they were game, in every sense of the word. Their partners, however, took a different view and would scowl at him whenever they came within hailing distance. Gordon would nod and laugh in agreement, as if it was all a huge joke. Pat almost enjoyed the performance more than he did.

'You are a very wicked man,' Pat told him. 'Isn't he, Crabbie?'

'He could get us all in a lot of trouble,' I admitted. 'It's not a cattle market out there, you know.' Gordon stretched his legs.

'Isn't it?' He put his hand on Pat's, squeezed her knuckles. 'It is true what you say, Pat. When it comes to women, I have no scruples.' He threw up his hands. 'You don't understand the temptation here, for a man of my disposition. Such a land of plenty. Such a land of opportunity.'

'But in Canada, there are pretty girls there, surely?'

'But it is so cold there.' He wrapped his jacket around him. 'They wear woollens and coats, like this, all year, even in bed. While here, come the spring . . .' He took his jacket off slowly, in a manner I can best describe as vulgar, and dropped it to the floor. Pat giggled and looked at me, as if to say, why don't you ever talk like that. I thought it best to change the subject. I beckoned Greville over. I hadn't seen him for a couple of months. He'd put on weight since the last time I'd seen him, but then, so had I.

'Greville, I'd like you to meet Gordon Lonsdale. Wheeler-dealers the both of you. Gordon's big in bubblegum dispensers, slot machines. All over Soho.'

They shook hands but Gordon didn't stand. Greville didn't like that. They looked each other up and down, like dogs on a beach. You could almost see the hackles rising.

'Nice place you have here,' Gordon growled. 'Is it difficult to become a member?'

'Quite difficult, yes. You have to come recommended.'

Gordon's gaze fell back to the dance floor.

'Perhaps we could come to an arrangement. I could offer you some of my machines, for your foyer, or cloakroom. We split the takings. In return . . .' He fixed his eyes on his host. 'Would you be interested?'

'I think not.' Greville dusted his hands. 'It's not quite slot-machine country, Kensington,' and walked off. I tried to excuse him.

'Not like him to be so short,' I observed. 'Bad day in Bulgaria, perhaps.'

Gordon took his eyes from the girls for a moment, and raised an eyebrow.

'Travels all over the place, does Greville,' I explained. 'Every time he goes away he gets closer to the Kremlin.'

'A man's got to follow the dollar,' Gordon acquiesced. 'Even to Moscow.'

'Ever been?'

'Bubblegum in Russia? Far too decadent. What line is he in, your Mr Wynne?'

'He advises firms on how to deal with the Soviets. Organizes trade fairs: steel manufacturers, electrical outlets, you name it, he can find a market for it. He's even sold them a bottle-washing business. Vodka bottles, no doubt. '

'Russia frightens me,' Pat said.

'Frightens you?' Gordon affected to look surprised. 'I wouldn't have thought anything would frighten you.'

'It doesn't seem to care who it tramples on. This communism thing. It's like a religion. It's like they're the believers and we're the infidels. Our lives mean nothing to them.'

'It's not like a religion.' I spoke sharply. 'It's the most ungodly thing on the face of the earth. That's why we have to fight it, every step of the way.'

Gordon flicked his cigar ash onto the table, brushed it from his knee.

'You know what you should do,' he said, 'if you really to want beat the Russians. Forget your spy planes and your secret agents. Forget your nuclear missiles and submarines. Girls, that's the answer! Girls, pretty ones, between the ages of eighteen and twenty-five. Make them your politicians and your ambassadors and your trade delegates. Put them in the United Nations and the Peace Corps. Dress them in tight skirts and send them over on clouds of perfume. Send them everywhere, East Germany, Warsaw, Moscow. The cold war would be over in a matter of days.'

'It's a radical thought,' I agreed. 'I'll put it to Eden, next time I see him.'

*

The weeks came and the weeks went. Every now and again, we'd all go out on the town, Pat, Maitland, Gordon, Gordon with a girl or two in tow, a secretary from some firm he did business with, one of the students at the language school he attended, on some occasions, one of those nightclub girls of his, but they were a bit too rich for my liking, what with their hard eyes and showy mouths and half-indecent conversation. After a couple of hours I would leave him to it, and take Pat home before returning to the Cavendish lean-to. No room for hanky-panky there. Still, it suited me.

Pat, however, was chafing. She didn't push it but I could tell what she was thinking. How much longer were we going to go on like this, with not an engagement ring in sight, not a bann called? I knew I had to do something. I had the time on my hands. All I needed now was the inclination. I was just about to take the plunge when it happened. I walked into the office after rather a demanding night.

'You're late.' Maitland sounded put out.

'Went round to Gordon's,' I confessed. 'He taught me how to make Eggs Benedict.'

Maitland wasn't interested.

'I've taken on an old friend of yours,' he said. 'Starting today.

Accounts. Supply maintenance. You might like to pop your head round the door, make yourself known.'

I did as I was told, knocked on the door and walked in. Smithy was sitting behind a cheap desk, his shoulder pressing the telephone to his ear, while he doodled on a sheet of lined foolscap.

'Commander! There you are!' and banging the phone down, stretched out his hand. 'I bet you never expected to see me again.'

'One lives in hope,' I said. I was rather short.

He indicated the chair opposite. I sat down, not knowing what to think. He looked different from before. He still had the beanpole look, but the green had gone. There was experience behind the eyes, experience and authority, and, yes, Pat was right, just a touch of honest deceit. Oil on troubled water, I said to myself, and wiped my hand on the back of my trousers.

'So. You been put out to grass too?'

His mitt went up and he started to tug the lobe of his left ear. I might have known.

'It's a useful little hidey-hole this, a good place for the likes of you and me to see what's what every once in a while.'

'How do you mean?' He stood up and walked to the window, tapping a cigarette out of his case as he walked.

'All that carry-on down at HMS *Vernon*, Crabbie. A passing cloud, nothing more. Sensitive times. It's best if everyone keeps a distance.'

'I don't follow. My severance papers, they've all gone through.'

'Yes, but it doesn't mean you have been overlooked. We were all very taken by your handiwork, Malta, that little episode off Stockholm, even, dare I say it, Suez, the discretion you showed. Marsloe was very impressed, despite the fiasco afterwards.'

'Marsloe!'

'We work very closely with the Yanks these days. We have to. It's all so much more fluid now. We do theirs, they do ours. Deniability, that's the name of the game.'

'How is Tony?'

'He's fine. He has a young family now. He sends his regards.'

I couldn't quite believe that I'd forgotten about him, and those rival years, Tony and Minella making eyes at each other, Paola standing in our doorway, arms folded, while we listened to her sister's murmured goodbyes on the steps below, unseen water lapping at our hearts. How she glowed from the light of our lantern, how seemingly tranquil her pose. Suddenly I longed to see her again and suddenly I knew I never would. All the people in one's life; how quickly the waters can close over them.

'Has he ever been back?'

'Back?'

'To Venice?'

'Yes, I think so.'

'Surprising he never got in touch, considering.'

'Well, as you know, in our line of work, it doesn't pay to advertise.'

'So you and he are still . . . ?'

'You might say that.'

'And here? Isn't it a bit too hush-hush for these walls, if you don't mind me asking?'

'You mean Maitland?'

I nodded. 'One of your lot, is he?'

He laughed. 'Maitland! Not exactly. Maitland's Maitland. A businessman. He goes here, he goes there; he sees things, he hears things, he makes contacts. He's not in, he's not out. He's Maitland. Like you're Crabb. It's how we like it.'

He took me to lunch. The Ivy. He ate well, Smithy, they all did. It was part of the deal. Patriotism has no price. You didn't earn much, and the possible deprivations were considerable, so food and drink, and the other comforts of life, were always on hand when required. The Ivy, the Westbury, Bentley's just off Piccadilly, they dined in them all.

We sat down at a table in the corner, the service laid out so that he would have an unobstructed view of anyone who entered. He knew how to listen, did Smithy, running his fingers attentively over his thin little moustache. We spent the first two courses chatting about HMS *Vernon*, faking interest in men we'd both known. We ordered dessert. I had sherry trifle, he the chocolate soufflé. I told him about Tobermory, the trouble we had.

'You're still fit, then?' he asked, looking at me as I poured on the cream.

'Who wouldn't be, gadding about on these pavements?'

'Only we'd heard that you'd been hitting the bottle lately.'

'No more than any other salesman. It comes with the territory, Smithy.'

'Quite.' He lowered his voice. 'The Russians, you know, are becoming quite active in your chosen field.'

'I take it you don't mean coffee bars.'

'Submarine warfare, two-man torpedoes, it's right up their street, unseen skulduggery. They have a whole division devoted to that sort of thing now, special forces, land, air, sea. Spetsnaz, it's called. Frogmen, submariners, in the early stages mind, but . . .' He scooped into his chocolate pudding. A dark, wonderful smell rose from the table. I began to wish I'd ordered it myself. 'It's not only that. The surface craft too. There's some designs coming out of Odessa that quite curdle the blood. Atomic propulsion, moveable propellers, we don't know what. We need someone to go down, take a look at it all, when and wherever we can. We'd pay you, of course, not a lot, but every little helps.'

I took a bunch of flowers to Pat's that night. It didn't do much good. When I told her, she hit the roof.

'They're using you, Crabbie. Getting you on the cheap.'

'So what if they are? I'm still needed, there's still a point to me. I'm still serving my country.'

'You and your patriotism. Look where it's got you.'

'You don't do it to get anywhere, Pat. You do it because it's right. I thought you understood that by now.'

'I do.' I could see her softening. 'It's just, I thought that was all over, Crabbie. I'd thought we'd done with that, that we had a new life now.'

'So did I. But duty calls.' And though I said it, I knew what she meant. I thought they'd done with me by now. I was an older horse, with an ache to my bones. But if there were fields to plough, who was I to refuse my harness.

So that was it. We didn't have to meet in Harrods or the Brompton Oratory or by the third duck on the Serpentine anymore. I could go for a two-month stretch and not see hide nor hair of him. Then I'd come in as usual and he'd be standing in the doorway, hands in pockets, grinning at me as I climbed the stairs.

'Got something for you,' he'd call out, and I'd tip my hat to Maitland, and follow Smithy to the back. He'd take me out to lunch, give me my orders, a rail ticket, a pass, whatever was needed, shake my hands and push off. I'd go back to the office and get the agenda for the rest of the day.

'How was Smithy?' Maitland would ask and I would say, 'Oh, you know Smithy,' and he'd nod and we'd get down to the business in hand. But how much he knew Smithy, the Smithy I knew, I could never work out. Until that last time.

We'd started to go further afield. As often as not the trips were three-, four-day jobs, getting out there, doing the recce, coming back. The Swedish coastline, up Finland way, the bloody Baltic. 'Why can't you find me somewhere warm,' I once complained, 'like Tangiers, or the Isle of Capri.' Smithy wagged his finger. 'If you want to look at that Russian bear, close up, it's best to go when he's in his lair, sleeping,' so and that's where we went, Sebastopol, Odessa, all the distant ports that no one has ever heard of, where there's nothing but ice and flatness and a skyline of dark cranes and oil refineries. Sometimes we left a calling card, for the sheer hell of it, sometimes we left them behind whether we wanted to or not; an oxygen tank jammed in the stanchions, a frogmask ripped off by the tide, and once even a mini-submarine, its propellers caught in wire netting. It was like the Italians all over again, a game of cat and mouse, only it was more callous now, with less respect. We were fighting shadows, not men.

And then came the *Sverdlov*, one of the new Soviet destroyer classes. That year she was taking part in sea trials off Spithead, but before that she was going to pay a goodwill visit to Portsmouth.

When Smithy told me, he practically pulled his ears off, he was so fired up.

'It's too big for one,' he informed me. 'We need another diver. Can you recommend anyone? Not from *Vernon*, though, too near home.'

Could I recommend anyone? He didn't have a phone, of course. I tracked him down at one of his men's clubs, working part-time behind the bar. I shouldn't have asked him really, but I felt sorry for him, out there in the sticks, driving lorries, breathing petrol.

'Knowles. Do you recollect that bomb under the bed you once referred to?'

'Indeed I do, sir.'

'Well, there's a very important bed arriving in Portsmouth in a day or two. The powers that be want a couple of chaps to give it the once over, test its springs and what not. They've roped me in, asked if I knew anyone suitable. I didn't of course, so you'll have to do. How about it?'

There was some muttering at the other end. That's the trouble with cohabitation. You're never your own master, however hard you try. He came back on.

'I'll need my pyjamas, presumably?'

'Yes, the ones with the polka dots on. To distract attention from me.' He chuckled.

'I'll have them freshly ironed.'

I met him off the morning train. He came sauntering down the platform with that stoker's swagger of his, just like the first time we met. The sunlight seemed to pour down upon him, a golden halo. I shook his hand. It didn't seem enough somehow.

'Knowles.' I took his bag. 'How's the freight trade? You're looking good on it.'

'I packed it in months ago,' he told me. 'Not much to hold a man, tooling up and down the A1, save tea and fry-ups. I'm a swimming-pool supervisor now. I thought you knew.'

Did I? I couldn't remember, couldn't remember if he'd written to tell me, or even when I'd last spoken to him. That's the trouble with men and war. You make all these promises, about friendship, about life, about the direction you want your world to take, and then, when peace comes, it all just evaporates.

'Pay well?'

'Pay lousy, sir. That's why I'm here. I'll be glad of the cash.'

I was disappointed, but kept my peace.

'Come down to London, why don't you?' I offered. 'I'll talk to my friend Maitland. You remember Maitland? Maybe he can find you some suitable employ too.'

'What, like selling stuff, like what you do?'

His face brightened, and for a moment we both saw the two of us working together again, Sydney by my side, hauling me out of trouble, sticking a coffin nail in my mouth. Then I tried to picture him in the London that I inhabited, the London of Pat and Maitland and Gordon and nights at the Trojan. Sydney wasn't coming to London.

'I was thinking perhaps more backstage. The warehouse, or deliveries.'

'You mean a stoker again?' He took his bag back. 'You took me away from that, sir. I didn't think you'd be looking to chuck me back in.'

'I didn't mean it like that, Knowles. I only . . .'

'I know what you meant, sir. When all's said and done East is East after all.'

Smithy met us at *Vernon*, shovelled us through a side gate. He didn't take to Sydney at all, didn't like his accent or his roll-ups. He doled out his money as if it was contaminated. We spent an awkward afternoon in each other's company, in the training offices, waiting for darkness to fall. I wished I'd never asked him. We went in about half nine, two-piece frogsuits, skullcaps, black veils, netting over our heads to break up the silhouettes. It was a complete shambles; badly planned, objectives unclear. They hadn't thought about the tides or our approach. The area was lit up like Regent Street on Christmas Eve, and we had to do the whole journey under water, against the outgoing current, and loaded up like a couple of Boy Scouts on a hiking holiday. By the time we got there we were exhausted. We clumped about in our size elevens with lamps and photographic equipment and not a clue what we were looking for. Just as we were about to give up, Sydney found himself swimming up into a large circular hole at the bottom of the hull, a sudden surge of water, as if some device had been switched on, sucking him in. I dropped everything and wrapped my arms around his legs, my face pressed against his groin as I pushed hard against the hull. I could hear the rumble of an engine and he began to slip from my grasp. I reached up, found a grip on the belt of his suit, and held him fast, his arms flailing uselessly above me. The lower part of his suit started to peel away in my hands, and I had no choice but to reach up again and dig in, around the fork of his flesh. He was my Sydney and I would not let him go, not now, not ever. There was never a man for me that bettered Sydney, Sydney plain and true. If Sydney was going to go, then I was going with him. There were worse ways to meet my Maker. Then, as abruptly as it started, the rumble ceased, the water went slack and we tumbled out. We surfaced about fifty yards clear, Sydney with his trousers round his ankles, me with a lungful of Portsmouth harbour. Searchlights raked the water and there were guards running up and down the length of the ship, yelling as if we'd set the bridge on fire.

'How did it go?' Smithy asked as we hauled ourselves out.

'How did it go?' Sydney tore the mouthpiece from his neck and threw it to the ground. 'Might as well have asked us to walk up the gangway and knock on the effing door,' he said. He turned to me. 'I'll not be doing that again, sir, not for you, not for him, not for all the effing tea in China,' and despite the language, I was inclined to agree with him.

Smithy slid away to make a report. Sydney and I spent the rest of the night kipping on the floor, though my eyes barely blinked. We didn't talk much. It came to both of us, I think, that despite what had happened, there was not much to talk about. Yet there was of course. There was almost everything to talk about, but we weren't the men to say it. The ceiling was as dark and immeasurable as the ocean, and I lay there, thinking of the man next to me, his uncomplicated grasp of life, my unspoken feelings. I wanted to wake him, to apologize. Of course Sydney could work in Soho, of course he could dine with Gordon at Bianchi's or share a table with Maitland at the Trojan, of course we could work together again. But I didn't. There are some sleeping giants you can't wake.

We left, unseen, before the milkman was up. Smithy drove us to the station. I carried Sydney's bag and walked him to his train.

'Come up with me, why don't you,' I declared as he held out his hand to take it from me. 'I'm sure we could find you something.'

'Best not, sir. Family ties and all that.'

'Yes. Family ties.' I opened the door and flung the bag inside. Sydney followed, lifting the bag onto the luggage rack. It had his old Service number stencilled on the side. I dug into my jacket pocket. Smithy's fifty quid lay in a little brown envelope. I slipped out two fives.

'Buy something for me, Sydney. Something for your family. Something they can look at, something that says, that's from the Commander.'

I thought he was going to protest, but he didn't. He took the notes and clenched them in his fist.

'Swimming-pool attendant, eh?'

'For the present, sir.'

'Then I'll know where to find you, when I'm in Preston.'

'That you will. Only there's no jumping or diving allowed, sir. Only the swimming.'

'Well, then, not much hope for Preston, then.'

He pulled the door shut.

'You never know, Sydney.'

He looked at me and winked.

He knew.

Fourteen

Rosa came in with a face as long as a parson's prayer book. Her sister had died, and she was off the next day for the funeral.

'Does she live close by?' I asked, dread filling my boots. She raised her hands in the air.

'Dresden.' The word came out flat, unadorned. She scurried off to fetch my midday bowl of soup. They do a half decent broth in here. Proper meat and potatoes.

But Dresden. Suddenly I was terrified. By the time she got back I'd got it into my head that I would never see her again, that she'd beetle off over the border and never come back. I knew it flew in the face of reason, that she had a husband and son to take care of back here, but I simply couldn't get it out of my head. I'd be left here alone with only the view of the Mayeruv Gloriet for company.

'I'd think twice if I were you,' I said when she returned. 'That city is worse than poison.'

'You have been there?' She couldn't disguise the curiosity in her voice. Another snippet to enliven her dinner table. She set the tray down on my lap. I grabbed her wrist.

'You don't want to go there, Rosa, not if you can help it. It's like the rest of East Germany, full of treachery.'

'But my sister! I must!' She shook her arm free. I knew what she was thinking. 'Why am I arguing with this old fool? What's he got to do with my life?'

'Take no notice of me,' I muttered. 'Of course you must. It's just without you I think I might simply float out the window and leave this old crate quite empty. How long will you be gone?'

She bent down and put her hand on my cheek. There was a wetness on my skin. She must have been crying, bless her.

'Six days,' she said, 'and when I get back,' and she pointed to the Mayeruv Gloriet.

'You mean?' and she nodded, running her hand over my head, as if to set the clock ticking.

Six days; one day for every week of mine, not that I saw much; the railway station, the inside of an ambulance, the small room in the doctor's surgery, looking out onto some quiet residential area. When my working days had come to an end, they paraded me before a panel and asked me where I would like to end up. In the hands of the Almighty I answered, a reasonable request considering the hours I'd put in, but they affected not to understand. Vladivostok, Leningrad, a grade-A rabbit hutch on the outskirts of Odessa is what they had in mind. All very tempting, but I had a better idea. The closest I could get to Him on high without actually having to turn my toes up.

'How about Italy?' I ventured. 'Say Venice.'

'Venice?' Clipboards quivered. They were quite taken aback.

'Or if not there, then somewhere remote. A little monastery in the hills, perhaps.'

One of the clipboards stuck a finger in my direction.

'You do not like the country that has given you a home for all these years?'

I tried to explain.

'It's not that. But after a while a man needs his memories warmed, don't you think?'

They withdrew to consult. Venice. I'd hardly given it a moment's thought, and now she danced before my very eyes. Sulphur was in the air, milky water lapped at my feet. I saw myself sitting incognito, under Paola's tree, watching her children play in the square. They'd be grown up by now, that is, if she ever married. She might not have done. Perhaps we could become friends again, visit those churches, the ones closest to her heart. There'd be an understanding between us, with none of that other nonsense getting in the way. Why, I might even propose to her!

You might think it odd that I didn't want to return to Pat and Len and the rest of the crowd, but when it came to it, I faltered. They'd only ask a lot of damn-fool questions and I didn't want any of that. I was tired of investigations and being passed from pillar to post. I wanted to be a welcome stranger again. Paola wouldn't ask questions. She'd accept my return as God's will.

It was all arranged. I was to be accompanied to East Germany by two security officers. From there certain paperwork would be done, then a train to Trieste, and after that I would be on my own. It was rather a roundabout way of doing things, but never mind. They were covering their tracks, wanted me to come into Europe at an angle, so to speak. I sat on the long journey in almost total silence. It seemed so unlikely, that I would be seeing Venice again. Had it changed, the colours, the sounds, the smells? No, of course not! Soon the city would envelop me like a warm bath. I smiled at my guards and we all drank a toast to my good fortune. As our glasses rang together I remembered Eugene and his Polish comrades and their last train journey full of similar hope, and I thought perhaps this was how I was going to end up too. So be it. I had another drink and let the train rattle on regardless. But no such station appeared.

I can't remember when it began exactly, but by the time we crossed into East Germany I was starting to feel a little below par. The truth was, about six months beforehand, I'd had a bit of a nasty twinge in the bathing-costume area. Nothing that a few stiff drinks hadn't put right, but on that journey, sitting stock-still hour after hour, I began to feel this lump moving about my insides, like a billiard ball trying to find a pocket. I'd rub my stomach, lie on my side, draw my knees up, anything to settle it down, but with every jolt and jostle of the tracks it became more insistent. By the time we reached Dresden I felt it was about to jump out of my navel. As I stood up, it rolled this way and that, tipping me off balance. One of the guards caught my arm.

'Nothing to worry about, old chap,' I assured him.

I sat back. I was pale and sweaty. I felt like a greenhorn adrift in the Bay of Biscay. Between them they carried me to the station waiting room, and shooed everyone else out.

'There's no need for that,' I told them. 'It's not catching.'

A doctor came and poked and prodded as doctors do. Before I knew it I was strapped into an ambulance, a regular bone-shaker, and carted off. I tried to get up, but they held me down.

'Easy, Commander, easy.'

'Easy! I'll miss my connection!'

Then the doors opened and I was lifted into a room at the side of what looked like someone's home. More prodding.

'You will be all right,' the doctor said, and patted my knee.

I knew it was bad news then. Good news and they treat you like you're an affront to their profession.

'Rest,' he said. 'You need much rest.'

'I can rest where I'm going,' I insisted, but they weren't having any of it. He explained my condition. Lumps where there shouldn't be.

'Cut them out,' I suggested. 'Only use a sharp knife.'

He shrugged his shoulders. 'There are too many.'

'I know a fellow in Harley Street. He might help?'

He smiled. 'You need rest. You need diet, grow strong again. And then.' He pointed to a poster on his wall. 'Karlovy Vary,' he intoned. 'The water there is very good for patients with your condition.'

Water! I might have known it.

Six weeks I stayed there, and then one day when the leaves were falling, they drove me here and here I have stayed. It could be worse. I could be in Swansea. I could have another mayor banging on about his clock.

Rosa was gone for five days, not six, but every one of them seemed like a week. The replacement staff did their best but I was implacably rude to them all and thoroughly ashamed of myself because of it. I just couldn't help myself. On the sixth day Rosa appeared rolling a wheelchair down the ward with a checked scarf and an old officer's overcoat draped over its arms.

'Twenty minutes,' she said, and strode away.

It was early. I shaved carefully and fished out my best shoes. When she returned I was sitting, all dressed up in the chair, waiting.

'You are sure?' she asked.

'I may not walk too well, Rosa,' I told her, 'but I still have an independent air.'

Once out the main entrance, she bounced me down the steps and pushed me down the drive like she was running in an egg-and-spoon race.

'Careful!' I cried out, but she took no notice. Once outside the gates she stopped to get her breath back. The Mayeruv Gloriet rose before us, a fresh cap of snow on its head.

'Now, Rosa,' I admonished her. 'Don't let's rush this. I want to get to the very top.'

'Top?' she queried.

'The Mayeruv Gloriet.'

'The Mayeruv Gloriet?' She laughed and shook her head. 'It is too far, too many steps.'

'But you promised.'

She laughed again, as if to a child who's misunderstood.

'Outside, I promised,' she countered. 'Outside, to the waterworks. Come.'

She started to push again. So that was it. I'd been living on half-digested promises for the week. I grabbed the wheel.

'I don't want to go to the waterworks. I'm sick of water. Water, water everywhere and not a drop to . . . Oh, Rosa. I want . . .' I held my arms out, like a boy does when he's running into the wind. I tilted them this way and that. 'I want to . . .'

She bent down on her haunches and grabbed my arms, held them still. 'OK. OK. We go,' and span the wheelchair half-circle in the slush.

We left the chair at the foot of the steps. I had to stop at every other step, to get my wind back. Rosa kept looking at her watch, urging me on. Halfway up I had to sit down.

'It's no use,' I told her. 'I can't go on.'

In the end she got two lads to carry me up in a bath chair, and plump me down in the round observation tower. Across I could see the sanatorium and my two tall windows on the second floor.

'Are those my windows?' I asked her.

'Yes.'

'And I'm not there. I'm here.'

'Yes, you are here.'

'Now, even when I'm there, I'll be here. Though it's not much of a view.' It was an ugly thing to say.

'It's all we have,' she admitted.

I got to my feet, stood beside her, holding on to the rails. I could smell smoke from a train, and something else in the air, sulphur. Venice! I touched my nose.

'The waterworks,' she explained.

We stared out for some time. I could see why people came up here, though, to see the town, where it begins, where it ends; how small it is and yet covers everything, love and life and lonely death.

'Your sister,' I asked her at last. 'Did she leave you anything?'

'Nothing. She lived with a bad man.'

She stared ahead. How sad that should be her sister's epitaph. What would Rosa's be? What would mine? He didn't live with anyone at all? I reached out and put my hand upon hers. I hadn't really thought of it before but I had a little nest egg put aside, from all my years in the Russian navy. It was supposed to be waiting for me when I got to Venice. God knows where it was now. When I got back I vowed to write to the authorities, tell them that when I go, they're to hand it over to her. Every last rouble. Whether she'll get it is another matter. There's something untrustworthy about bureaucracy, whatever the country.

'Come on, Rosa,' I said. 'I've a letter I want you to post. And be sure you put the stamp on the right way. Some people can get very fussed about that sort of thing.'

★

I decided not to tell Pat until the last minute. I'd made up my mind, though, as to what I was going to do afterwards. Pack it in. This was going to be the last time. I'd run my course. This old fish was tired of flapping his fins.

'Easter's just round the corner,' I said to her one day. I was in her kitchen, peeling potatoes. We often ate there together now. We'd prepare a little something, go to the public house and come back for something nicely overcooked. 'I thought I might propose again. A young man's fancy and all that.'

'Don't be silly, Crabbie. You're not a young man. Pour me another gin.'

I did as I was told.

'Anyway, what makes you think I'll give you the right answer. Remember the notice Len has behind the bar. "Do not ask for credit as refusal often offends." '

'Who says it's to you?'

'Who else would have you?'

'I iron my own shirts. To a prospective bride, that's quite a selling point.'

She came up and kissed me on the cheek. It felt happily familiar, comfortable like a pair of old shoes.

'Come on, Easter Bunny,' she said, untying my apron. 'It's time we hopped to it, you and I,' and we went to the pub and stayed there all afternoon. I can't remember what happened to the meal. Afterwards I went home and wrote the letter. On the day I go, I thought, that's when I'll give it to her.

March ended. Edmund Bentley died at the close of it. I'd always admired him, not least for inventing the clerihew.

Sir Christopher Wren
Said, 'I am going to dine with some men.
If anybody calls
Say I am designing St Paul's.'

It always brought a smile to my face, that one.

The Friday before I was due at Portsmouth, I came to the office to find Smithy sitting behind Pendock's desk. Maitland was standing beside him. He'd shown no sign of knowing, so I played it that way.

'This one of these city takeovers you read about?' I joked. Smithy smiled, but there was no humour in it. I felt a cold hand upon me.

'I've come to buy some furniture for my new flat. Maitland's offering me a deal even better than Roosevelt's. And I need to see you. We both do.'

'Oh?' I looked at them.

'Sit down, Crabbie,' Maitland said, 'and close the door.'

'Wrong order, Maitland, but very well.' I closed the door and drew up a chair. The office was strangely silent. He must have sent everyone home.

'Ready to rumba?' Smithy asked.

'I suppose so, though I've just realized you're sending me down after budget day. Scuppers my chances of having a cheap pint or two if they put the price up.'

Maitland put his hands on the desk. He was sweating.

'When you come back, Crabbie, I'll stand you as many pints as you can drink at today's prices for a whole week. What do you say to that?'

'I'd say you'd been out in the sun too much.' They looked at each other. Smithy tugged his ear. Here we go.

'The thing is, Crabb, we haven't told you the whole story. They'll be on the lookout for you, you know that.'

'Of course I know that.'

'The thing is, we'd quite like it if they found you.'

'Sorry?'

'In such an eventuality, with their security arrangements, men in the water and so forth, lookouts on deck, a frogman, even one of your skill, could well be captured. That's what we'd like to happen to you, if at all possible.'

I thought I must have heard them wrong.

'They shoot spies, if I recall.'

'Actually, Commander, that is what they never do. Usually they stash them somewhere uncomfortable, like the Lubyanka. They become currency, barter, to be traded with, as and when.'

'I'm not liking the sound of this much.'

'But you're different. They know you, we've made certain of that. Those little items left behind? They know who you are, your expertise. What would they do, do you think, if one day they put out their fishing line and hauled you in.'

'Chuck me back, I'd imagine.'

'On the contrary. They'll congratulate themselves on their good fortune. They'll examine you, question you as to who sent you, and for what purpose. They'll ask you about our set-up, the chain of command, what else you've done, what else you plan to do; what goes on at Teddington and at *Vernon*, but they know most of that anyway, know too that you're not the type to volunteer such information. So then they will look beyond that, to what other use to them you may be. And there, maybe, they will find a perfect fit. Who better to advise them on the formation of their new underwater units than the legendary Commander Crabb, who better to train their new squadrons, conduct their sea trials? And so, if we read them correctly, they will offer you an alternative. Death by dishonour, which they will not carry out, or life in the uniform of an officer in the Russian navy. It's our hope that you will be dragged into the service of the Soviet Union.'

'Are you out of your tiny mind? Me work for the Soviets?'

'If you please. Serve them with honour, learning their capabilities, their dispositions, their future thinking.'

I was beginning to see the method in their madness.

'You mean spy on them? Send messages back, that sort of thing.'

'Far too dangerous, all those dead-letter drops and miniature cameras. Just do your job and keep your ears and eyes open. And then, when the time is right, we'll spirit you away.'

'How long are you thinking of?'

Smithy took a big gulp.

'Four years, five at the most. Then we'll bring you out. Someone like Greville, through one of his trading exhibitions.'

'Wynne? Is he in on it?'

Maitland butted in.

'Oh, Crabbie, don't be so naive. Import, export, all those European trade exhibitions he attends? You're in on it, I'm in on it, he's in on it. Anyone who's anything is in on it. It's what keeps us going. God, imagine if we didn't have any of this, that all we had was work. What sort of life would that be? God bless Russia and world domination, that's what I say. May her days be long and plentiful.'

'And let all her children be red ones?'

'Something like that. It keeps the blood flowing, you know that as well as I do.'

I said nothing. They waited.

'It's a bit of a tall order,' I said at last.

'It's a very great sacrifice,' Smithy acknowledged. 'When you come back, due recognition will be shown. I think we can safely say that. The Crown would be very grateful.'

So there it was, the cloak they were asking me to throw down, the safe path Her Majesty must walk. I thought of Visitini's young widow, and Sikorksi's daughter, how great their sacrifice, how meagre mine. What choice did I have?

'But wouldn't they suspect me? A plant, isn't that the right word?'

'Only if you offer yourself. But you will not. You will merely lead them to it. You are the forgery. Let the experts decide as to how genuine you are.'

'And if they don't bite?'

'We'll exchange you in a few months. A surfeit of black bread will have been your chief discomfort.'

They took me through it for two hours, where I might be sent, the dangers involved. They didn't want to rehearse me too much.

'How will I know?' I asked at last. 'When the time comes to get me, how will I know it's for real? They're bound to try and trick me every now and again, aren't they.'

Smithy put his finger to his lips.

'Remember the King,' he told me, 'the words he used, the words only you and I and the King know. When you hear those again, then you can be certain. If you don't hear them, even if it's Maitland here come to get you, you'll know it's a set-up, that he's working for them, not me.'

Maitland blushed. I nodded. There was reassurance in that, a wholeness, the old King reaching across to his loyal subject.

'So what now, then?' Smithy brightened up. His shoulders slackened. Business over.

'Have a good night out, take Pat somewhere special. You won't tell her, will you?'

I shook my head.

'I think that's best. She mustn't know anything. You can see that.'

'Yes, I can. But it's bloody unfair.'

Smithy nodded. 'This is not written in stone, Commander. Take the weekend to think it over. Tell Maitland here. I'll be down in Portsmouth. If you're there on the 17th, all well and good. If not . . .' He looked at his watch. 'I must flee.'

He wrote a cheque out, and left. Maitland and I stood there, not saying anything. I'd known him for twenty years and I hadn't known him at all. And Pat and Smithy, did I know them? Did they know me? When it came down to it, who knew anyone?

'How long have you been in on this?' I asked him.

'Best not to ask, Crabbie.'

'No, best not, I suppose.'

'Now take the day off. Don't try and tie up any loose ends, bar bills, landladies, I'll settle them later. Carry on as normal. Make appointments that you won't keep. A dentist or something.'

'I'm meeting my publisher next week.'

'Good. Ring them to confirm it. Sound keen.' He picked Smithy's cheque up, scanning the entry.

'Would you credit the man,' he said. 'He's put the wrong year. '55. You'd think he'd know what year it is, wouldn't you? Now I'll have to wait until he comes here next. God knows when that will be.'

He flapped the cheque up and down. He seemed to be waiting for something. Then I understood.

'Hand it over,' I told him. 'I'll get him to change it before I go.'

He walked me to the stairs and stood there as I made my way down.

'Cheerio, then.'

'Cheerio, Crabbie.'

He turned and stepped back into his office and was gone.

★

So that was it, done as they'd always done it, almost without noticing. The next five years of my life taken away, with barely a handshake to seal the deal. Just like the war. Paddling canoes up to Bordeaux? It's nothing much. Parachuting behind enemy lines, sailing into the jaws of the Arctic, riding two-man torpedoes into Gibraltar harbour, it's nothing much. Five years of your life? You'll get over it. Count yourself lucky to have five years to spare.

Pat was away, visiting some school chum of hers. I had a few days to kill. It wasn't hard to know what I wanted to do. I went to the Brompton Oratory and heard the boys sing. Did they sing in Russia? I suppose they did, but it wouldn't be like this, not music that you drink, music you could drown in, music that simply washed over you. I went walkabout one night, the streets of London like a meadow to me, full of scents and scampering life, and in every hollow a haven, a snug, a smoke, a bar with no one in it at all, stools for strangers, chatter for unknown friends. Twelve pubs I visited, ending up at the Nag's Head. Len found me a spare bed and in the morning brought me a cup of tea. It was hard to take it, and say not a word. One afternoon I bought a stick of salami and some cooked polenta and took myself to the National Gallery and spent a couple of hours in front of the Canalettos, taking surreptitious bites out of Italy from a brown-paper bag. He could draw straight lines, Canaletto, but it wasn't the Venice I knew, too clean, too still, too man-made, though the bones were there. If I stared hard enough I could almost breathe life into it myself, see the waters stir and the boats move. There was Belloni, old and stooped, shouting at me from the little bridge on the Angeli. There was Maria Visintini seated in her own gondola, tall and erect and wealthy now, but still dressed in black. And there was Paola standing on the little jetty by the Zatterre, our children gathered about her skirts, waving to me as I drew near. If I looked close enough I could even see myself. I had been there once. I could be there still.

Afterwards I went to Harrods Food Hall and bought a fish. I took it home in my arms and cooked it and talked to it as I lifted its flesh to my mouth. I kept its head on and looked into its eyes.

'That's where I'm going, chum,' I told it. 'I'll be as cold and quiet as you.'

April 17th, the day after Budget Day, Pat and I met up in the Nag's Head. I could have gone to her flat, but that would have given her too much room to swing me about. I couldn't say anything at first. I sat next to her and put my hand on her knee. She brushed me away.

'Crabbie! You're a bit frisky this morning.'

I put my hand away and smoked a cigarette. Twopence on a packet of twenty. Not that I should care.

'What do you think of these new Premium Bond thing-a-me jigs?' she asked, trying to cheer me up.

'Monte Carlo politics,' I snapped. 'They'll be raffling off the Crown Jewels next. Never thought you'd get that from a Conservative government..'

'I don't know what's so wrong with them,' she countered. 'Saving money, perhaps making a bit.'

'It's turning us into a nation of gamblers, Pat, people who want something for nothing. Forget the money, what about the country, Pat? What about the country?'

'What about the country? Seems all right to me.'

That shut me up. It seemed all right to me too.

'What is it, Crabbie?'

There it was. The time had come. I took her hand. I know one shouldn't.

'The fact is, Pat, I've a little job on.'

She pulled away. 'Crabbie!'

'Nothing untoward. They just want me to pop down to Portsmouth, that's all. Take a look at something.'

'What sort of something?'

'There's this ship coming in. Want me to take a shufti on the q.t.'

'What ship?'

'Use your loaf, Pat. The one Khrushchev is coming in on. They want me to take a look at her backside while he's taking tea at No. 10.'

'Are you mad? Whose idea was this?'

'Just a quick flip of the fins and then it's all over.'

'It's Smithy, isn't it?'

'Just a quick flip of the fins.'

'It is, isn't it?'

I nodded.

'I knew it! This is madness, Crabbie. Think of the security that will be there.'

'We've got to know what they're up to, Pat. We can't have the Russians stealing a march on us. We rule the waves, remember.'

'But why you? You haven't done any diving for nearly a year!'

And I couldn't tell her. For the first time in my life I wanted to open my heart to her, to tell her everything, all my silly little trips and my moments of vanity; Smithy and Suez and meeting Mount-batten in a room above Admiralty Arch. I wanted to tell her what the King had said to me, and the way St Augustine looked when he saw his vision out the window. I wanted to tell her about Paola, not just the bare facts, but the unspoken flesh of it, and how I ran away. I wanted to tell her everything, knowing that once done, I would never have to mention any of it to her again. I wanted to tell her that I was going, that five years was not such a long time.

'Would you come with me, Pat, down to Portsmouth?'

'What, so that I can get on another train back to London?'

'Just this once, Pat.'

She looked over to where Len was polishing his glasses.

'Go on,' he said. 'Indulge the old fraud.'

So we caught a cab to Victoria and travelled down together. We had a compartment to ourselves, and I held her hand like a young soldier going to the front, and looked out the window. The last time I saw England.

'That picture you have, Pat. Of you and the dog. Could I see it?'

'It isn't very flattering.'

'Even so.'

Shaking her head she took it out. There she was sitting on the wall in her stripy sweater, with the little dog and a grin on her face. Where was that happy world in which she lived? Was the world ever happy like that? Or was it like the photograph itself, only an image, bound to fade, remembered only in moments of forgotten time. I couldn't stop staring at it.

'Take it, if you like it so much,' she said. 'Put it by your bed. When you get back it'll be the first thing you see.'

I folded it into my wallet. She put her arm through mine and snuggled up.

'And when you get back to London we'll have another picture taken, if you like, an engagement picture. How about that, Crabbie, an engagement picture, and we'll have a party, with Maitland and Gordon and Sydney and all your chums from the Nag's Head, and we'll set up home and settle down. But we'll still go out of a night, still have fun. It won't be a nine-to-five marriage, Crabbie, I promise. What do you say?'

I could feel tears in the back of my eyes.

'Crabbie?'

'Damn smut,' I said, and got out my handkerchief.

'And no cottage in the country, Crabbie. We're not country folk, you and me, I can see that now. And no shelves either. We'll get a man in.'

'That's what I'm afraid of,' I said. 'That you'll get a man in.'

'Crabbie!' She punched me on the arm.

And then we were standing on Portsmouth station, and the up-train was firing its boilers on the platform opposite. Pat held onto the lapels of my coat.

'This is the last time, Crabbie. You promise?'

'Cross my heart and hope to die.'

'And you'll come back to me, just as soon as you can. No hob-nobbing in the wardroom.'

'As soon as I can, Pat.'

'I'm frightened, Crabbie. I don't know why, but I'm frightened.'

I held her then, like couples on stations do, close, unable to speak.

Journeys are such uncertain things. Her train hooted. Whistles were blown.

'You'd best go now. Toodle-pip.' I shook her free and kissed her, once, on the cheek. She smelt of perfume and tears.

'See me in your dreams,' I whispered and walked away, never looking back. Oh, that I'd had the courage to.

*

Smithy was waiting in the tea shop. He had a plate of scones in front of him, and a large slice of Dundee to the side. He was drinking tea with a slice of lemon floating on the top. He prodded the plate in my direction.

'Help yourself,' he offered, 'though the jam's not up to much.' He fussed about with his napkin and helped himself to another. I took his precious cake and sank my teeth into it. Nice and moist. He pretended not to notice.

'Someone said they saw Pat at the station.' His voice was light, but careful.

'Someone?'

'We like to keep an eye on things. She all right?'

'Over the moon, Smithy. She's planning our wedding. Thinks I might be there. She's traditional in that way, silly girl.'

We walked to the Sally Port Hotel, and checked in. Rooms 17 and 20, at the very top. I took the larger. Smithy didn't appreciate it, but under the circumstances he had no weight to throw around. From my window I could see Vosper's yard and the South Railway jetty, where the *Ordzhonikidze* would berth in the morning. The harbour was a forest of cranes and masts. I wanted to climb up there and hide in the branches, like any boy might, watch the whole thing from way up top, and not come down again until they'd all gone home. I was sick of diving.

About eight thirty I went downstairs. The Porthole Bar they called it. You can imagine the decor. I was just about to order when Smithy bundled up behind me.

'My shout. What'll you have? A Bell's?'

I looked at him.

'Have you read the label lately?' I said, and chose the only single malt available. Tact was not his greatest asset. We drank in silence. I ordered another. Smithy was all for getting an early night.

'You go ahead,' I told him. 'I need a breath of fresh air.'

So I had a last look at the town I'd taken for granted for so many years. For a long time Portsmouth *was* England. London, Oxford, Bristol; it knocked them into a cocked hat. The naval station and arsenal, Drake, Nelson's flagship in dry dock. Why, even Dickens was born there. It was our Venetian lion, half in, half out of the water. It guarded us, a symbol of our strength. It was the right place for the Russians to come, to see us in our old glory, the right place for a salty Englishman to take his leave.

I got back about nine thirty, lightly pickled, and summoned up a final whisky. 'Afore ye Go' indeed. Back in my room I opened up my wallet and propped Pat's picture against the glass by the bed. I might not have told her the whole truth, but I'd got as close to it as I could. There was my letter there too and I burnt it in the little grate and washed the residue down the hand basin in the corner. I took off my shoes, peeled back the cover and slipped into bed. I didn't undress for I thought I might need to go out again, to be alone for the last time in the land of the free. I put my hands behind my head and stared at the ceiling, and the shadows on the wall. Downstairs I could hear the clatter of plates, and through the window came the smell of fish and chips. Someone coughed in the back yard.

'Ted,' a voice called. 'The barrel needs changing.'

I heard a trapdoor open and a man grunting as he went below. I remember singing to myself, 'They're changing barrels at Buckingham Palace, Christopher's drinking a pint with Alice'. I closed my eyes. I could practically feel the newspaper warm in my hand, batter grease oozing through. I licked my lips and sprinkled salt and vinegar on it. I laughed and fell asleep.

Next morning we left before anyone was up, the harbour masked in thick mist, a lather of soap on its face. We got to *Vernon's* main entrance about ten to six, Ariadne looking lost and bewildered, as if neither of us should be there. I tipped my hat to her as usual and walked down the length of the football field. Lofty Gordon was at the far end messing about with the goalposts.

'Crabbie! What on earth are you doing here? Today of all days.'

'And what's that supposed to mean?'

'Nothing.' He stared at Smithy, then back at me. 'Free tonight?'

'It's possible.'

'The Boar's Head at Havant, if you've a mind. That is if you haven't anything else diverting on.' And he walked away, whistling the 'Internationale'. I turned on Smithy.

'You didn't specify dress, then. No black tie, no dickey suit?'

'Come again?'

'The invitations you sent out. Bloody hell, Smithy, I thought this was meant to be hush-hush. Does everybody know?'

'Rumours, Crabbie. There's nothing they like more.'

At the divers' room I checked my equipment, my favourite frog-suit hanging in its old place. I fingered its neck, testing the strength and flexibility of the rubber. It was a second skin to me, my Pirelli. The next time I removed it, there would be a different Crabb underneath, slithery like an eel, easy to admire, hard to grasp.

'Everything OK?' Smithy asked, anxious to be off.

'Everything is just bloody perfect,' I replied.

We returned to the hotel and sat down to breakfast. We had the best part of a day to kill. Smithy was nervous, couldn't eat a thing.

'What would you like?' the waitress asked me. 'Bacon, eggs, kippers, Quaker Oats?'

'Train smash,' I said, thinking of an old friend. She knew what I meant. This was a naval town. Smithy's brows locked together. I didn't bother to explain.

I ate at my own pace, eyeing the morning crossword. The spinster at the table opposite burnt her tongue on the porridge. I fetched her a glass of water and went back to my paper.

'Don't take all day,' Smithy complained. 'She's due any minute.'

'Twenty-seven across. "The Gods of Aintree". What do you think?'

'Crabbie!'

'National Gallery. Clever, eh?' Smithy tut-tutted while I wrote it in. 'Teams in the market' took a while, but I got it in the end. Marxist. Rather appropriate under the circumstances.

By the time we got to the quayside, the mist was breaking up, and the *Ordzhonikidze* was gliding in on a pool of morning light, grey and somehow golden, like something out of *Swan Lake*, floating towards us as if pushed by an unseen hand. She was beautiful and big, though much of her upper deck was covered in canvas, hiding her radar and other refinements. I felt suddenly small, a pebble to be thrown against a granite cliff. Smithy must have sensed it, for he put his arm around me.

'Think of all those sailors of old, all those Columbuses and Cooks. Think of what they must have felt like, sailing to uncharted land. Think of what they learnt, the treasures they brought back. They left under a cloak of anonymity or indifference. They were gone for years. They returned heroes.'

I try to picture him, the lines on his face when he said those words, but I can't. I wasn't looking at him. I was staring at the *Ordzhonikidze*, thinking how swift and spirited she looked, how noble and determined, how improper it was for a man such as me to climb aboard, deception in my heart. It didn't feel quite right, to steal upon this honest, decent ship. For a ship is a ship, and the men who man her sailors all, whatever their creed. This wasn't war anymore, least not any I'd fought. This was being what you weren't, speaking untruths. Heroes, indeed. A hero is someone you look up to, who stands straight in the world, fights cleanly, as honest to everyone else as he is to himself. There was nothing honest or upright in this. Yet this is what my Queen, my country, was asking me to do.

We watched her dock, the gathering crowd curious but not effervescent. They knew who was on board, Mr B and Mr K, bears in a cave, half asleep but soon to come into view, large and sturdy, with little beady eyes and clumsy paws, and the scent of Stalin still hanging on their coats. Then the gangway was lowered and the band of the Royal Marines struck up. A man appeared, hatless, his right hand, palm open, raised in salute. The crowd craned forward, with a rush of breath. There was no cheering. With his little pointed beard and fussy glasses he looked like a maths professor.

'Which one's that?' a woman next to me asked.

'That? That's Bulganin.'

'No wonder they shoved him out first. Look what's following. Ugly looking pudding, isn't he?'

He emerged short and squat, with a kind of roll to his gait that was unlike most men. It was as if he'd only learnt to walk recently, or was made out of materials that didn't quite match up to the actions required. His suit didn't hang like a suit should either. It seemed draped over the wrong sort of frame. His face was lumpy, like a root vegetable, with pressed-in eyes and a stuck-on nose, and a mouth gouged out with a penknife; a face bred in the soil. He raised his podgy hand and turned in our direction, looking us over, as if to gauge our intentions. Then he ducked, like a burrowing animal, quickly and instinctively, into the safety of the waiting car. He was like me, embarking on a journey into the unknown, uncertain as to the reception that might await him. Smithy tugged at my arm. It was time to leave.

I was due to dive at around five, when the tide was running high. I insisted on Smithy buying me lunch, roast beef and all the trim-mings. It wasn't much good, though, the meat tough and bloodless. It had been waiting around too long, served up a little too late. Remind you of anyone? After one or too mouthfuls I found I wasn't hungry after all. Smithy sensed my anxiety.

'You can always say no, Crabbie. No one will think any less of you.'

'Do you know,' I replied, chewing on a large piece of gristle, 'I don't believe that's true. It's what fellows like you depend on, the importance of our peers' esteem.' I threw down my napkin. 'But as you've offered, I'm calling it a day.'

'What?' I'd never seen it before, the fork held halfway to the mouth, suspended in time. I grinned, happy at last.

'I've changed my mind, Smithy. I'm not going.' I waved my hand in the air. 'Waiter!' I shouted. 'How about another bottle?'

Smithy laid his knife and fork on his plate and looked around, hands knuckling the tablecloth.

'Crabbie, are you serious?'

I held his stare for a moment. I was pleased to see a little green coming back to his cheeks. I could say it, I thought. I could say, yes I am serious, and catch the next train to London. Smithy wouldn't stop me. I'd be back up before opening time. I'd give Pat a bell, and we'd go out, and halfway through the meal I'd pop the question, flowers, ring, knees, the works. We probably wouldn't stop celebrating for a week. I didn't have to shed a rubber skin to be a new Crabb. All I had to do was walk out of there. But what could a new Crabb do in this world, what had he done? Smithy understood; there wasn't room for a new Crabb. It was only the old one that was of any use.

'No, I'm not serious, but it rather proves my point. Now, let's hear no more about it. What shall we talk about? Do you know we're importing potatoes from Belgium these days? What happened to Jersey Royals and King Edwards? What are we going to get now, King Ferdinands?'

I kept it light all afternoon. By four we were back at HMS *Vernon*, getting ready. A staff car took us to the King's Steps in Portsmouth Dockyard, about eighty yards from the ship. Smithy helped me on with my gear, dusting the inside of the suit with chalk, lifting the breathing gear over my shoulders. I entered the water at just after five, the tide running fast. The cold gripped me like an unfriendly hand. I began to swim through the jetty's dark blurred columns. It sounds easier than it was, with the current tugging at my heels, and instead of moving easily under my own steam I found myself struggling against the pull of the water. Before I knew it I was whipped off course, the pillars acting like sluice gates in a lock, the tow dragging me sideways, knocking me this way and that into the pilings. It was like driving dodgems in the dark. Then I was caught fast, the bulk of my gear snagged in a tangle of wire and rope, the weight of water shaking me to and fro against the stanchion, like a terrier at the kill. There was nothing for me to do but to slip my gear off and swim to the surface, but I had to wait for the strength of the water to ebb before it was safe. Twenty minutes later I was back where I started from, exhausted. Smithy was standing on the running board, a pair of binoculars trained on the target. He almost dropped them when he saw me climb up the steps.

'We'll have to wait until tomorrow morning now,' I told him. 'I've taken a fair old battering. I couldn't do it again, not today. Besides, the light's fading. No telling where I'd end up.'

Smithy drove me back with ill grace, grinding the gears as well as his teeth. He must have sensed it, for walking back to the hotel he tried to jolly me up.

'You're just trying to wangle another dinner on expenses, that's what it is,' he joked, but I was tired of Smithy's company and he of mine. He'd done his job. Now, he couldn't wait to see the back of me. As far as he was concerned I'd already gone.

I ate on my own, a plate of ashes. By nine o'clock I was in the Bear's Head, trying to hold my own with Lofty and a couple I knew, Crawford, I think their name was, decent enough chap, nice wife. I can see them now, the three of them sitting on bar stools and me standing in the middle, watching them as they talked of families and houses, and the new helicopter pad that was being built. It was about continuity, life as a boat journey, picking up passengers on the way, ports of call, friends of the quayside, there to greet you, there to wave you away. Come next Thursday, they'd be here again, no doubt. It's what you want in life, an evening with friends, a little money in your pocket and a nice wife. Doesn't seem much to ask. I talked as best I could, about the furniture business, the book I was writing, but my heart wasn't in it. Every now and again I'd catch them looking at each other. They sensed what it was. Air and water.

When I got back, Smithy was nowhere to be seen. I went to my room. There was no clatter tonight, no murmur of voices, no smell of fish suppers. The day had come and the day had gone. The guests had left and the town had drifted away. Only the ship remained, shrouded, mysterious, bathed in ghostly light, sleeping on a moonlit pond.

I went down to the lobby and pushed the pennies in, dialled the number. I could hear it ringing, picture her, sitting in bed, reading a magazine, see her patting her hair before leaning across to pick it up.

'Yes?' That's how she always answered. Never 'Hello' or the number. She always expected someone to have something immediate to say.

My finger rested on the A button. One push was all it would take. One push and the world would take me back again.

'Yes. Is anyone there?' Her voice was touched by cigarette smoke and just a hint of gin. I wanted to throw stones up at her window, wanted her to throw stones up at mine; something to break the spell.

'Gordon, is that you? I've told you, the answer's no,' and she started to sing, the 'Marseillaise' bless her, at the top of her voice. And I joined in. Not the words, just the tune. Seems a funny thing for an Englishman to sing the French national anthem in the dead of night, but I sang it back to her as best I could, only she couldn't hear.

'There. Satisfied?'

I pressed the button.

'Pat,' I cried, 'Pat, it's me!' But she'd gone.

*

We were back at the King's Steps at half six, the tide running at half strength. By seven I was ready, the morning sun bringing firmer shape to the Russian ship.

'If they don't bite,' I ventured, 'at least I might get a dekko at their propellers. It would be a shame to come back empty-handed.'

Smithy nodded in an abstracted sort of way. He looked terrible. Indigestion, he claimed.

'This is it, then,' said I.

'This is it, Crabbie. Good luck.'

I shook his hand and walked down into the water.

What more do you need to know about that trip? How easy it was, how the water seemed to part before me, how young I felt, how clean, how clear-headed. They said in the papers that I was too old, out of condition, that my years of smoking and drinking had rendered me unfit for such duty, but I felt not a flicker of fatigue, not a tremor of hesitation. I felt like my counterpart Buster, bound by a restless energy, ready to swing from branch to branch, holler my presence over the treetops. There was a lightness to my bones, a strength in my body, and I swam straight and true, four fathoms below, to a new future. I was leaving England behind, and part of me was glad, for since my return I'd never felt happy with it. England was a bubble of breath rising up through the water. She would grow, this England, have children. I could see them already on the pavements, the quiff of their hair, the way they stood on street corners, insolence and ingratitude in the eyes, the young women staring back, giving as good as the men, adjusting the back of their skirts, smoking in public. The days of how-do-you-do's and whist drives were over. They would bump up against the Russian ship, just as surely as I would, a mine or a lifebelt, it was their choice. Those who lined the streets that morning knew that, not waving flags nor cheering, but Londoners standing in silence, not simply to have a look at him, but also to say, this is what you're up against, chum, ordinary folk like us, and he, staring back, would have understood, for he felt the same, fierce in the defence of his own home, suspicious of being caught unawares, a collar thrown around his neck, made to look foolish, the world's dancing bear.

I swam on, the tide flexing its muscle, but content to let me ripple through, blurred shapes to my right and left, like rain falling on a watercolour. I was close.

I surfaced momentarily to get my bearings. A pool of sunlight flooded over me, dazzling in its intensity, the *Ordzhonikidze* rising up, like a citadel of the deep, young men calling down from the ramparts. For an instant I imagined I was back in Venice, looking out of my little window, the sun in my eyes, and my boys below me, calling up from the barges. They were perfect, those young men. They had that beauty you find in sculpture; the proportions, the muscle tone, ready to wrestle their way to glory like young gods, with only the javelins and chariots absent. At school I'd always been taught that the love of man for a man was greater than the love between a man and a woman, and that the Greeks sculpted the human form in recognition of that superiority, but I'd never understood how it could be until I'd seen those boys. They were so beautiful, even the way they laughed, their black hair falling over their eyes, their arms folded across their golden chests. They were out of this world, and as I tipped up and plunged down again, I realized that I was out of this world too. I had turned away from it, ignored it, and now it was far beyond my reach, just a globe of blue and white, floating in eternal darkness. I could reach out, I could cover it with my hand, blot it from the sky, but its light would always seep through, reminding me of its presence and the distance between us.

Then I fell into their embrace, coils of limbs about me, muscular hands under my arms and between my legs. I was flesh. They carried me aloft, passing me from hand to hand, like a troupe of dancers with their ballerina, the world in bow ties and tiaras watching my performance. I pirouetted, my toes pointing to heaven. There was shouting and clapping and offerings thrown at my feet. I was magic now. Abracadabra.

Now you see me.

Now you don't.

Fifteen

I was shown into the same room again. No Serov this time. Another man was sitting there. Another man, another bottle, another glass. I pushed the offering away.

'Not after what happened last time,' I said.

'There is no need to worry on that account,' His voice was thick, in no doubt. 'This is my personal bottle. For security reasons. I never used to drink at all, but Stalin forced it on us all. He wanted to turn us into drunkards, for us to make fools of ourselves. We obliged, naturally, weekend after weekend, in that dread dacha.'

I looked at him again. He bowed his head. He was fatter than me, coarser, but we were both small men. He had a sort of brute determination about him, open and direct. His face was of a naturally sunny disposition, but when shadows passed over it, the skin darkened. He was dressed in plain blue serge and, rather charmingly, held a hat in his hands. I don't know why but I warmed to him, despite his reputation. I like a man who knows how to carry his hat.

He placed it on his lap.

'Premier Khrushchev,' I said. 'I am honoured.'

'First Secretary Khrushchev,' he corrected. 'The rest will come later.' He grinned and rubbed his hands together, as if they were cold. 'I wanted to see the famous Commander Crabb for myself, before we sail.'

So, I was going with them. I tried to speak but my throat had closed up. He understood well enough. He put his hat on the table. I wanted to snatch it up, cram it on my head.

'You blame no one for your predicament?'

'Only myself.'

He swatted the pretence aside.

'If you must. America sends its spy planes, your government sends divers. In the air and under the water, it is a constant battle. The Americans are flying over us all the time, past the Urals into Siberia, photographing our cities and military installations. They go from Wiesbaden in Germany. From Germany! We have both grown used to it. They think they are invulnerable, flying so high. We know that they are not. One day we will catch them. But first we have caught you. The question is, now that you are here, what are we going to do with you?'

'Crippen seems to want to keep me for a pet. He's been a bit lonely while you've been away. Trouble is, I'm not very house-trained. You could still send me back if you like.'

'And if we did, once you are safe, you would cock a snoop at us, say what a fool the First Secretary was to believe in your innocence. I am not a fool. You do not survive Stalin's republic by being a fool.'

'I can see that.'

'In time everybody will. They will not like it, but they will see it, plainly on my face. Suppose we granted your request. I do not think there are many in your government who would welcome your return.'

'If I kept my mouth shut, I dare say they'd get used to it.'

'But how could they be sure you would keep it shut? Your government has its KGB, believe me. Do you know what I think? I think you are safer here with us. Here you can talk to your heart's content. Freedom of speech. You see! We believe in it too.' He laughed and clapped his hands. 'Say goodbye to your homeland, Commander, as I must do soon. I have enjoyed it here, the crowds who lined the streets, the laying of the wreath, remembering your dead. The men took their hats off as I passed. Some booed. You know what I did? I booed back. One man shook his fist. I tapped my head. Many attempts have been made to speak to us in that tone. The British, the French, the American, the Japanese, all shook their fists at us during the Revolution and we cleared them all out. Then came Hitler and we cleared him out too. It is time you stopped behaving this way towards us, otherwise one day we might wipe you off the face of the earth, like a dirty black beetle.'

He was trying to rile me, but I wasn't having any of it.

'I hope you didn't tell Her Majesty that. She's rather fond of the place. As its countrymen are of her.'

'As you should be. She may be your Queen, but to my eyes she was first and foremost a wife and a mother, just the sort of young woman you'd meet along Gorky Street on a Sunday afternoon.'

I couldn't quite work out whether that was a compliment or not. He was grinning as he said it, his turnip skin all wrinkled, his beady eyes twinkling like harbour lights in the dark.

'Up to a point. Not many would go back to a quarters like that, though, I imagine. Is that where they put you up, the palace?'

'We stayed in a hotel, Claridge's. All the time I thought, why do they not give us a house? Is it an insult to put us in a hotel and not one of your stately homes? When Peter the Great came to England, they gave him a mansion.'

'Which he proceeded to wreck, if memory serves. "Gutted" was the word my old history master used.'

'And they think I would do the same, like one of your teddy boys?'

He banged the table. The anger seemed only half feigned.

'You've read about them, then?'

'Oh, Commander. Our papers are no different from yours. We only hear the very worst of you.' And he squeezed his hands and heaved with laughter.

'Our rooms were bugged, of course. I talked only to my valet, about my clothes, what I should wear, whether the colour of my tie was correct. Your secret service must have thought that I am a very vain man, but as you can see I have nothing to be vain about. I needed my dress to be correct, that was all. Everyone was expecting a bumpkin. But we can be gentlemen too, even though we are communists.'

He brushed at the lapels of his suit. He might have a face like an old sea boot, but he probably spent more time in front of the mirror than Pat.

'So, I was told of your arrival by letter, not by phone. I knew before Eden. I made a joke about it that night, "certain underwater rocks", and I could see him trying to work it out. I did not bother to enlighten him. He would learn soon enough. I congratulate you, Commander. Of all the people involved, you made my visit fun. True, there were more important matters to discuss than your little swim. The Prime Minister and I are leaders; we could not waste our time arguing over such trivialities. But there was a big joke here, the two of us talking of world peace and treaties, when all the time you were captive on our ship. And by that time Eden knew too. And so we sat there, a world to organize, both of us knowing that the other knew, both of us knowing that we knew each other knew, both of us knowing that we knew that each other knew that we knew that we knew.' He rubbed his hands. 'Oh, this world of mirrors, Commander. It demands good eyesight and a clear head. Sometimes we must do things which on the surface appear unworthy of us. I myself have done terrible things. Every day at the washbasin I look down to the water and expect it to turn red.' He gripped his elbow. 'I have blood up to here. But others . . .' He pushed his hand hard under his chin. 'But I cleared them out, even Beria. I have served my country faithfully for thirty-two years, twenty-nine of which I spent surviving the reign of Joseph Stalin.'

'You did better than me,' I told him. 'I barely lasted twenty-nine weeks.'

He looked at me, nonplussed.

'That's what I called the wife,' I told him. 'After she sentenced me to Siberia.'

He smiled.

'You are not married now, though?'

'You know I'm not.'

'Yes, I know. But I wanted to hear you say it, so you might realize, in your own voice, where your interests lie. A proposition has been put to you, has it not?'

'Not one that made any sense.'

'You are a patriot, yes?'

'I'd like to meet the man who says I'm not.'

'Good. I approve of patriots. We are a nation of patriots, us Russians. Is that not a good thing?'

'Can't argue with that.'

'So on the one hand we have Russian patriots and on the other men such as yourself, British patriots.'

'There are patriots the whole world over, First Secretary.'

'But some patriots are more important than others. You can be a Dutch patriot, but it does not matter one way or the other, except to another Dutchman. In some countries men must bear greater responsibilities. I want you to be a patriot, Commander. Your country needs us, Commander. Can you understand that?'

He pushed back his chair and stood up. The interpreter half rose out of his seat, uncertain as to what he should do. Khrushchev pushed him back down and spread his hands out on the table, his face close to mine. He began talking rapidly, the Russian streaming out of his mouth, our interpreter trying to catch up in the infrequent pauses, languages slipping in and out of each other.

'Imagine if there was no Soviet Union. Imagine if there was no other great power in the world other than the United States. What do you think America would do with such an opportunity, with its planes and its missiles, with its money and its oil and its wheat? What would happen to the rest of us, what would we become, listening to their Frank Sinatras, watching their John Waynes, chewing their gum; the whole world bowed down before America's altar, singing the hymn of Wall Street. There is no part of the world that she would not try and own. She is like a disease, this America. Smallpox, cholera are nothing to what that country could do, the rapidity with which she can infect whole nations. Stalin knew this too, but he was a bully and like all bullies he was afraid of standing up to anyone stronger than himself. I am not a bully. I am not afraid. I will stand up.

'It is our duty to become a great power, to play America at her own game. But we need to catch up fast, otherwise it will be too late. America will overwhelm us all. Once it was a contest between communism and fascism. Now it is a contest between a culture which wishes to turn everything into a department store, and one which believes not everything can be bought and sold. It is not an issue of democracy but freedom from the rule of money, the right not to consume, not to become part of a market place, to be bought and sold and bartered over. So we must cut corners, become experts overnight in a hundred different fields. Fortunately there are men and women from many countries who see the necessity of what I say, who see the justness of our cause. Your Mr Burgess, Mr Maclean.'

'Bloody traitors,' I said. 'Should have been shot, the pair of them.'

'Traitors to Britain, maybe. But to the world? They helped to make us equals.' He paused. 'There are others. Shall I tell you what we will achieve next year? Something extraordinary. Something no would suspect in a hundred years.'

'What is it, then? You off to the moon?'

I don't know why I said it. Something to do with my namesake, perhaps. He went to the moon in one of his matinees before the war. Khrushchev's face darkened. I'd stolen his thunder.

'Have I said something wrong. First Secretary? Only it's every schoolboy's dream, to fly a rocket to the moon.'

'Not the moon, and not a rocket, but what we call a *sputnik*. We will fire this –' he held his hands around an imaginary ball – 'this . . . *sputnik* into space. Round and round the earth it will go, a symbol of our power, the strength of our cause, communism encircling the globe. *Sputnik* will become one of the most famous names in the world, more famous than Rolls-Royce. Later we will send up a dog. Then a man. That is just the beginning. The Americans have their rodeos, their cowboys riding wild bulls, but we will have men riding the bare back of the earth! Is that not a thing to marvel at? You who dive to the bottom of the world must appreciate that. And we will have done it first, stolen a march on our American rivals – for all their new kitchens and fancy cars.'

His eyes shone with pleasure.

'We are catching up fast. Our new plane, the Tupolev, is one of the first jet passenger planes in the world. I could have come on it, but the designer was afraid that if something bad happened to me on the way out, something bad would happen to him on the way back.'

He laughed, thick grained, like water in a muddy field.

'So, we came on this instead. And on the way I celebrated my sixty-second birthday. So.' He pointed to the glass. 'So drink to my health. And I will drink to yours.'

He poured them out. Would you believe it. Bell's.

'To your future, Commander.'

I picked up the glass.

'Many happy returns, old boy. And may all your troubles be collective ones.'

He stood up, pulled on his coat and buttoned it up.

'We sail within the hour. I must go and wave your country good-bye. You will be kept here, while you decide what to do. You will be quite safe, until that decision is made, I give you my word.'

'Do you think I could see it just one more time?'

'See?'

'The home country.'

'On deck?' He shook his head.

'I won't try anything. I won't speak out or draw attention to myself. You have my word.'

I held out my hand. He looked at me for a long time.

'The night before I arrested Beria, I rode home with him in his car as usual. When we came to Granovsky Street he bade me good-bye and shook my hand as I got out. I thought, You scoundrel! This is our last handshake. Tomorrow at two o'clock we'll shake you up pretty good. But your handshake is different. I take it, gladly.'

He grasped it hard. His hands were thick with flesh but not flabby, short stubby fingers made for tearing off hunks of black bread. I could imagine him at the Mansion House or Buckingham Palace, faced with all the flunkeys and the cutlery, wondering which knife to pick up, which glass to drink from, from which direction to ladle up his soup. No wonder he stood in the mirror and talked to his valet. A man like this could easily be made to look a fool, and a man like this would not like that. What fear of humiliation he must carry. I felt for him then, sensed his nervousness.

He released his grip.

'I must send a last goodwill message to your Prime Minister.' He half turned. 'Have you anything you would like me to tell him?'

He said it with a smile. I rather liked him for that.

'You could ask him to cancel my milk.'

*

They put me in a baggy sailor suit, Gert and Daisy pressing in on me like two sides of a meat-paste sandwich. There were men and women standing on the quayside, countrymen of mine, wishing him bon voyage. I wanted to lift my arm, not to make contact, but simply to exchange something, a gesture to one of my own, but I did nothing. I'd given my word. I stared down at them all, wondering if anyone from HMS *Vernon* might be amongst them, Lofty or the Crawfords, even Smithy taking a last look. There were Englishmen there, English men and English women, English like me. I saw boys I had been, young men I had left behind, older men that one day I would be, all of them born in England and hoping to die in England, as all Englishmen should. And I think I became aware then, that for me, this was not to be. This was the last time I would see my country. Serov was right. England had deserted me. No one was going to come and get me. Not after five years. Don't ask me how I knew. Maybe it was the way Smithy had gripped the wheel on the way back after the first attempt, like someone trying not to show you've outstayed your welcome. Maybe it was in Maitland's offer, the ways his eyes slid over mine as he said it. Maybe it was Pat coming down with me, as if she knew in her heart I was not coming back. It's funny, that, how one can know things without it having any form. I knew I was made for diving, the moment I stepped on that ladder, knew that my life would be spent under water, my nose rubbing against the ocean floor. I wasn't cut out for dry land. The Russians were going to throw me back into the water, where I could slip free, move again. My gills were flapping at the very thought of it. I thought of Len and the bar and the nights Pat and I had spent at the Trojan. I thought of Maitland and his little office in Seymour Place, Anthony leaning on his desk, Giulio with his young buck eyes

239

and how his hair shone in the hiss of the coffee bar. I thought of Gordon winking at me as he whispered to one of his moxies, his dough hands kneading her flesh. I thought of Pat's perfume and the cab rides and how I would stand back when she unlocked her door. Over on the quayside they were untying ropes from the bollards, letting them splash down into the sea below. I thought of all the water that had enveloped me and the number of times I had come up grinning, Sydney pushing a wet cigarette into my mouth.

'Take me down,' I said. 'I've seen enough.'

*

Isn't air just about the sweetest thing, the smell of it after rain or breathed in brittle through the cold? Even now, when Rosa comes and opens the window and lets me take a lungful I can almost see the bubbles rising up, floating out to meet their companions beyond, above these rooftops and fir trees, above the snow and the cold and the coal trains that smudge the sky, to the something blue and beauti-ful that warms the heart. But perhaps my breath is too heavy for that now, too full of old gases. If I behave myself perhaps Rosa will take me out again, sit in the park, feel the bubbles fall out of my mouth, drop to my feet, where I could stir them in the snow. Perhaps I could bend down and squeeze them into balls, throw them onto the folk out walking, pepper them with an old man's breath. They would skip and dodge them with delight, to see such a sight, an old man playing in the snow like a young child. Perhaps someone would stoop down and join in, my breath and all that it contained, thrown back and forth, children after school, a young honeymoon couple, factory workers coming off their eight-hour shift, blackened faces grinning. When I was gone, the whole town would remember me.

'Remember that old man,' they would say, 'his lively dance,' and they'd go home wondering who he was, and those funny words he threw, all squashed up.

They never came for me, see. I was right. I couldn't work it out at first. When I saw the photo I thought that they must have known about the whole set-up. I half expected Serov to drape an anchor round my neck and chuck me overboard. Then, when nothing happened, I concluded that Smithy must have known there was a plot afoot to capture me and had seen how he could play that to our advantage. That made sense. So I did as I was told. I was stubborn, but not without a certain amount of wit. I enjoyed it, speaking as I would have spoken, seeing them come round to Smithy's way of thinking, the two of us playing the Russians for fools. They offered me what Smithy said they would, and I accepted. I joined their navy. I learnt Russian, worked alongside them. They were good fellows, most of them. No surprise in that. Odessa, Vladivostok, the Baltic Sea Fleet, I worked and waited, four years, five years. Sometimes I forgot I was waiting at all. They were keen, the lads, and there was much to do. There was a pattern to it I could appreciate. Even the salutes and the ritual drinking. In 1960 I was posted to Estonia, two years later to Sebastopol. Still no one came, not a Maitland nor a Greville, nor any other of Smithy's midnight messengers waiting in the wings. And then it struck me. What if it wasn't the Russians who had been spun this tale, the Russians who had been sold this fake. What if it had been me? What if Smithy and Maitland were working for the other side all along, selling me this line because it was the only way to get me working here? I can't prove it, of course, and besides, no one gives a hoot anymore. I did my bit, that's all, remembered the King.

People might want to know what my life in Russia was like. The truth is, it all passed me by, being someone else. Korablov would tell you what it was like, but Korablov seems to have retired hurt these days. I went in the water, I came up again; I ate my food, slept in my bed, saluted when I had to. That was my life, in, out, in, out, washed clean of everything that had gone before the moment I was pulled out the water. I had swum not a river of forgetfulness, but an ocean of it. There was nothing more of Lionel Kenneth, the small boy who'd watched the lifts go up and down and dreamed from Beachy Head. I was Lieutenant Korablov and he was but minutes old, no past, no future, only an eternal present: dragonfly days. No dreams at all.

There was only one time when the past nipped me in the ankles. We were helping out an icebreaker whose rudder had got into difficulties. There was nothing for it but for someone to hop overboard and see what had to be done. My superiors didn't want me to go. I'd freeze to death, they said, but they didn't understand. I didn't have much blood left in me by then, and what was there had lost its warmth a long time ago. So I stood my ground and demanded a treble ration of vodka, and as I downed it I could feel a bit of the old devil within me, feel the sour taste of him, rising up to my mouth. I never liked it much, vodka. It always had the taste of death for me, of bodies and cold and a frozen kind of hell.

'Are you trying to poison me, Knowles?' I shouted out. 'I could have you up on the mat for this.' There was a second of silence and I looked at them in turn, searching their faces for Sydney's ugly mug. Then they started laughing, clapping me on the back, imagining I was simply someone who could not take his drink. Just to prove them wrong I took another double, and went in over the side, did what I had to do. They were quite right, of course. I nearly froze to death. Perhaps I did, for when I look back on it all, I can't remember having any, what were they called, feelings after that. Still, it wasn't a bad life. They liked me well enough, my lads, left me alone when I wanted to be alone, drank with me when I wanted to drink, knew enough about me not to ask questions. There was a woman at the base, a signaller, Sonia, who the boys ragged me about, but though she liked me well enough, I didn't have time for that sort of thing anymore. I'd learnt my lesson. There was nothing there. I had nothing to give, you see.

*

Maitland died in Ireland a couple of years later. I never did find out how, but something wasn't right. Gordon Lonsdale was caught spying for the Russians in 1962 and sentenced to twenty-five years. He wasn't Canadian at all. His real name was Konan Molody and he had a wife and children back home in the mother country. Peter Kroger was part of his set-up, as was his wife; they got twenty-five years apiece too. Dear old Greville was arrested by the Russians trying to smuggle Colonel Olag Penkovsky out of Russia in the same year. They gave him eight years. They gave Penkovsky the bullet. As for Anthony, well, everybody knows about Anthony.

Greville and Gordon were swapped on April 22nd 1964. The two of them walked out across Checkpoint Heerstrasse just after dawn. It was a short walk, no more than fifty feet, Greville had a black Mercedes waiting for him, Gordon a yellow one, with Russian number plates. Gordon had served two years of his twenty-year sentence, Greville eighteen months. I was still serving mine.

They walked towards each other in the morning silence, car doors open, engines running, two huddles of men ready to receive their progeny. Halfway across they stopped. Greville, British to the core, raised his hat.

'Good morning,' he said.

Gordon walked on. He never had time for such niceties, and he was home now, Greville too, but in truth I don't think men like them, like Maitland and me, ever really had a home. After the war none of us quite understood what a home could be. We'd already made ours in broken bunkers and gutted farmhouses, hung tarpaulin over the windows and frayed pin-ups above camp beds, and found that home enough. Front-door bells and three-piece suites might have looked like a home, but it was a grate with an empty fire. There was no heat there, no flickering life. These things – life, heat, a little danger – smouldered elsewhere, in the arms of Gordon's good-time girlfriends, in the hidden compartment in Greville's exhibition stand, and yes, on the end of a pair of swimfins.

I never heard or saw my name again, save the one time. 1964. I'd long given up. I had become Commander Korablov, training divers and frogmen for special task duties. I'd just popped into the bar we frequented, after a long training session. It was winter and if there was blood in my veins it had long since frozen over. I ordered up a cup of hot sweet tea.

'You're not going to drink that, are you?'

I looked over, and there he sat. He had one of those Russian hats on, stuck over his ears, but I recognized him well enough. Not a flicker on my face, though.

'Commander Korablov?'

'The same.'

He stood up.

'Molody. I have something to show you.' He pulled out a sheet of newspaper from his pocket and unfolded it. There was an article all about me and lying across the crease, a series of pictures: one of Pat, and one of Sydney, and one of a grave, with an inscription upon it.

IN

EVER LOVING MEMORY

OF

MY SON

COMMANDER CRABB

'AT REST AT LAST'

'What is this?' I said, pushing them away.

'Something I brought back from England,' he said. 'An English Rose caught in thorns in an English graveyard.'

'Why are you showing this to me?'

'You have never been to England, I understand. I thought perhaps you might like to see one of their prize flowers.'

I pushed it back.

'You thought wrong. I went to England once, on the *Ordzhoni-kidze*, and didn't like it. It is full of dead men.'

He smiled and tapped me on the back.

'Just as you wish, my friend. Are you a gambling man?'

'Isn't everybody?'

He smoothed the paper down again. 'She is very tenacious, this rose. She waits for a man who never comes. Ten years, she has been told. Ten years and he will be back. Some say this is nonsense, but she believes one day he will. What do you think the likelihood is of that?'

I looked at the picture. There was nothing I recognized.

'I wouldn't bet on it,' I said, and walked away.